60 1

Upendra Namburi is a sales & marketing professional who has launched over twenty new products and participated in setting up three new businesses. He is an engineer by accident and an MBA by design.

He has contributed to leading newspapers and online publications and is an evolving blogger. He has written on a wide array of subjects including payments, loyalty and marketing. He has also been invited by several management schools across India to speak and interact with students.

Having realized that we are all in a constant rush, set up against timelines and deadlines in this often transactional life, he has captured that essence in a new genre of 'contemporary Indian life thrillers'.

He is on the passionate voyage of writing the numbers triumvirate of novels titled *31*, *60 Minutes* and *8*. His novels touch upon the various facets of urban India, including corporate life, obsessions, love and relationships. His debut novel *31*, was a bestseller and also on the longlist for the Tata First Book award.

He currently resides in Gurgaon with his wife and 'The Prince', his mischievous son.

westlan

61, Sil
Chenr

No. 3
Layc

93,

Believe in your passions.
Follow your passions.
Live your passions.
Never let go.

Relationships are not defined by their outcome. Friends are not defined by their utility. People are not defined by their actions. Motives are not defined by choices. Identities are not defined by designations. Love is not defined by rationality. Right is not defined by wrong. Black is not defined by white. Reality is not defined by facts. Victories are not defined by defeats. Truth is not defined by lies. Suffering is not defined by pain. Morals are not defined by the rights. Guilt is not defined by punishment. Journeys are not defined by maps.
The truth lies in the shades of grey.

Contents

Acknowledgements

To

My prince and son, Yashvardhan, my window to innocence and truth.
My wife Nirupama, for being beside me unconditionally.
My brother Pradyumna, for his sheer conviction in my writing.
Mom, who understands me like no other.
Dad, who defines friendship.
&
Those who have been with me through this wonderful journey.
Amruta Dongray, for her insane passion and brilliant original verses.
Niranjan Mendonca, who convinced me that I was on the right path.
Payal Mathur, my lodestar and rock of support.
Prasanth Mohanachandran, for his sheer effervescent presence.
Rashi Mendes for her unbounding enthusiasm.
Rupali Mehta for her refreshing perspectives.
Sridhar Kuchibhottlla, for the insightful conversations and views.
Umesh Kotwani, who embodies persistence and courage.

Gautam Padmanabhan, Paul Vinay Kumar, Krishnakumar, Sanghamitra and the entire team at Westland who always give it their all.
Sharvani for the intense debates.
And Anuj Bahri, who can inspire like no other...

And countless others who have inspired and blessed me with their sheer presence in my life.

Chapter One

THE PREVIOUS DAY

I had torched them
one by one
will I have to burn
to be left alone

It was the last cigarette. Maithili tugged at it repeatedly, but it refused to budge from the safe confines of its white box. She huffed, exasperated, and turned the pack around and shook it till the cigarette fell.

'Damn!' she yelled and bent over to pick up the nicotine stick that had landed next to her feet, on the ledge. It was a calm evening and the rays of the setting sun lit up her hand. As she grabbed the cigarette and hoisted herself up, the heel on her left shoe gave away. She clung on to the pole behind her with her right hand and heaved her body back towards the terrace, away from the steep drop that lay in front of her.

With one foot angling for space on the ledge and the other suspended dangerously in mid-air, she let out a manic laugh, realizing that she had dropped the cigarette. One more, in a long, endless series of mishaps. She watched the cigarette descend rapidly, teasing hundreds of patients in their hospital beds; that fleeting resplendent sin that could not be theirs, as it whizzed past them.

The cigarette eventually landed on a black and yellow, twenty floors below. She pulled her left leg back and let it rest on the ledge, two feet away from the right leg and straightened her back. With no nicotine fix in sight and the sweet swing of tequila receding, the pain was unbearable.

Her grip around the pole slackened and she urged herself to walk down the ledge towards the far corner. Her feet moved forward, though nervously at first and her hands spontaneously extended themselves above her shoulders, balancing her lean frame. The warm breeze brushed against her cheeks and she gently tilted her head and raised it towards the sky. Her feet continued in their path forward, unmindful of the steep fall.

She had expected to be nervous, but the walk was far smoother than she had hoped. She felt numb. What did she want up here? Did she want to feel fear or didn't she? Did she want to complete this walk or not? Did she really want to just jump? Did she want to make love to him or did she just want to slice him slowly with a sharp blade? She felt this intense disdain and spite for men, specifically the men who had meant anything to her. They had all hurt her. None of them ever understood her, or had even tried to understand her. They were so susceptible to her façade—a mask that shrouded her real identity—that she ended up fooling even herself. It had all blurred.

Her heartbeat picked up pace. The trembling had started and a wave of nervousness swept through her body. She was experiencing fear again. This was good. She felt alive. But did she want to be alive?

Her feet toed the corner of the ledge. Now she needed to make a choice. Move to the left and follow the ledge, or turn around and move back towards the pole. And then it struck her. She didn't have to wait for a strong breeze or even a passing bird to nudge her off the ledge. She was just one step away from flinging her body into the air. One last flight! One last plunge and she would be away from it all. Nothing to look back on. No more decisions. No more contradictions. No more flaws. No more regrets.

She was feeling confident again. Or was it false bravado? She was always a little uncomfortable whenever she felt confident. Fear and nervousness were welcome allies. She just couldn't figure out happiness. It unsettled her—not knowing how long it would last. She couldn't grasp the dizzying extremes of joy and fear that were sweeping her today. How could she even feel happy? Was she pretending to feel happy? She couldn't make out the difference anymore. Could even the gentle breeze and the setting sun trigger such emotions in her? This was strange. Was this all that it would take? Was she losing it?

She yearned to experience true, authentic joy and the passionate embrace of a loved one. Her heart yearned to be shattered again. Her body longed for the warmth of another, someone she could cling on to without fear or demands. Another body, just a body, that could be by her side. She just needed to be assured that there was indeed blood running through her veins and that she was alive. Nothing more... nothing less. She wanted to just feel human. But not too human, of course. She couldn't afford to make that mistake.

This was an illusion. The ledge and the terrace were playing tricks on her mind. This couldn't be. Just one step forward. Just one step, and it would have been the best moment of her life. No more medication or therapy. No more relatives tormenting her. No more conniving men, mutating into various strains of indecency.

And then she laughed. At least if she was to jump, it wouldn't have inconvenienced anyone else. After all, she was jumping from a hospital. The morgue and crematorium would have been next door. None of those men would want to see her mangled remains. She didn't want them to see her like that either. She switched on the camera on her phone and looked at herself on the screen. Her mascara was running and the breeze had played havoc with her hair. She said to herself, 'I should have had a hair wash...they can't see me like this...' As she switched off the mobile, she admired her finely manicured nails and her long slim fingers. She always believed she had pretty fingers, but didn't recollect receiving compliments for them.

She slid her fingers into the pocket of her jacket and felt the reassurance of the metal object that had been gifted a few months earlier. She wrapped her hand around it and her finger felt its way to the trigger. It was a small handgun and she was frustrated that she couldn't recollect the brand or the model. She had always been finicky and particular about minor details.

'Damn!' she shouted again and pulled the gun out of her pocket.

It was a beautifully sculpted piece of metal which shone brilliantly against the sun's dwindling rays. She admired her name that had been engraved on the barrel. It was a single action revolver. She had wanted a semi-automatic, but had been enamoured by the romantic notion and appearance of this quaintly destructive contraption. She turned her hand and pointed the muzzle towards her till she could see down the barrel, placing her thumb on the trigger.

She stood there staring down the barrel, well aware that there wouldn't be anyone to prevent her from pulling the trigger. She wondered if even a single tear would be shed, knowing fully well that there would be more than a few who would be relieved to have her gone from their lives.

She thought to herself, *'Do I even have the guts to do this? Do I really want to hurt them?*

Do I have it in me to take my life? Do I have a reason to live? Does anyone even care?'

She laughed, knowing that her desire to die was weaker than her desire to live. She was repulsed by herself. She placed the gun back in her pocket and pulled out a piece of paper.

She unfolded it and read the numbers once again. It was a payment advice for ₹30 crores marked in her favour. She had sold her stake in a company that she had set up four years earlier. It had been a volatile, turbulent and emotional journey. The venture had drained her out, and there was a tremendous emptiness that pervaded, now that she had given up the one thing in her life that was indisputably hers. It had been a brutal but necessary call that she had taken, knowing well that emotion had no place in business.

The venture had propelled her confidence and her competitiveness had driven her, ensuring that the business was a success. She had had investment bankers and venture capitalists eating out of her hands. It had been a rollercoaster ride and it was now over. She had cashed out. Or had she bailed? Was it an emotional decision after all? Now she wasn't sure. She had felt a sense of loss…in fact there was more loss in the last few months than she could take. She realized that the venture had battered her and sapped her out. It had been her source of strength and purpose and a reliable emotional anchor. And now the purpose was gone. She wasn't sure why she had even gone through the torture.

Hate and vengeance had fuelled and driven her to this point. But the sudden awareness, that she had not gained what she had been truly seeking, made the money and the fame inconsequential. She still had a minority stake in the company, but she knew that she wouldn't be calling the shots any longer. She wasn't at the reins. She didn't steer or lead anything. She was afraid that she would need to be led again, or possibly even be dependent on someone, once again in her life. The venture had been her pillar of strength.

And then the journey back from Dubai, a fortnight earlier, flashed through her mind. The reluctant call that she had made to her father, well after a decade, from a hospital room. The questions and paperwork that she had to complete, the lonely flight back to Mumbai and the disturbing sight of her uncle at the airport.

Then the deluge of relatives and ghosts from the past who had engulfed her when she was recuperating in the hospital room in Mumbai, more curious to know what had happened than how she was. The slew of therapists and doctors who had wandered into her room to prod, question and assess her. The straining of the one meaningful bond she had with Roshan, and the quest for its relevance and definition. Mountains of inane medications and redundant therapies, severe bouts of loneliness in the midst of friends and relatives in the hospital room and the questions on their faces when she was being discharged… The pangs of pain and fear that overwhelmed her, on being released from the hospital, into a quagmire of anxiety, panic and disgust for everything around her.

And then there was Priyanka's meltdown.

She flung the phone at the ant-like cars creating a ruckus on the street below her. The mobile crashed against the windscreen of a crummy sedan and the traffic screeched to a grinding halt.

She smiled. *'What the hell? Why not?!'*

2:30 pm
FRIDAY

after the pleasure
there awaits a grave
legitimacy is for the faint

The tension in the board room was palpable. Vikram was a perfectionist and he was busying himself with every tiny detail of the launch function. The invitee list had been discussed for the second time in the day, and the new television advertisement had been screened to five different audiences over the last two days. Vikram had just concluded two meetings; the first with Mark—Global Marketing Head for BCL—and the second with Vikram's immediate boss, Richard, the Asia Pacific CEO. They had contradictory points of view on several aspects of the launch, as on almost everything as well. Agastya had already taken his second analgesic for the day.

The television advert had already gone through three rounds of editing, and now, Vikram was having second thoughts about the housewife depicted in the film. There had been a fierce debate on whether the model should in fact be wearing a blouse with sleeves, rather than the sleeveless one in which she had been shot.

The model was a new find and Agastya wasn't comfortable with the choice that had been imposed on him by Vikram. It had been a subject of furious contention between the two, but Vikram chose to go against the recommendations of the advertising agency and use the model he wanted. She was going to be the face of the brand in national media. There was even a proposal to have her face appear on the packaging, but the idea had been deflected by Agastya. He realized that his discomfort would likely have stemmed from a conversation with either Mark or Richard earlier in the day, and was now doubly intrigued at how he would manage the situation.

It amused Agastya that the Chief Executive Officer of a multi-billion dollar organization didn't have the autonomy to decide on the sleeve length of a model's blouse. But he realized quite well that it wasn't about the sleeves. It was merely another turf for the politics of power and an easy territory to play their role in the affairs of BCL.

Agastya viewed the commercial yet again, frowning at the model's expressionless and nervous looks. He just had to move on. Surely the quality of his new detergent would outshine the dull face of his new brand, who he planned to replace soon anyway.

The team from the advertising agency, managing the BCL account, had been working for over 40 hours without a break. With the press conference slated for 3:30 pm, the film production and editing crew was getting nervous about the last minute changes and modifications being demanded by their confused client. The creative head had already walked out in a huff and Michael, the Account Director from the advertising agency, was playing the role of mediator between Agastya and the senior BCL management team, whose demands for the film were, by this time, getting ridiculous.

Agastya was trying to pacify his CEO, Vikram Rajyavanshi, repeatedly assuring him that the modern Indian homemaker dressed in a sleeveless blouse, as represented in the film, was in line with the target audience for their new premium detergent, Sparkle, which was going to be officially launched later in the evening. He didn't want to remind Vikram that the same sleeveless blouse clad housewife was already up across two-hundred hoardings and waiting to be unveiled later in the evening. That was a nightmare that he didn't even want to think about.

Instead, he scanned the press conference schedule before it went in for the final print.

3:30 pm	Vikram Rajyavanshi, CEO – BCL, India
3:35 pm	Mark Phillips, Global Marketing Head – BCL
3:40 pm	Richard Hendricks, President – Asia Pacific – BCL
3:45 pm	Product Launch & Unveiling
3:50 pm	Question & Answer Session

The agony in finalizing the agenda had amused Agastya. He had watched as Vikram struggled to determine who should speak first at the press conference—his immediate boss Richard, or the Global Marketing Head, Mark. The mental tussle had taken its toll on Vikram and seemed to have fractured his equation with both of them.

Agastya had been working on the Sparkle launch for over two years. It was slated to be the grandest, and by far the most expensive product launch ever conceived by BCL in its hundred–year presence in India. BCL was a global soaps, detergents and personal care products conglomerate with business lines ranging from personal care, foods and beverages to household items and garment care. Their sales turnover had crossed the ₹30,000 crore mark in the previous year, but they had been struggling in both, growth and profitability.

BCL had been losing market share in the detergents segment for over two years. Most of the damage had been done by their arch rival, Stark, which had been offering aggressive consumer promotions, backed by a blitzkrieg of advertising, discounts and incentives to the retail trade.

The rivalry between BCL and Stark was now corporate legend. Agastya found himself in the crossfire of perhaps the fiercest periods of competition between the two organizations in the last two decades. Stark was on a rapid growth trajectory, and had been investing heavily in the Indian market. It was a distant second to BCL in India, with its sales turnover having crossed the ₹12,000 crore mark, but it had its sights on outrunning BCL in India.

The marketing budgets for Sparkle outstretched the profit rationale. Sparkle was slated to be the first in a series of product launches that had been earmarked by BCL for the subsequent twenty-four months. Most of the new products were under wraps, with only some key management team members being privy to their development plans. Most of them were offshoots of their global brand stable, but Sparkle had been indigenously developed for the Indian market, with BCL registering patents for some of the innovations in process and formulations. This would have been one of the few products that had been developed in India with a global ambition. Both Mark and Richard had been keen on taking Sparkle to Africa, Asia and possibly even North America over the following twelve months.

Sparkle would be the flag bearer and the new showcase brand for BCL in India. It was their new beacon of light, bearing on its shoulders the passion and hope of driving in the next wave of growth in the Indian market.

The company was going overboard with the advertising, promotions and events that had been planned for this product launch. With a ₹30 crore–blitzkrieg planned for the first four weeks, the company had budgeted over ₹110 crores for the first three months on this product. There was a lot resting on the market response for Sparkle for everyone involved—Vikram, the entire senior management team and the prospective shareholders. Agastya was also banking on this product's success in propelling him on the global stage at BCL.

They had to make this work. The entire FMCG (Fast Moving Consumer Goods) industry was looking towards them. BCL had been a stellar performer in the past, which needed a shot in the arm. Sparkle was it!

Agastya handed over the agenda document to Sebastian, the Group Product Manager for the detergents business, reporting to him.

'This is the final one. Just print it and don't ask anyone else for their suggestions. Got that?' he spoke in a hushed tone.

Sebastian had been the CMO-in-waiting far longer than he would have liked. At forty-seven, time wasn't on his side and reporting to a much younger Agastya irked him. He had commenced his career with BCL as a management trainee and had had successful stints in sales and marketing, but all his assignments had been within BCL's India operations. Agastya had been an unusual hire for a senior-level posting, in that he wasn't from the BCL family, and Sebastian had found himself in an unpleasant corner. He didn't know of any world beyond BCL and that fact was now proving to be his disadvantage in an otherwise spotless career.

Sebastian nodded and rushed out of the conference room.

Across the table, Vikram stood up and stretched his arms.

'That's it! Let's roll with this. No more changes. We will have to show this to Mark and Richard before the press conference though and take them through the changes.'

'We love the lady's bare arms, Vikram?' Agastya was crossing his fingers under the table, but he had to make sure.

Vikram laughed. 'Yes. Let the country admire her slender arms in their naked glory, and I hope Richard takes a fancy to them as well!'

Agastya nodded. He was exasperated but knew that he had to keep everything together for another few hours. He was also relieved that he wouldn't have to alter the hoardings, the millions of sales–fliers, posters, danglers and glow signs that had already been dispatched across the country.

The sales teams across three divisions had been gathered into a single project team, to manage and coordinate this launch. Most products took over fifteen days to reach the shelves of the over 2,00,000 retailers that they had across the country. But on this occasion, Vikram had wanted it done in forty-eight hours!

The sales team had already gone flat out in pre-stocking Sparkle, with all the display materials, within the warehouses of large supermarkets and department stores. Once the press conference was over, the teams would move into action on the field and place the stocks on the shelves.

Agastya thought this was unnecessary, but Vikram appeared to have some deep rationale behind the move and wasn't going to budge from it.

This was also not the smartest move, as it was quite likely that when the advertisements hit the national press, the stocks would not be freely available at all retailers, but Vikram had been adamant. It had puzzled Agastya, but he was at the end of his tether. It was just a matter of a few more days, and then all this would be water under the bridge.

The profit margins on Sparkle were under pressure even before the formal launch. He had taken on an aggressive promotional pricing for the new product and was betting that it would help him gain market share and get some critical volumes for the company. He shook his head and decided not to let this distract him. He had to focus on the press conference and the launch party later in the evening . This was a big day for him. He had to gain the trust and confidence of Mark, who had been watching his work on Sparkle for the last several months rather closely, shredding him for the slightest error.

Mark had involved himself with several strategic aspects of the Sparkle launch in India, including the package design, communication plan and pricing, which was surprising considering his position in the corporate hierarchy. There had been arguments between Agastya and Mark over several conference calls, but the latter finally seemed to relent. If Sparkle didn't make a splash in the Indian market, and quickly at that, Agastya was sure to be fired.

'Sure, Vikram. Will meet you at the Oberoi at 3:15?'

'Let's leave together at 3:10.'

Vikram had to have the last word.

'Must feel good to launch Sparkle on your birthday eh, Vikram? We definitely have a twin celebration on for tonight?'

'Sure!' Vikram smiled.

Agastya turned to the client director from the advertising agency.

Client directors had the thankless task of managing the client's requirements, conveying the briefs to the media and creative teams within their advertising agency and then selling the output from the stubborn creative teams back to the client and vice versa.

'Have you checked the venue since the morning? Everything in place?'

The client director nodded nervously.

Agastya turned towards the TV screen. There was a flurry of activity with reporters holding their earpieces in place, outside the Bombay Stock Exchange (BSE) building in

Mumbai, trying to get their grip on some new breaking news. The trading volumes on the Sensex seemed to be increasing rapidly. He couldn't hear the announcements being made by the luscious news reader from the other end of the room. His feet carried him back towards the large LED screen. He was getting an uneasy feeling about the markets. It was a gut instinct.

The phone rang and he answered immediately.

'Nandita … I'm in a meeting. Let me get back to my room and I will call you back.' He disconnected abruptly, anticipating that a conversation with his wife could have gone on forever.

He pressed a number on his speed dial. The person on the other end picked up within the first ring.

'Ags! What have you done to the markets?'

Manish Shah, an investment banker and a childhood friend, had been his accomplice and ally in the stock markets for several years. They had been through the good times and not–so–good times on several occasions. Geoffrey's had been their watering hole on several evenings after taking a heavy beating on the bourses. They would flush down their agony with chilled beer and whiskey shots, discuss their strategies for the next day and return to their homes, brandishing false smiles and firm resolves that the following day on the markets would be theirs.

'What's happening out there, Manish? I have been stuck in meetings. What have I missed?'

There was a frustratingly long pause at the other end, as he heard fingers slamming down on the keyboard. Agastya needed to get back to his trading position in the office. His hands were itching, his pulse was already picking up pace; he was aroused by the thrill and uncertainty of the stock markets.

Manish had introduced Agastya to the fascinating world of stocks and day trading. It had started off as a pleasant distraction to kill time in long meetings and conferences. It eventually evolved into a passion. Agastya now knew that he was addicted to it. It became evident that his increasingly extravagant lifestyle depended on it. He knew he had crossed over from passion into affliction. It also became apparent to his peers and friends, that this was an interest that he pursued with a religious fervour even during the workday. He had rescheduled meetings, shuffled reviews, juggled conference calls and taken days off when the markets were turbulent and offered the greatest uncertainty to feed his ever increasing lust for thrill and even "pain", as he often referred to it. The unpredictability of the stock market prepared him for the uncertainties of business and the politics of office life. It helped him develop an interpersonal style that was laid on the foundation of constant surprise.

The stock market also offered an alternate dimension of competitive play and rivalry with his peers and friends. Now they had scores to settle and bets to wager on their wins in the markets. It had taken them beyond their acquisitions of apartments, holiday homes and SUVs. Now, it was about their ability to maneuver the chaotic inconsistencies of the markets and their ability to gather information from the movers and shakers who influenced the prices. Insider information, market rumours and analyst reports were constantly interspersed between market share reports, advertising plans for soaps and promotional budgets. The online trading screen was always on, and the Bloomberg application on the BlackBerry kept him up to date when he was away from his desk. Even the lift and the washroom areas were not spared, as every moment was crucial in tracking and studying the nuances that determined stock movements.

SMS tips and BlackBerry messenger conversations spread throughout the day, and an early morning summary of the North American markets had become the morning mantra. The opening of the Far Eastern markets synchronized with the milk and paper delivery in the mornings. Saturdays and Sundays actually became dreary, as he missed the thrill. His fingers itched for the keyboard and his mind yearned for the opening bell of Monday morning. Cards over the weekend and a beer at Geoffrey's in the evening had become the norm. Good days were few and far in between. Long term was for a day and short term could last even a couple of minutes. He liked seeing the constant movement of his stock portfolio. Of late, the downward movements of his portfolio value seemed to charge him more than the upward ones.

'Manish...you there?'

'Listen, Ags, will have to call you back. My boss is on my case and I'm taking a beating in the markets. Catch you later.'

Agastya clicked on an icon and scanned the prices of his stocks. He was hoping to grab a few minutes before heading out for the launch, to scan his portfolio. He had been dying for some action since morning, but had been tied up with Vikram and the advertising agency. He could feel his stomach growling and realized that he hadn't had lunch.

Agastya loved the thrill of the launch, and Sparkle would now be his sixth and most significant product launch in his career. As he entered the lift lobby, he could see Sebastian frantically screaming at someone on his phone, gesticulating wildly.

The lift doors opened.

'Hi, Agastya. How's it going?'

Nitin Chandra, the ever effervescent national sales head for BCL looked exhausted, not having slept for more than eight hours in the last three days. Another BCL veteran, he had grown up the ranks in the sales system and, at fifty-one, had made a definite place for himself in the multinational. A street fighter and a hands-on manager, he had earned the trust and loyalty of his team, and those who felt otherwise, usually found themselves shunted across to a rural assignment in the North East. He took pride in his "non MBA" status, and quite often seemed to go overboard in his deliberate choice of non-management words. He wasn't one to shy away from getting his hands dirty and revelled in adversity.

The Sparkle stocks had been delayed in their dispatches from the factory, and Nitin had been making sure that each and every distributor across the country received the stocks in time for the launch. The large retailers were extracting their pound of flesh, charging huge amounts of money for display and advertising space within the stores. They knew that the global top brass, Richard and Mark, were in town and that the BCL team would pull all stops to impress the two with their sales and distribution prowess.

'Sparkling!' Agastya smiled and entered the elevator. The button for the third floor had already been pressed.

'All set for the big day?'

'As set as I can ever be. How were your discussions with V-Mart, Nitin? Have they agreed to the corner aisle displays?'

'They are playing hardball. Our friends at Stark have been pumping money there for the last six months and have blocked most of the prime retail spots. I'm going to need some more funding from your marketing budget on this one. I've already busted my budgets. I'm running dry!'

Agastya had been avoiding this conversation and was relieved to see the doors opening on the third floor. It was now common practice for the sales teams to cry and seek additional budgets from the marketing team at any given opportunity.

'Let's connect after the press conference, Nitin. We will need to discuss this in detail. You will have to make your sales promotion budget work harder for you.'

Nitin winked at him and sprinted away towards his cabin.

Agastya noticed a series of MMS messages popping on his mobile. As he walked towards his room he noticed that his team was scurrying around the office creating quite a commotion. He noticed a familiar person walk into his room, but turned towards his team instead.

'Guys!' he screamed.

The twenty odd people who were there, froze in their steps and looked up at him.

'Just going to take a few seconds. We need to make it happen today. I need all of you to pay attention.'

He looked at them authoritatively. 'Today is important.'

Some people in the group nodded their assent while others listened closely.

'We need to be unfailingly meticulous. This is now on the global stage. Anurag?'

'Yes, sir!'

'I don't want any surprises with the press. Have you planted those questions?'

'Yes, boss. I am heading to the venue right now. Will receive the press at the venue.'

'Good. Rashmi, you're in charge of the launch event. The buck stops with you.'

'Yes, sir. It's covered!'

'Hemant! What about the hoardings?'

'They'll be unveiled just after the press conference. We've got ten of them on Marine Drive. Checked them in the morning.'

'Lakshmi. The inventory report. Pick it up from the sales guys.'

'Nitin Chandra's team is keeping the numbers guarded. Only he has access to the all India numbers.'

'Get in touch with the regional sales heads and take the numbers over the phone. I need to know how much stock has been sold into the trade and I need that in the next ten minutes.'

Lakshmi hesitated. She knew it would be impossible for her to get the numbers and wanted Agastya to have a chat with Nitin.

'But, boss...'

'No ifs or buts, Lakshmi! And what about Mark's retail visit tomorrow?'

'Nitin's team is managing that one. Don't have those details yet.'

'You should have told me, Lakshmi. I would have spoken to Nitin about this.'

'But... I did email you...'

Agastya shook his head.

'That's it, guys! All the best and let's get cracking.'

The tension between the sales and marketing teams was a constant feature, and in this case with their two driven and ambitious leaders it was even more amplified. Both teams were quite often stuck in the crossfire between the egos of their bosses.

He turned around abruptly and rushed towards his cabin. He opened the MMS messages and smiled.

He clicked on the second MMS, which opened only to reveal them both in a tight naked embrace, their lips locked in a hotel room. The date and time were clearly visible on the bottom right hand corner of the image and appeared to have been taken from a laptop that had been placed on the table opposite the bed.

This had been taken a month earlier in a boutique hotel in Bengaluru. Agastya was there, attending a marketing conference and Maithili had flown in from Mumbai. She had gained access to his room, convincing the hotel staff that she was his wife and was in town to surprise him. He had been drained out from the early morning flight and a distinctly boring and dreary day of presentations and uninteresting interactions.

The champagne had been ordered and the lights had been dimmed as he entered the room at around 9 pm. A wine tasting event after the conference had accentuated the fatigue. She was lying in bed, tucked in tightly under the cotton duvet. They downed several bottles of champagne and made love.

There was a part of him that wanted to call her and make love to her that very instant. There was another part of him that wanted to slap her and throw her off a cliff. They hadn't been in touch since they had met in Dubai a few weeks earlier.

Maybe he believed that being with only one woman was a norm, and how could Agastya, the rebel, the contrarian, be bracketed within a societal norm. Maybe he just wanted more, because it was out there for the taking. Maybe he wanted to question the definition of morality. Maybe he felt there was no need to restrict or inhibit any part of his life or senses.

He looked at the picture once again and then closed it. He glanced at his watch and decided he needed to wrap up quickly.

As he approached his cabin, his personal assistant Rebecca stood up behind her desk.

'Agastya. You have a visitor.'

'Visitor? Now? I don't have anything on my calendar.'

'But she insisted that she had spoken with you.'

'Who?'

'She's inside your room.'

'Inside?'

Rebecca followed him into the room as he walked across to his desk.

'Hi, Maithili.'

He walked around to his side of the desk and placed the laptop on the table.

She remained seated and didn't respond, but smiled as her eyes met his.

She was dressed in a black tailored suit with a pink blouse and was wearing subtle pink lipstick. The dark tan Louis Vuitton bag that he had gifted her for her birthday, which he had forgotten, was placed on her lap. She seemed to have changed her hairstyle, and the brown streaks interspersed with her jet black hair complemented her long, slim face and her fabulous figure. With the four-inch heels that were an integral part of her attire, she levelled up in height with most Indian men, which discomforted many, but not Agastya.

She had been a banker, but had quit four years earlier to start a venture with her colleague. They had sold out to a larger firm and had gone their separate ways. Maithili was now dabbling with her bonanza and was in the process of raising funds for a new Internet venture that she had conceptualized.

She had managed to raise the first two million USD, but needed another two million to be confident that she could pull the enterprise through for the first eighteen months at the minimum. Her partner in the new venture had developed cold feet, and she had been searching for a new partner entrepreneur ever since.

'This is a surprise, M!'

He looked at his watch and nervously twitched.

She was holding his family photograph with Nandita, Rishikesh and Ananya. It was their vacation photograph taken in Goa the previous year. It had been a good vacation, and he had managed to scrimp and save some time away from the stock markets and work, to focus on the family. It had also been precipitated by the fact that it was a long weekend and the stock markets had been closed for that Monday. Maithili had flown in unannounced to Goa, and checked into the same hotel in a suite above theirs. She had called him from her room and suggested they meet up. Agastya had been petrified with her proximity to his family and checked out a day earlier from the hotel, citing an office crisis that needed to be resolved. They had managed the classic family photograph earlier that morning before their unscheduled and early departure.

She hadn't been inside his office earlier, though she was well acquainted with his secretary Rebecca, who would fix appointment slots at convenient times for their meetings, which were mostly at the Thai Pavillion at the President.

Maithili had a particular fondness for Thai red curry and Agastya soon acquired a taste for it. The staff at the restaurant, also maintained their discretion, as he often went there with Nandita as well. He wasn't really sure why—it was either the food or a secret thrill to challenge the staff on their discretion.

He would also pick the same table and order the same items from the menu. It was some kind of a mental game that he would be playing with himself, questioning and challenging his relationship with Maithili, and bringing it dangerously close to the life he lived with this wife. He knew it was warped, but it became a habit after a while.

'Nandita is looking very pretty.' Maithili smiled.

Rebecca was standing there holding several folders and copies of the final product presentation that he had asked for earlier in the day.

'Just leave those on the table, Rebecca. Thanks.'

He connected the network cord to the laptop and seated himself as he drew his eyes away from Maithili and turned them towards Rebecca, who was now carefully arranging the folders and presentation copies into two piles on the edge of his desk.

'Can I get you some tea or coffee, Maithili?'

'A black coffee please. Thanks so much, Rebecca.'

Rebecca smiled and left the room.

Maithili placed the family photograph back on the table and stood up.

'Goa is a great place.'

Agastya was checking his phone for incoming emails. They had been flooding in and he didn't even have the time to scan them. He was struggling to distinguish the important ones from the cursory emails that continued pounding the inbox.

'Agastya. You won't even smile?'

He had been avoiding eye contact. He was unsettled by her presence and the incidents of the past few months flashed before him. He wasn't prepared to see her or have a conversation with her.

'M … this is not a great time …'

'I wanted to wish you luck for the product launch.'

'Thanks for your wishes, M, but please leave now …'

His fingers were trembling as he randomly pressed keys on his BlackBerry to divert his energy and gain his composure.

'Why are your hands shaking?' she smiled

Agastya didn't respond and continued glancing at the emails without reading them.

'I was hoping to hear from you, Agastya.'

Agastya was agitated.

'M! What are you doing here?'

'Just wanted to catch up on some good times.'

She pulled out two photographs from her bag and placed them in front of him.

'What are you doing, Maithili?'

'Do you ever wish we could just pause? Or just head back in time and start all over again? Don't you miss me, Agastya? Not even one call after I got back from Dubai?'

Chapter Three

TWO YEARS EARLIER

lust is cursed
a cursed addiction
in the skin
indelible splinters

Geoffrey's was rather crowded for a weekday evening. Manish, waving out to him, was seated at a table on the far corner on the other side of the bar. As he walked across he could see four management trainees from BCL seated on the high stools at the bar, sipping beer and cribbing about their orientation programme. He smiled to himself, hoping they hadn't noticed him. He had already met them earlier in the day and didn't want to intrude on their evening.

As he approached Manish, he noticed that he was seated between two women. He was instantly struck by the looks of the one to his right, dressed in a grey suit and a white blouse. She was immaculately dressed, wearing a Rado watch and a ring with an exceptionally large ruby perched on it. A Hermes scarf adorned her neck, barely covering a string of white pearls that hung delicately above her bosom. Some red berry lipstick seemed to be the only make-up she was wearing and her Bvlgari perfume welcomed him six feet away from their table. Her eyes were dark brown, her dark hair politely touching her jacket collar. She had radiant skin, with nails perfectly manicured.

Manish got up and greeted him with a handshake.

'Hi, Agastya. You're late!'

'Hi...'

He couldn't take his eyes away from her lips and seemed unapologetic as he continued leering at her.

'Please meet my friends.'

The lady in the white blouse extended her arm out to him, grasping his hand in a firm handshake which was confident, yet sensous.

'Hi. I'm Maithili,' she said, in a deep voice with a tinge of huskiness.

He held her hand for a moment longer than necessary, when he noticed that the woman to the left of Manish was also awaiting her turn with an extended arm.

He shook the other woman's hand and seated himself beside her, facing Maithili.

They had ordered a pitcher of beer and the waiter quickly appeared with a mug for Agastya and poured draught beer into it.

He kept looking at Maithili and noticed that she didn't seem to mind the attention. She seemed very confident and there was something about her presence and poise that seemed fascinatingly appealing to Agastya.

It transpired that the three of them were classmates from school. Maithili, an IIM grad, had been an investment banker and had recently set up a new venture in the Internet education domain.

Manish was in his element, regaling them with a slew of jokes and nostalgic anecdotes, ensuring the two women were in splits with his impersonations of their professors from school and their other classmates. Agastya remained silent, sipping his beer slowly, unable to take his eyes off Maithili.

She spoke with a mild British accent and contributed to the conversation from time to time.

'Agastya, you're very quiet today. What happened? Took a beating on the bourses?'

He didn't much feel like talking, but decided to be courteous.

'Not really, Pathak. It's been a great day, and it's getting better in fact ...'

Maithili interrupted, 'Where do you work?'

'I haven't been accused of that for several years now! But yes, I do go to BCL on weekdays.'

She laughed, revealing her fabulous set of glistening teeth. She could easily have been a model for one of his brands.

'And what is it that you keep yourself busy with at BCL?'

'I bide my time pretending to be their chief marketing officer.'

'Which other sins have you committed, Mr CMO?'

He could sense the sarcasm as she nonchalantly dismissed the importance of his corporate designation.

'Guilty of being married, with two gorgeous children.'

He wasn't sure why those words came out and he bit his lip. She wasn't wearing a wedding band, and there was nothing else on her that gave away her marital status, but then it wasn't necessarily the norm to be wearing one either these days.

'Is that all?'

'Well, also of being brutally honest. Not everyone can handle it.'

She looked intrigued. Manish turned towards both of them.

'Ok, guys, you'll need to excuse us. I need to head home, but don't mind me.'

'What happened?'

'My uncle is on his way to New York, and has decided to invite himself over for dinner. I can't leave my wife alone on this one. He is my uncle and you know how these things are.'

Agastya looked at Maithili, hoping she would choose to stay back. He couldn't remember the other woman's name and didn't know how to ask her to stay.

Deciding to try his luck anyway, he turned to her. 'What's the rush? Why are you leaving as well? Stay back.'

She blushed, and he wasn't sure why.

'I would love to, but I don't have my car today and this joker stays next door. Don't want to let go of a ride in this crazy traffic.'

He usually recognized a lost cause when he saw one, so he turned towards Maithili again. She remained seated.

He got up and let Manish and his friend leave. Maithili remained silent. The management trainees on the other end of the bar seemed to have noticed him and made a hasty retreat from the bar.

Agastya called out to the waiter and ordered two rounds of scotch.

They were soon talking and exchanging notes on their lives. Maithili was from Delhi, had graduated from St Stephens and post-graduated from Cambridge. She then took a year off and backpacked across Europe and North America. On returning to India, she worked with an NGO for over a year before completing her MBA from IIM Ahmedabad. She came from a family of means, as she put it, but didn't reveal much about them. Her sister lived with her in her apartment in South Bombay, but she evaded any other questions on her family. It was of course, understandable, given that this was their first meeting, but Agastya was intrigued nonetheless.

The waiter arrived with the scotch and placed the glasses on new coasters that he had brought along with him.

Agastya raised his glass, 'To life?'

She smiled, raised her glass and nodded.

'Cheers.'

His BlackBerry had been vibrating furiously, seemingly facing a relentless attack of emails. He retrieved the phone from its cover and clicked on the office email box. They were launching a new advertising campaign for their hand-wash and a furious war was underway between the media planning team at the advertising agency and his communications head. He had told them both to come to him with the final plan, but they had decided instead to keep him in the loop on their frivolous exchange.

He put the phone on silent mode and pushed it back into its black leather cover.

'Do you find it difficult to switch off from work?'

She hadn't taken her eyes away from him and seemed to be studying his every action and movement.

He pushed his back on the leather sofa and slowly rotated his neck. The doctor had warned him of the challenges he was bound to face with his demanding lifestyle, but he hadn't got down to taking any corrective measures. He massaged his neck with his right hand, delaying a response.

'Why do you ask?'

'Just…'

She wasn't letting go of it either.

'Let's just say I'm passionate about what I'm interested in and what I do with it.'

'Does everything come easy to you?'

'I wouldn't say that… How about you?'

'They could always get easier,' she laughed and then continued.

'So what drives Agastya?'

'Several things. My work…'

She was looking directly at him and her eyes were drawing him in. They seemed to be saying much more.

'Are you interested in me?'

Agastya wasn't prepared for the candour. It actually unsettled him. Was she playing around with him?

'Why do you ask?'

'Do I make you nervous?'

She was getting at his ego and knew that she was yanking his chain.

'You fascinate me.'

'Oh cut the crap. I thought you'd be more of a man than that!'

Agastya tried suppressing the flare of anger he felt. She had penetrated his calm exterior. He wasn't used to being spoken to like that, and by a woman, and one that he had barely met. Yet here he was, getting drawn to her. Her words amused, offended and aroused him all at once.

Was he losing his objectivity?

He leaned towards her, resting his elbows on the table, and held his hands together.

'Yes, you do look smarter than that…'

'That wasn't for me, Agastya, that was for you. I needed you to hear those words for yourself.'

Her mystique kept increasing leaps and bounds. She was affecting him on so many levels, it was almost cruel. It was almost as if she had figured him out. It unnerved him.

'Are you always like this?'

'Like what?'

He shook his head. The duel was getting fascinating every second.

'Candid!'

She rested her elbows on the table and moved her head closer to him.

'Life is too short, Agastya, for playing with words. Let's get the awkwardness out of the way. Doesn't that make so much more sense?'

He suddenly felt at ease. He got the feeling that he could be just himself. No apologies or defense mechanisms. No pretenses.

They remained silent for several minutes and just looked at each other, blatantly unmindful of the people or the commotion around them.

'Let's get out of here.' It wasn't a question.

He had wanted to ask *where to?*, but then realized that would have been too obvious. He also realized that he couldn't let go, he couldn't digest the fact that he was not the one with the upper hand nor the one in control. This was a game, and as in chess, sometimes it was important to take a step back before moving forward.

'Is it going to be a long drive?'

'You ask too many questions. Meet me at the lobby.'

She touched his hand with hers as she got up and held onto it for a few seconds. She was feeling his fingers and his palm.

'Quite soft for a man,' she winked at him and left.

She stopped suddenly, almost as an afterthought, then turned around and came back to the table.

'Don't ask for the bill, I've got a tab here.'

'A tab at Geoffrey's?'

He took a sip from the glass and placed it back on the table. He noticed her speaking to some people seated at the bar, then walking towards the exit. There was a distinct grace in the way she carried herself. He could sense the sophistication and class, but there was also something unfathomable about her. He couldn't understand the dichotomy of confidence and nervousness that seemed to rest calmly beside one another.

He stood up, picked up his jacket and held it in his hand. He looked around the bar, relieved that there was no one else that he knew there. He checked his emails as he walked out towards the exit and handed over his coupon to the valet standing outside the gate.

She had lit a cigarette and was speaking on her phone. There was a distant look about her.

Agastya's mobile rang as the valets drove in both their cars at the same time. It was a call from Sebastian. He moved back into the lobby.

'Boss, need you to clear the budget for the month. The finance guys need the final numbers.'

He despised the fact that he couldn't switch off from work even when he wanted to. He also realized that he should have delegated some more powers to his team members, but there had been several gaffes over the recent months for him to be able to let go right away.

'Have you reworked the final week TV spots?'

'Yes, boss.'

'Send it to Finance, but tell them there may be a small iteration in the morning, just to be on the safe side.'

'Agastya… There was a hesitation in his voice.

'What happened?'

'Stark has launched another promotional offer.'

'How much this time?'

'They're giving 25 per cent off on Klay!'

'25 per cent off?!'

'It's for a one month period…'

'Even Sailesh should know that's crazy!'

'I know, Agastya…'

'Ok, do the workings tonight. Let's meet early in the morning tomorrow.' He could sense the resentment in Sebastian's tone but disconnected anyway.

As he walked to the driveway, he saw Maithili sitting in his car. The valet walked up to him.

'Sir, the lady has asked you to take her car…'

Maithili drove his car slowly past him and winked. He was hoping that this was a joke, and remained standing even as the valet had walked to her red Audi A8 and stood holding the car door open. His BMW was now being driven onto Marine Drive and within a few seconds it was speeding towards the Air India building. Agastya rushed to the Audi and sped down after her. She seemed to have picked up furious pace. He could barely see the rear lights of his black BMW as it crossed the Air India building. As he approached the signal near Pizzeria, the light turned red. He raced past the NCPA apartment complex and realized he had lost sight of her. He had a few nervous moments, till the signal turned green and his foot pressed hard on the accelerator.

He raced the car, nervous that the police would be in full force in the vicinity of South Bombay. He looked for his BMW as he crossed the Trident hotel and wasn't sure if she had driven towards Mantralaya or had taken a U-turn back onto Marine Drive. He reached for his mobile and noticed three missed calls from the same but unknown number. He dialled back.

'Hello?'

She laughed. He couldn't mistake that huskiness for anyone else.

'Where are you?' Agastya cringed as he realized almost how desperate and pleading he sounded.

'Missing me already?' she laughed.

'Missing my beamer for sure. Do you often go on joyrides?'

'Not in such a civilized manner though… now… why are you slowing down? Let's go for a drive.'

'Where would you like to go?'

'Just race me to Wilson college. Surely you can give a lady a head start of a few seconds. Even you can be chivalrous enough for that!' She disconnected.

Agastya had parked the car outside the NCPA. He took the U-turn and noticed his BMW moving slowly. It was about 100 metres away, opposite the Trident hotel. She would have spotted her red Audi approaching and she accelerated again.

He looked around for the police and noticed a patrol van on the other side of the road, gradually on the prowl. Maithili seemed to ignore the patrol van and continued accelerating the car. His mobile rang.

'Now don't tell me you're just a load of hot air,' she teased, before hanging up again.

Full force on the accelerator, Agastya struggled to get used to the gear changes, but was quite impressed by the pick-up he achieved in the car. The scotch had kicked in and he was now in the mood for some thrills. He wasn't going to let go.

The cars were soon speeding down Marine Drive with both of them crossing 100 km/h within a few seconds, swerving and aggressively cutting lanes. The traffic was quite light for this time of the night, but even the few cars present on the road presented sufficient obstacles for the two rapidly accelerating cars. They both had to constantly change gears, steer clear of struggling taxis, ferocious SUVs being driven by plump businessmen, sedans with blaring music and inebriated teenagers.

His nervousness was mounting as his speeding BMW nearly collided with multiple cars in the rash manouvres down Queen's necklace. He struggled to come to grips with the Audi's steering and his nerves. Her recklessness seemed almost deliberate.

The BMW scratched a taxi as it swerved from the right lane onto the middle in an attempt to overtake it. He could see the taxi driver flinging his arms outside the cab and attempting to chase down the car, but soon surrendering, knowing quite well that he didn't stand any chance against the German hulk that had just overtaken it.

As Agastya sped down the road, the seconds on the digital clock on the dashboard seemed to be lapsing slower than usual. He was getting an incredible thrill carelessly steering and accelerating the Audi, and imagining making love to Maithili. His left hand groped for a cigarette in the jacket pocket that he had flung on the seat. He was relieved when his fingers quickly felt the familiar and welcome feel of the carton. As he quickly extracted the carton, he flicked open the lid with his teeth. He rejoiced as he glanced at one stick of nicotine sliding its way out of the box and to his lips.

He had taken his eyes off the road for a fraction of a second to admire his nicotine-rolled conquest. As he focused back on the road he could see that Maithili had now crossed 140 km/h in a wild frenzy while the speedometer was displaying 122 km/h in the Audi. He wasn't struggling as much as he thought he would have at this speed, in his inebriated state, in her car. And then the law of averages kicked in. He couldn't find a lighter in Maithili's car and realized that he had left his own at Geoffrey's. Cursing himself for not carrying a spare lighter in his jacket, he spat the cigarette from his mouth and slammed on the accelerator in disgust.

He was sure that there would be a convoy of police patrol vans in hot pursuit, which would have only been a punctuation to the fantastical evening that he had just had, but was surprisingly disappointed by the inefficiency of the Mumbai Traffic Police department.

As he approached the Charni Road junction flyover, he slowed down the car near the traffic lights. The BMW however appeared to be operating with a mind of its own.

He picked up speed again as he crossed the signal, knowing quite well that he had lost the race. He still needed to make a dash for it, when he saw the BMW swerving recklessly as it struggled with the braking. Something had gone wrong.

The BMW veered to the left and hurtled onto the pavement and then to the beach, crashing through a coconut vendor stall. The sudden braking, rapid change in surfaces and the side shift resulted in the car being flung sideways into the air. It rolled over on its side at least twice till it finally crashed and landed on its head.

A stunned Agastya slowed down his car and halted beside the pavement, remembering to switch on the emergency lights. He was in a state of shock and the effects of the scotch seemed to have been drained out instantly. His heart was beating quickly and a sense of panic soon consumed him. He wanted his life to rewind to Geoffrey's and wished that he had just blocked Maithili as she drove away in his car.

He opened the door, looked behind him for approaching traffic and ran towards the car. He could see Maithili unconscious in the driver's seat. The air bags had burst open, enveloping her head entirely. Several passersby had already rushed to the accident site but stood around waiting there, forming a ring of sheer uselessness around the car.

He pushed them aside and pulled at the door. He could see Maithili writhing in pain. He reached inside and unbuckled her seat belt, gently moved her head away from the air bag to pull her out of the car. He could feel the wet blood stains on his pristine white shirt but couldn't figure out where she was bleeding from.

He placed her head on his lap and stroked her hair. She was breathing, but heavily. The crowd around them was gaining strength, but nobody was stepping forward to help.

She weakly pulled his head towards her and whispered, 'Your place or mine?'

As a few constables approached them, the crowd made way. With the light now hitting them, Agastya could clearly see her bloodied face.

Chapter Four

2:34 PM
TODAY

a battle turns to war
we wash our dirty linen
with sweat and blood

'How goes monogamy, Agastya?' The sarcasm was distinct.

She stood up on her heels. He had always been impressed by her height. She stood tall and had an excellent posture. She walked towards the glass wall that separated his large cabin from the rest of the office and drew the blinds. She then walked up towards him and gave him a peck on the cheek. The cabin door was still open and Maithili seemed to get a rush from the open display of passion.

'So, Agastya…'

'Maithili. What's with the messages?'

The tension was palpable.

'You really don't have the luxury of time.'

Agastya noted the seriousness in Maithili's voice and sensed that there was more to it than just humorous banter. Her words were meticulously articulated, almost like she had rehearsed the lines. There was something about her eyes when she spoke. He couldn't decipher whether it was rage, anxiety or something else entirely. Her hands were clasped together and tucked around her knees, as if in a bid to keep them steady. She had one leg crossed over the other, and was slowly rotating her foot in the air.

She was nervous and possibly even confused, but her sense of determination was more than apparent.

'What are you doing, Maithili?'

She paused and smiled at him, and then blew him a kiss.

'Now, listen carefully my dear. You don't have time on your hands, trust me.' She paused again. 'You got that?'

He nodded hesitantly.

'I want some money. I know precisely how much your portfolio is worth and the details of funds in your various accounts with the bank. I have also tracked down your second account. Is that clear?'

It frustrated her to see a slight smile emerge on Agastya's lips, but she waited for him to nod. It also gave her fraction of a moment to pull herself together and catch her breath.

'I've also changed your Internet banking passwords for both your accounts. So, trust me, you won't be able to send money anywhere for a while.'

She paused again, to see if her words were having any effect on him at all.

Agastya was livid and yet amused with her words. He still wasn't convinced of her seriousness, but her words were beginning to aggravate him. If this was a joke, which he was guessing it was, then the timing just wasn't working for him.

He looked at the photographs that were lying on the table, which had been taken in a room at the Trident. Agastya had slipped out for a long lunch break and Maithili had access to a suite at the hotel. They drank wine, made love, listened to music and laughed, like they never had before. It had been a wild, carefree day for both of them. He had given her access to his trading accounts and even allowed her to try her hand with some quick trades and was thrilled when her fluke punts turned out to be winners.

'Now, if I were in your place, I would get cracking and make some moves quickly, my darling!'

She placed on the table the tablet she had in her hand, the screen upright and facing him. She switched it on and the display flashed the Sensex statistics with the quotes of the stocks in his portfolio.

There was an email from Nitin.

Hi Vikram,

Stark is introducing Velvet, a new product priced 20 per cent lower than Sparkle. It's going to be launched in a nationwide campaign later today. They've imported the product from their factory in Malaysia as they have decided not to wait for their local manufacturer to kick-start operations.

We need to act fast!

We have scheduled a market visit for Mark at Q-Mart tomorrow, and Stark will be handing out thousands of free samples to all customers walking into the mall. They've also got front page ads in all newspapers for tomorrow.

I'd already tied up with a major store for some in-store promotion, but Stark has tied up with the mall. The whole mall will be up with their new campaign by tomorrow morning, unfortunately, just in time for Mark's arrival.

I can't even change the schedule, as the Q-Mart CEO has been slotted to meet Mark & Richard at the store itself! Sailesh Rao has really come after us this time.

This would be a major blow for us, Vikram. I don't think Mark will be too impressed with their guerrilla tactics! Our reputation is at stake.

Nitin

Agastya was aware of the launch of the new detergent range by Stark, but their information suggested that it was at least another ten weeks away. Stark must have pushed it forward to coincide with Mark and Richard's impending visit. Sailesh Rao, the CMO at Stark seemed to have taken every effort in making this a true stealth project. He had taken them all by surprise!

The global rivalry between BCL and Stark, and their leadership teams was quite often more about thwarting each other than focusing on their individual business growth. This had become a compulsive distraction for the senior leadership team within BCL. BCL had even announced special rewards for any market intelligence and reconnaissance efforts for gathering information about Stark. The system appeared to have let them down on this occasion.

Agastya had met Nitin a few minutes ago in the lift , and he hadn't even mentioned this to him. He must have been typing this on his BlackBerry even as he was speaking with him. The bastard!

Agastya dialled a number on the intercom.

'Sebastian!'

Sebastian appeared from his neighbouring cabin in a few seconds.

'You read the email?'

Sebastian looked at Maithili, whom he hadn't seen or met earlier. He was hesitant in responding to Agastya's question, but the situation and circumstances left him little choice. He was trembling. Sparkle was his baby. He was the group product manager for the premium detergent range. This was a debacle!

'Agastya, I just found out about it!'

Sebastian caught a glimpse of the two photographs lying on Agastya's table, before his boss hurriedly turned them around and slid them inside a file.

'I'm trying to get all the information I can, boss, but ...'

He was hesitant to respond with specifics with another person in the room.

'But what, Sebastian?' Agastya wanted to yell, but realized he had to hold back with Maithili in the room. He looked at the watch. They had barely an hour to go for the press conference.

'Boss...'

'Please call the agency team from upstairs. Get them into the conference room on our floor. Call the media teams and ask them to hold the press ads for tomorrow.'

'Yes...'

'Please call back the press conference agenda and ask the PR team to rush back from the Oberoi to my room this very instant.'

Sebastian rushed out. Agastya could see the BlackBerry buzzing again. It was Vikram.

'Why didn't we know about this earlier, Agastya? This is ridiculous. And who marked this email to Mark? How does he have a copy of this already? He's already called me...he's coming here from the hotel. Where are you?'

The words were being volleyed with great ferocity. He could sense the tension and anger, but Agastya wasn't sure why Vikram believed that he was solely responsible for the market intelligence malfunction. Nitin was just as responsible for sourcing information from the market as he was.

Agastya stood up from his chair.

'In my room, chief. I'm just coming up.'

'No, I'm walking across to Nitin's room to get the facts. Come up with something, Agastya...we may need to call off the press conference!'

'It's too late, Vikram. The press must already be on their way. They already know Mark is in town and he's had some one-on-one interactions with a few journalists in the morning already. We can't bluff them either.'

'Just figure something out. Get us out of this mess.'
Vikram disconnected.

Agastya massaged his forehead with his fingertips. How in frigging hell had this happened?

This could be the end of his career at BCL! But how would he have known about this? Mark would have him for dinner on this one .

Agastya called up Nitin. The line was disconnected. He must be with Vikram. He wanted to leave the room and walk across to meet them when his mobile rang again.

It was his wife, Nandita.

'Nandita! Not now!'

'Who's this Maithili? She wants to meet me later today for coffee. She says it's very important.'

'Not now, Nandita.' He disconnected.

'What the hell?' He thought to himself as he stared at Maithili.

His head was now spinning, sinking back into reality only at the sight of Maithili sitting across the table.

'Sweetheart, you're looking distracted from the situation that you're in. I think you should remain focused. Don't you?'

'Maithili, cut the crap. Let's chat about this tomorrow. Ok? I will have to call in security otherwise ...'

Maithili undid a button and leaned towards Agastya. Her pink bra was now in clear view and he could see the pearls resting on her bosom as they bridged across her prominent cleavage.

'You think I'm kidding, don't you? You want this, don't you? Don't fight it. Don't resist it, sweetheart!' She laughed out loud, looking around to ensure she was audible outside the cabin.

'You need to understand something, Ags. You have more to lose than I have to gain. Think about it.'

She got up and showed the mobile screen to him. She had drafted a message for Nandita with the MMS pictures attached.

'It will take me less than a second to press the send button... and your life will be over... got that?'

The gravity of the situation was sinking in. She was serious. The intensity in her eyes was unquestionable. Any doubts that he may have had, had been demolished in the last few seconds. This was blackmail and extortion!

'Maithili, you do know what you're doing, right? And even if I were to call the bluff... how much money is it that you want now?' Agastya was buying time, as he mentally ran through his options and potential outcomes.

Maithili sighed. 'Fair point, Ags! It was a mere 15 crores that I was looking at, for today. I was expecting it, actually. So, you want proof of intent?'

Agastya didn't offer any response. He sat still, with his eyes locked in a duel with Maithili's.

'I've asked Nandita to meet me at the Oberoi at 3:30 pm today.'

'You know Nandita?'

'Of course! Through you.'

He was in a state of panic. His whole world seemed to be turning upside down.

She handed over his stock trading password, which she had scribbled on the back of a movie ticket. It was a ticket to a movie premiere that they had attended earlier last year. She had worn a pair of CK jeans and a white linen blouse. He could still remember the perfume that she had worn that day and how he had kissed her in the theatre. She had arranged for corner seats on the last row and had held onto him tightly, without a care for the world. She had kissed him several times and even unbuttoned his shirt as she placed her hands on his bare chest throughout the movie.

After the show, they had driven to a cheap hotel in the suburbs, drank cheap rum and made love. It was also then that they had argued profusely as he insisted on dropping her home, whereas she had wanted him to spend the night with him. She pulled at his hair and scratched his back with her fingernails as she tried to hold him back and pin him down against the bed. He had slapped her and thrown her naked body on the floor as he struggled to put on his clothes. She had flung the rum bottle towards him and had barely missed his left eye.

The argument had quickly blown up into a physical fight as they hurled themselves at each other. She was bleeding from her lips and he noticed blood drops on his shirt, only to realize that he had a deep gash on his forehead. It took them over forty-five minutes and two calls from the hotel's front desk to calm down, wear their clothes and reach a nursing home to get stitched up.

They hadn't met for several months after that incident, but then a chance meeting at a mutual friend's party had reignited the affair. It had barely taken a few moments of social interaction for them to fling themselves at each other, and then there had been no looking back until the recent pause. She had raised the incident on a couple of occasions, when she was inebriated, but not at too much length. It however was clear that the night did weigh down upon her and did linger on her mind, and she was drawing upon the incident to fuel her spite and vengeance. But he wasn't clear what had driven her to this stage. What had precipitated this behaviour and why would she throw everything that they had for this?

It wasn't about the money. It was never about the money for Maithili and despite her tough exterior, she remained extremely emotional. She had made a significant amount of money selling her business. She was rudderless and constantly sought an emotional anchor. Maybe she felt she was losing out on her one, not necessarily meaningful, but long-lasting relationship. The despondency and helplessness was possibly driving her to this behaviour. Her need to take control of the situation was to assuage the emotional void that she was attempting to fill.

Should he just appease her for now? Should he just put her at ease and commit to the relationship and explain how it would have to co-exist with his marriage with Nandita? Should he just tell her that he would always be there for her, and that this was just a low phase they were going through? Or should he urge her to commit to her live-in relationship with Ismail and his son?

But, he also knew that with the anger that he was currently feeling, his words would appear quite hollow and she would see right through him. She would never believe him. They knew each other too well.

Was there actually something else on her mind? Or was this just a bluff? Poker had never been one of her areas of strength, and she despised the game whenever they had played it. She seemed to be in this for real. Her eyes constantly reinforced that determination.

There was surely something else.

He was looking at a scenario where he would have to pay her within the hour, or face the consequences. There didn't seem any way of escaping that.

He logged into his trading account and clicked on the portfolio summary option. He noticed that his fingers were unsteady as they pressed the keys on the keyboard.

He saw the numbers on the screen but was unable to register or comprehend what they were saying to him. His whole life seemed to flash by him. His wedding to Nandita. The birth of their first child. The first time she had walked out of the house.

The stakes were too high. Should he just come clean to Nandita and tell her everything? What could happen? She would freak out, throw tantrums, possibly walk out with the children.

But he could always get her back. They loved each other too much. She couldn't live without him. For the kids at least. For despite the progressive exterior that she meticulously maintained, she was a traditional woman at heart. Family and the family name meant the world to her. Indiscretions weren't new in her family. Harems and mistresses had been common vocabulary in their family sagas. This shouldn't really shock her as much. But, he also knew that Nandita was a determined woman, and she could possibly have digested these indiscretions from an arranged marriage. Not one in which the marriage was outside the caste and based on love. He would have no excuse for this, and maybe her stance would also be influenced by incidents of adultery and divorce in their social settings and friends and family circle. Divorce had become a relatively acceptable phenomenon within the upper echelons of South Bombay society.

And then it finally sank in. He risked genuinely hurting her. They did share a bond, which spanned beyond the legal boundaries and necessities of marriage. They had been friends before they became lovers. They continued to be close confidantes and even respected each other's judgements and viewpoints. They also offered each other space in the relationship. They pushed each other and also comforted each other. Would this one precise and sharp blow break the bond they had? Would it really shatter everything they had built all these years? Would it break down the bridge of trust? Or was it strong enough to withstand this one storm?

So, what if he were to come clean and tell Nandita everything? Damn Maithili…damn the affair…damn the wild parties and escapades. This was just an adventurous meaningless streak in his life. It didn't have any future. It didn't mean anything. It had been but a phase of experimentation and irrational physical actions that he had indulged in. It didn't really mean anything.

His head was spinning. How would Nandita take all of this? His gut feeling said she would explode. And even if he were able to manage Nandita, her father, the colonel, would surely lynch him alive and hang him out to dry. Nandita's father, Colonel Chauhan, had been with the armed services and now ran a public relations firm. In essence he was a fixer. He got things done and was discreetly powerful within government and corporate circles. Based in New Delhi, he would visit them once a year. It had been an amicable agreement reached between father-in-law and son-in-law. The colonel had not approved of the marriage but with Agastya's blossoming career, had decided to leverage the opportunity to his best interests. Agastya would open doors for him in corporate Mumbai and the colonel would reciprocate within the government.

The colonel had always watched over him like a hawk—it would surely be a blow to his Rajput pride and ego. They hadn't been on the best of terms of late and had a fundamental disagreement on his hedonistic lifestyle, amongst other things. And then he did owe the colonel over ₹7 crores from his earlier escapades in the markets. They had agreed that it wasn't important for Nandita to be aware of the loan. If he were to cash out his position in the market, he would have been insolvent and the colonel would have ensured that he would become a pariah in corporate India as well. He had seen the colonel at work—how he could meticulously and ruthlessly take down a person once he got after them, decimating the individual at every level.

He had known that his illicit odyssey with Maithili would only further jeopardize his situation if it ever came to the colonel's notice, but then that only accentuated the thrill.

Time was against him. Maithili wasn't even giving him breathing space. She just sat there, staring at him. He had an insane urge to just get up from his chair, hold her by her hair, drag her across to the window and fling her, crashing through the glass, and see her collapse and smash on the road below, possibly falling on some passing cars on the way, that would drive over her body and ensure that only a mangled corpse would remain. And then he could get back to managing his portfolio, his wife, his children and the damn product launch by Stark!

He was used to pressure and taking decisions in extremely demanding situations. But this was different. There were different strands of his life that were now getting intertwined and interconnected. His career was going to be determined with the response to the sudden launch of Velvet by Stark.

His marriage was on the stress line with the risk of Maithili exposing his affair. His life savings and wealth were about to be decimated in the matter of under an hour. He would be back to ground zero. Over leveraged... well technically infinitely leveraged, if the denominator were in fact zero with zero liquidity! His marital, financial and professional lives had got precariously interconnected and juxtaposed. Surely... for once in his life... he would need to prioritize! The avid multi-tasker and "ultra-flexible" Agastya had his back against a wall.

This was new territory.

'Agastya. You're usually quite quick. Age catching up with you?'

'I'm just admiring your pearls, Maithili!'

'Only the pearls?' she laughed lightly.

'You've got so much more, Maithili...'

'And so do you, Agastya. At last count you had just over 11 crores liquid across your accounts. You see, you just need to make another 4 odd crores in the next hour.'

'That's very generous of you, my dear. You've just gone bloody insane!'

'But the way the market is today, and looking at your grandiose selection of stocks, I would say you're on quite a shaky wicket, unless you act fast!'

'You do know, my dear, that this is not possible? Where do you think I'm going to get another 4 crores from in the next one hour? Why do I get the feeling that you don't really want the money?'

'There's nothing more I would like than to see you burn in hell, Agastya. But, I also want to see you sweat on your way there!'

'It's not possible, M! Just move on and meet Nandita for all I care! There's got to be something feasible, and this isn't.'

'You're quite a gambling man, Agastya! Not up for this?'

'There's a time and place, M! This is neither.'

'Just like Dubai?'

Sebastian walked back in again with Michael, the advertising agency account director in tow.

'This is crazy, Agastya. What do you want to do?'

Maithili smiled at Michael as he walked in. Michael raised his eyebrows and hesitated before speaking with Agastya, finding it difficult to steer his eyes away from her cleavage. Agastya just shook his head.

'Michael. Can you please wait outside for a minute? I'll join you there.'

Michael left the room, closing the door behind him as he left.

'Maithili! You can't be in this room. It's not right.'

'You really want to discuss about "right" with me, Agastya?'

'Just wait in the room next door, ok?'

'But that would make you comfortable, Agastya. I really wouldn't want that, darling!'

'You do want your money, right?'

'I want so much more, and the funny part is I will gain less if you actually give me 15 crores. This is a strange world, Agastya! I'm not moving from here. I just want to see the pain and agony you will go through in the next hour. It's going to be worth so much more than that measly money you're going to be giving me!'

Agastya rose from his chair, walked across towards Maithili. He held her arm, raised her from the chair and then guided her to the meeting room adjacent to his office through a glass door.

He guided her to a leather sofa that had been placed near the window.

'I need to address something, M. Please wait here!' It was more of a desperate plea than a request. She was amazed at her meek submission after her lofty words and realized, to her disgust, that Agastya continued to have power over her and an aura about him that continued to hold her in its grip.

He rushed out of the room, drawing down the blinds on the glass door and closed it behind him as he walked back into his office. He stood for several seconds, taking deep breaths as he closed his eyes. He dialled Rebecca on the intercom.

'Can you please ask Michael to come in?'

Michael opened the door even as he was placing the receiver back. Michael looked around and the curious search for the missing lady from a few moments back was apparent.

'Why didn't your team know about this, Michael?'

'How would we know, Agastya…'

Agastya interjected. 'Then how did Stark get the front page ads in all the papers?'

Michael was clearly uncomfortable taking on the verbal assault.

'Come on, Agastya, we've got the front pages! My media team has confirmed this…'

Agastya was struggling to restrain himself and maintain a polite demeanour.

'You had no idea about this?'

'We didn't, Agastya…'

'Speak with your media head. Stark cannot get front page with their ads. These damn papers can't play us like we're fools. I'll take all the Stark advertisements! Everything they've booked with News Times & HT for the next three months.

Block the bastards out! I want a frigging blackout of their ads. Got that?'

'It's not that easy, Agastya ... it doesn't work that way.'

'You need to make it happen, and tell your creative team to be on standby. We may need to change the advertisement as well.'

'This is too short a notice!'

'Just do it!' It was a stern response delivered in a dramatically lowered voice.

Sebastian read a text message on his phone.

'Boss, bad news.'

'What, Sebastian?'

'The press release has already been sent to the press!'

'Damn!'

'Get them to retract it. Feed the journalists something. Anything. Get those press releases back!'

He called up Vikram. Vikram disconnected.

They needed to take some decisions and very quickly.

Should they hold back the product launch, or go ahead with it? The product would fail for sure with Stark's Velvet being priced much lower than Sparkle.

He dialled Vikram yet again but got a busy tone.

'Rebecca, please find out where Vikram is. I need to meet him ...'

Agastya browsed through his BBM contact list and selected Sailesh.

'????!!!!!'

He received a response instantly:

'☺'

'Damn!' he murmured to himself.

What was Sailesh doing?

Chapter Five

THREE YEARS EARLIER

play I will
against a hand unknown
death strikes those
unwilling to move

It had been raining heavily and the Mumbai trains were expected to grind to a debilitating halt by late evening with the downpour flooding some vital sections of the city's lifeline. Offices were being cleared early as everyone rushed towards Churchgate and CST stations to catch the suburban trains back towards North and Central Mumbai. The taxis were running full and the connecting buses to the stations were already overflowing, with passengers even clinging on to the rear windows.

The monsoons in Mumbai could be romantic, but when there were torrential downpours, the city would grind to a paralyzing halt.

Agastya had flown in earlier in the morning from Hong Kong and had been booked into a room at the Oberoi. He had gone to Hong Kong for a meeting with the regional head of Pepsi, exploring potential assignments. He hadn't been too optimistic. It had been one of those meetings created by the Pepsi HR team to delude him into thinking that they were making every effort to find him a relevant assignment, but the brief meeting that lasted for just under twelve minutes was an expected but yet disappointing eyewash.

He was now getting desperate to close an assignment either within Pepsi or outside. He had knocked all the doors he knew within Pepsi, but his equity within the organization seemed to have run out of steam with a single incident. He felt like a pariah. He was a career Pepsi man and realized that he hadn't adequately expanded his network beyond Pepsi. He had never really needed to and felt restless and uncertain in these unchartered territories of anonymity and helplessness.

His finances were stable and he could have easily sustained his lifestyle and family for a couple of years even if he were to have left Pepsi, but it wasn't in his DNA to be just lying around. He was impatient. He needed to prove a point. He just had to get on with it.

He had a chance meeting with Richard Hendricks, the Asia Head of BCL at The Peninsula hotel in Hong Kong, where he was having lunch with a colleague from Pepsi. Agastya had worked with Richard in Brazil earlier in his career. Richard had been impressed with Agastya's astute business sense and his indomitable spirit. He had plunged him into situations and posed challenges which would have urged most seasoned managers to beat a hasty retreat, but Agastya had deftly weathered a deluge of challenges and delicate situations.

Richard had been appointed as the Asia Pacific Head of BCL six months earlier and had been restructuring the operations across his region. Three country heads had already been replaced within this short span and Vikram had just returned from a heated review session in Hong Kong a fortnight earlier.

Richard seemed to have a leisurely calendar for the afternoon and spent over an hour with Agastya, and before he realized, he had been set up for a meeting with Vikram the following day.

The Asia Pacific region contributed to over 30 per cent of BCL's global turnover and was growing rapidly. With the developed economies struggling to register even 3 per cent growth rates, Asia Pacific was the focus region for the BCL top management, and Richard's appointment from Pepsi had raised several eyebrows within BCL. His work and performance in developing economies was unparalleled and so were his contacts with the government bodies in the region. BCL had been planning to expand its operations rapidly in

China, and Richard's three year stint as the Head of Pepsi's business in China made him the ideal candidate for the role.

Vikram had his eyes on China as his next assignment and seemed to have it in the bag till Richard's appointment. Richard's views on BCL's, and hence Vikram's performance in the Indian market had been vocal and uninhibited. The BCL top brass in London seemed to be more compassionate and empathetic towards Vikram and the Indian market. Afterall BCL had been in India for over a hundred years and this was one of their oldest markets. It was almost like a family heirloom.

Agastya sat beside the window and reflected on his situation and the impending conversation with Vikram. He extracted his mobile from the jacket and checked for new messages. He noticed a text message from Richard.

'Sailesh Rao shortlisted...'

Agastya bit his lower lip, an involuntary reaction he had found difficult to shake off.

Sailesh Rao was a mathematics genius with a PhD from MIT. He had wandered from the world of academics to business management because of a chance meeting with a board member of Pepsi, and had taken up an assignment with the global strategic marketing team at Pepsi in North America, before he relocated to India to be with his ailing parents.

Their paths had crossed on several occasions. Sailesh had been working on strategic marketing initiatives with the Pepsi India CEO's office, when their first confrontation occurred. The situation had soon turned ugly and Agastya was moved to another assignment to contain the matter. However their duels and spates of disagreements extended to several matters including market share estimations, communication strategies and even channel margins.

Sailesh had been focusing on reducing the operating cost structures which was at a direct conflict with the expansionary and "market share grab" ethos that was prevalent across Pepsi. The recommendations stimulated by Sailesh from the CEO's office often throttled and suffocated Agastya's initiatives. Their public spats and ferocious email exchanges had become folklore within Pepsi, but with Agastya's rapid rise and stellar performances within the sales and marketing hierarchies, Sailesh often found himself lacking sufficient support from the CEO's office in rolling out cost saving measures. With global pressure on increasing market share, Sailesh found himself waging a lonely battle in a sea of professionals who were obsessed with increasing the topline and revenue at any cost. An acrimonious and public showdown at a marketing strategy meeting had been the nadir of their hostile relationship, transcending the realms of professional courtesy and chartering into the choppy waters of personal animosity.

Sailesh had, however, ensured that a series of measures had been rolled out, initiating an audit enquiry into Agastya's department, raising questions on Agastya's utilization of his marketing budgets and had forced him to acknowledge malpractices that weren't adhering to defined policies. It had resulted in yet another token action being taken against Agastya.

The resistance to Sailesh's cost–cutting initiatives gained momentum after the showdown and he increasingly faced extreme challenges in implementing his proposals across the organization. The battle lines had been drawn and he found himself constantly waging a lonely battle against the sales and marketing juggernaut of Pepsi.

Sailesh left Pepsi within a month of the strategy meet, as Agastya rallied his forces in a series of moves to thwart all recommendations and plans proposed by him. He took up an assignment with a rapidly expanding confectionery brand, Klaysons, in Singapore, and the reason for his departure wasn't subtle enough to be ignored. He had risen quickly within Klaysons and was currently its Asia marketing head and had been slated to become the Asia CEO in Hong Kong. But with a slew of restructuring measures and a new leadership at the helm, he had remained stranded in Singapore, unable to break away from the shackles and move up the corporate hierarchy.

In his late forties, time was running short for Sailesh to hit the "big league", as he termed it. Some wrong moves and inopportune events had drastically altered his career, but industry veterans vouched for his sharp business and marketing acumen. He was like none other, but just hadn't been as politically savvy or lucky as he could have been.

Agastya realized that he was entering a vicious web at BCL. He dialled a number on his mobile.

'Hi Sameer.'

'Hi, boss! That tip on Ferlite was a killer. You're a genius. Seriously, that was a master move…'

'Thanks. How're things at Klaysons?'

'The same old bickering and politics! It doesn't change. And now with the new global CEO, there is yet another set of changes. They've already replaced a few country heads and they're expecting some heads to roll in Asia as well.'

Sameer was a group product manager at Klaysons, India. He had commenced his career with Pepsi and Agastya had been a mentor to him.

'And how are you doing?'

'I'm ok, boss! Just wish that I had stuck around at Pepsi on some days.'

'Don't look back, Sameer. You can always get back to Pepsi with your track record.'

'Thanks! I might just take you up on that one!'

'What's happening with Sailesh?'

'I've heard that he put in his papers last month!'

'What happened?'

'They shortchanged him on the Asia CEO spot once again!'

'Where's he heading?'

'Not sure. I've heard from Gillette that they've offered him the India CEO post. But it's not confirmed. Also heard that he's eyeing something bigger, but back in India.'

'How about you?'

'Think it's time I moved on. Let me know if you come across something, boss.'

'Will do, Sameer. Don't rush into anything.'

'Thanks, boss!'

He disconnected and crossed his fingers.

He searched for a name on his mobile. He had been meticulous in maintaining his contact details over the years and had amassed over four-thousand contacts ranging from office colleagues, vendors, acquaintances—each and every person he had met, and in some cases even just quickly exchanged business cards with.

Each name had been indexed and marked with the name of the company, city and a quick reference word including the context of the meeting. It had been a foolproof system for a professional who had worked across three continents in four countries.

He finally found the name he was looking for and now hoped that the number was still valid.

He hadn't spoken with her for over four years now.

He could hear the mobile ringing and soon enough a voice broke the monotony of the inane ringtone.

'Hello?' Her voice was as appealing as ever.

'Hi…long time, Vaidehi.'

There was a long silence on the other end. The struggle was apparent, and possibly even deliberate.

'Hi, Agastya…'

'How're you doing, Vaidehi?'

'Let's just say I've stopped waiting for the phone to ring,' she laughed.

'How's Aditya doing?'

'He's alright. Becoming quite a brat! And your children?'

'Doing well, thanks.'

'You should meet Aditya if you have some time to spare.'

'I will. I promise.'

'That's been a promise for quite some time, Agastya. Not that you have any obligations of course!'

'It's not like that, Vaidehi. You were the one who made some choices and decisions. It wasn't me, remember?'

'I can see some things don't change. We still fight like it was yesterday!' Agastya could sense Vaidehi smiling on the other end of the line.

'If anything, that was one thing we were good at…'

'I was emotionally vulnerable then, Agastya. I'm not like that anymore. But…'

'Free for coffee?'

She held back. The hurt was there. He had hesitated making the call, but he knew that she could help him in this situation, if anyone could.

Vaidehi was the country director for Lewis & Stokes, a boutique placement firm specializing in CXO roles. Her firm managed several blue chip clients in India including Gillette.

They met over coffee at a restaurant near her office.

'You're working on the CEO position at Gillette.' It wasn't a question.

'Yes, why? You want to take a shot at it? It's quite late in the day...'

He smiled. 'No, I just need you to push the case for a friend of mine. You need to keep the conversation discreet though.'

'What's on your mind?'

Boutique placement firms had the opportunity of working on a select few assignments in a year and the fruits of their labour were monetarily gargantuan. The stakes were high, and candidates needed to be often cajoled and persuaded.

'I hear that Sailesh is in contention?'

'You should know better, Agastya. I can't discuss this with anyone. Especially about your good friends,' she laughed.

'But why is he evaluating the Gillette role in the first place? I was under the impression he had the Klaysons Asia CEO spot in the bag.'

Vaidehi shook her head. She had always been repulsed by his obstinacy but also knew how easily she had always given in to him.

'Maybe it's not happening...'

Agastya shot back, 'Why?'

'Some internal politics...'

'Of course, I understand, but I'm sure that you would like to close the position soon enough. You're not going to get anyone else to sit at the table as long as Sailesh Rao is in the race...'

Vaidehi smiled. 'What are you up to, Agastya?'

'Why don't you just drop the games and fast track the Gillette offer to Sailesh, because as I hear, he is playing you on this one.'

'I'm not referring to Sailesh, but it's not unusual for candidates to evaluate their decisions carefully, and they must. We don't believe in rushing. After all, we also need to make sure that they remain in the assignment for at least a year after they take it up.'

The high-end placement consultants had a contractual obligation of refunding their fees if the candidates placed by them exited within pre–agreed stipulated time frames.

'Of course. I understand. But sometimes it's about nudging the candidates into making the right decision. You know, just in case they are distracted.'

'And who is distracting Sailesh? Or rather, what is?'

'Let's just say that Sailesh has always had a fetish for soaps and detergents.'

'BCL?'

'Let's just say that they will be moving fast.'

'And, how would you know this? And what's in it for you?'

'Why don't we focus on you for today?'

Vaidehi laughed. 'You're a scheming bastard. You know that, right?'

'Yes, but I never figured you to be a quitter either.'

'What are you trying to say, Agastya?'

'I would give him till end of day to make up his mind for the said assignment, or tell him that the offer is off the table.'

'As simple as that?'

'You may also happen to mention BCL in the conversation?'

'What about BCL?'

'That as per your sources there is an offer on the table for another candidate?'

'He has his sources as well. It will take him very little time to figure that one out.'

'Just tell him that Richard Hendricks has handpicked this person.'

'The Asia Pacific CEO!'

'Yes.'

'And is that a fact or mere conjecture?'

'It would be the former if you were to guide him towards Gillette.'

'I might just lose him. He's quite a cool customer.'

'You do play poker, Vaidehi. Don't you?'

'Not as well as you.'

'You're not playing blind on this one.'

Vaidehi sipped her coffee and looked into Agastya's eyes.

'You're going for it, aren't you?'

'That's not of consequence.'

'What plans in Mumbai, Agastya? How long will you be here?'

'I am meeting Vikram for a drink later today.'

Vaidehi smiled.

They sipped their coffee as they both checked their emails.

'Agastya …'

'Yes?'

'Do you ever think what if … ?'

Agastya nodded. 'Yes.'

****

Agastya had expected his meeting with Vikram to be held at the Oberoi, but was surprised when he was invited for a drink at The Chambers at the Taj Mahal Hotel. A Mercedes picked him up at 5:45 pm sharp and he found himself at the lobby by 6:00. He was received by a member of the lobby staff and discreetly but swiftly escorted to the lift by the courteous manager who appeared to be in his late thirties. An attendant in the lift area, quickly escorted him to a private meeting room.

It was a stunning view with the Gateway of India, the fishing trawlers bouncing on the restless waves and the monsoons lashing away at the large French windows. He picked up a copy of the Forbes magazine and noticed that Vikram was on the cover. He was a part of a panel discussion on "Innovation in India" and was immaculately dressed in a sharp black suit and his customary red tie.

'Agastya?'

He turned his head around and noticed the large and imposing, six-foot-three-inch frame of Vikram Rajyavanshi. Agastya noticed a red tie around his collar and smiled. The thick moustache, deep voice and looming gait would make him stand out in a crowd. Agastya got up to wish him.

'Vikram, a pleasure to meet you.' He extended his hand and received a firm handshake.

'Likewise, Agastya. Please have a seat.'

Agastya waited for Vikram to seat himself on the sofa beside his before he sat down. They were now both facing the window. Vikram looked distracted and there was a pause for a few moments before the conversation recommenced.

'Hope I didn't keep you waiting too long?'

'I just came in a few minutes ago. Thanks.'

'I trust they gave you a decent suite at the Oberoi?'

'Oh yes, Vikram, absolutely, thanks for asking.'

'What would you like to have?'

The distinct formality in the manner of the conversation intrigued Agastya. The butler seemed to have sensed their readiness to order and appeared almost instantaneously behind them.

Vikram looked up towards the butler.

'Albert, my usual please.'

The butler nodded and looked towards Agastya, who was wondering if it was possible that his prospective boss was heading in the direction of becoming an alcoholic.

Agastya smiled. 'What would you recommend, Albert?'

The butler got the drift and politely responded.

'Sir would be having Chivas.'

Agastya was relieved and nodded.

There was a pause for over a minute once again, as Vikram checked the emails on his mobile and then finally placed it back in his jacket.

'You know Hendricks well?'

Vikram had avoided the otherwise mandatory preamble of pleasantries and decided to head directly into a conversation about his current boss, Richard Hendricks.

'I worked with Richard in Brazil.'

Agastya didn't want to delve too deep into his relationship with Richard Hendricks at this early stage of the first meeting.

'How long did you work with Richard?'

Agastya sensed hostility in this initial interaction. He felt that it may have been something that Vikram was carrying forward from office and decided to give him some latitude, but he also understood that Vikram wouldn't really appreciate being asked to meet a potentially "pre-selected" candidate by his boss.

'I was on a special assignment. It was more of a strategic advisory role for Richard in Brazil. We were restructuring the Brazilian operations. It was quite a complex process.'

Vikram nodded but had clearly drifted on to some other thoughts.

'I've read your profile...'

Agastya had an impeccable record but had had a rocky patch over the previous ten months. His life seemed to be going into a tailspin within Pepsi.

Agastya was hoping that Vikram would follow that up with another question or observation, but there were several moments of restless silence. Had he already made up his mind?

Vikram sipped the single malt and fidgeted with his BlackBerry again.

Agastya didn't like the initial few minutes with Vikram, and got the impression that Vikram had been pushed into having this meeting with him. Agastya tried to divert the conversation with aspects of family and children, but it didn't seem to thaw Vikram.

'Are you exploring other options within Pepsi?'

It was common knowledge that Agastya had had an altercation with the CEO of Pepsi's India operations, and had hit troubled waters. With the exit of Richard and some other sponsors from Pepsi, he had been finding it difficult to find a suitable role within the company.

Vikram was now going for the straight punches. Richard had indicated to Agastya that he could possibly be a top contender for the CEO slot, if he were able to turn around the business, but that was an implicit understanding, and a conversation that Vikram was oblivious of.

'I am.'

He didn't want to lean too heavily on Richard. It was vital that he build his own bridges and credibility with Vikram, and he had clearly started off on the wrong note.

'What's your view of our business in India?'

'You've got a strong bouquet of brands and your distribution infrastructure is undeniably spot on. I would imagine there is some opportunity in expanding into the premium segments and gaining some share there.'

Agastya realized that it was a simplistic response but he had been working on building up a comprehensive set of views that he had prepared for the meeting. Richard had shared some relevant details of the Indian operations, but Agastya decided to hold back for a little while longer.

Vikram continued to be distracted.

'You must excuse me. Can you give me a moment? There is a call I need to attend to.'

Vikram rose quickly and stepped into a meeting room on the right.

Agastya sipped his drink and took a few deep breaths.

Vikram walked back in a few minutes, but this time sat on the sofa opposite Agastya and facing him.

Agastya decided to up the ante and turn the tables around.

'Vikram … I'm sure that there's lots of talent within BCL. Any particular reason for looking outside?'

Agastya had heard of Sebastian, a group product manager, who had been groomed as the top contender for the role. However, a gaffe on a recent advertising campaign required him to be rapped on the knuckles and put into the freezer for a while. Sebastian was also reputed to be Vikram's eyes and ears within BCL. Vikram was clear that he required a resolute chief marketing officer at BCL, an individual who could steer a new path, outside his shadow. The appointment of a *pet* could have created ripples within his senior management team. He also realized that BCL needed a fresh perspective to reinvigorate the business.

Sebastian wasn't a babe in the woods either. He was an IIM grad and had been with BCL for a considerable and fruitful time. But there was that distance to be traversed on several dimensions, which hindered his climb to the senior management spot. Vikram couldn't convince Richard to overlook the advertising gaffe and both Mark and Richard seemed to be on the fence on Sebastian's candidature. He had been hoping to present a few duds from other companies and kill time, till they finally gave in to allow Sebastian's appointment. But he was in for a rude shock when he was referred Sailesh Rao's profile by Mark.

Sailesh and Mark had attended a leadership programme at Harvard and had remained in touch. Mark had often reached out to Sailesh to seek his views on market situations and strategies and trusted his judgement and gut.

'We are still looking within.' Vikram didn't seem to like Agastya's tone that appeared to mock him.

Vikram continued.

'Agastya...may I be frank?'

'Yes. Please...'

Agastya knelt over and placed his elbows on his knees and clasped his hands together.

'You've got an impeccable track record, Agastya, and we've got some major work lined up here in the next twenty-four months. But you're not from this industry. Beverages is a very different market from soaps and detergents. It's very different out here, but you would know that. This is an extremely critical position and quite honestly the fate of the company rests on how this role delivers. Our manufacturing is world class, our sales and distribution network is top notch.

We've got some of the best talent in the country working for us. Where we really need the firepower and some sure shot hitters is in marketing. That's been the missing link in the puzzle.'

'What's the story with your current marketing head?' Agastya knew the finer details but was curious to hear Vikram's perspective.

'He's taking up an assignment in Africa next month. It's been in the offing for a while. We had finalized a candidate six months earlier from within BCL, but things haven't turned out as we had hoped for. Mark and I have been discussing this at length. You know Mark, right?'

'Yes. The global marketing head.' Agastya nodded.

Vikram seemed to be under tremendous pressure from both Mark and Richard, which seemed quite unusual for a country head. Or it was possibly the fact that Vikram just wanted to play everything right for the assignment in China, and didn't want to upset either of them.

It was quite likely that Mark was pressurizing Vikram, by suggesting Sailesh's profile. Agastya was perplexed. He didn't figure Sailesh would settle for the CMO role at BCL, India. Though the BCL India business was much larger than that managed by him currently, Sailesh was quite established in Klaysons and could have made it to the Global Management Board, if the situation had worked out for him.

And then it struck him. Sailesh was eyeing the India CEO spot. This was getting trickier. It was also unlikely that Sailesh would be patient to wait it out for two to three years before he got the CEO spot. There was something brewing. Perhaps Vikram's assignment in China was to commence earlier than he imagined? Richard had reiterated to Agastya that it would be a two year wait at the minimum.

'Yes, I can understand where you are coming from, and I do understand how vital this role is. I have worked in some extremely challenging markets and business environments and I can say this for certain that it's going to need the entire senior management team at BCL to work on this together.'

Vikram sensed the deflection and smiled.

'You've got a penchant for high stakes?'

Agastya's fascination and indulgence in the equity and commodity markets seemed to precede him to the meeting. His performance had been exemplary and, in most of his assignments, he had managed to ensure that his immediate managers also gained from his financial acumen.

'It's important for all of us to have a passion outside work. The markets are an ideal place to hone one's skills in managing volatile and uncertain situations. I believe it's one of the world's greatest enigmas.'

'Enigma? With all the insider trading and scams going around, is it really all that enigmatic, or is it just a bunch of manipulated transactions?'

Agastya was tempted to take Vikram up on this debate, but was worried that it may just distract them from the purpose of the meeting.

'There are different points of view, but I'm just a student of the markets, Vikram.'

Vikram paused and looked towards him.

'Where's the market headed currently?'

Agastya wondered if he should refrain, but knew that the trap had been set up.

'I'm sure your bankers would be more attuned to your investment goals ...'

Agastya took another sip and realized that he had finished his drink.

'Another one?'

'Yes please...'

The conversation then meandered to exchanging notes on leadership styles, the global currency markets and Agastya's family.

Vikram looked at his watch.

Agastya figured that the meeting was drawing to a close. He had been scoping out Vikram and trying to understand him better. It had become quite clear that he was quite insecure and even threatened, and Agastya's nomination from Richard seemed to exacerbate the situation. He needed to appease him and gain his confidence.

'Vikram, I can sense the criticality of the position. Just in case this position was not to materialize for me, I could suggest some other people to you as well...'

This was quite unusual, and Vikram didn't hesitate in displaying his surprise and smiled.

'That's rather valiant of you.'

Agastya was offended with the term, but proceeded nonetheless.

'I believe in relationships. We can't allow jobs to rule our lives.'

Vikram laughed; Agastya seemed to have lightened the mood.

'And who would you suggest I should be having a chat with?'

Agastya sipped his drink. He was now playing Vikram, and was taking his time.

'Have you considered Anand Rathi from Prime?'

Vikram shook his head and leaned over. 'He can't seem to keep away from the bottle.'

Agastya was familiar with Anand's binges, which had become folklore in corporate circles. He paused for a few seconds and then slipped it in.

'How about Sailesh Rao?'

Vikram blinked and remained motionless for several seconds.

'How would you view Sailesh?'

Agastya paused for a few seconds and responded, 'One of the best there is out there. I'm sure you would have met him at some time.'

Vikram nodded and played along.

Agastya continued. 'He's a brilliant mathematician, strategist and a suave leader...though it's just a matter of time...'

'What is?'

'Haven't you heard?'

'What's that?'

'It's rumoured that Gillette has rolled out a final offer to him for the India CEO position. I haven't been in touch with him, but that's what I hear.'

Vikram raised his eyebrows.

Agastya paused and then spoke in a hushed tone. 'He's getting a major package as well.'

'I see...'

Agastya laughed. 'Sailesh can be rather cautious, which is good, but sometimes you have to take that leap of faith. I hear he's got over three offer letters from other companies that he's picked up over the last fifteen months. Klaysons keeps sweetening his deal for him to stay back each time. That's one more thing about Sailesh…he doesn't do too well with change. He likes to be in a familiar environment.'

'You know Sailesh from his days at Pepsi?'

Agastya realized that Vikram would have done his research and picked up on some market reconnaissance as well.

'Yes…' Agastya intentionally kept it brief.

Vikram looked at his watch again and opened an email that he had just received.

Agastya decided to check his mobile and opened a message from Vaidehi.

'Sailesh has taken the bait.'

'Thanks so much for coming over to Mumbai to meet me. We could have done this on a video conference, but it's just not the same as meeting in person.'

'I know. I couldn't agree more with you, Vikram.'

They both looked and felt as unsettled and restless as when they had first met.

Vikram gave Agastya a firm handshake.

'We'll be in touch. I have another meeting here. Trust you've got a car.'

'Thanks, Vikram. That's been taken care of.'

Vikram read a message on his mobile.

They both nodded and as Agastya was about to enter the lift, Vikram approached him.

'Agastya. Why don't you stay back tomorrow? I would like you to meet our head of HR.'

Chapter Six

2:40 PM
TODAY

one up, one down
tested are the brave
a chequered playground
springs shades of grey

Sailesh Rao's Office, Stark, Mumbai

Sailesh was standing beside the window overlooking the Bandra Kurla Complex. The surroundings had always fascinated him with the expansive skyscrapers in the backdrop of rotting slums. He read the message once again and opened the attachment. He had already seen it over a hundred times, but each time he opened it, a different set of emotions was triggered. Myriad emotions engulfed him—anger, betrayal, hatred, sympathy. He couldn't figure out where it had all gone wrong.

He had just come out of a crucial meeting, in which the CEO had grilled him exhaustively on the proposed plan. They had been at loggerheads for several weeks, in spite of the CEO having given his nod for the plan before he started on the project.

The illogical nature of the corporate world was far removed from the order of academia and research. He often wondered how it would have turned out if he had continued in research and teaching. He had been proud of his modest childhood in Hubli and his struggles as he scratched his way up with scholarships and grants from family members, all the way to MIT. He could have possibly become a management guru or even a senior leadership consultant, roaming the globe while constantly stimulating his intellect. He was now beginning to feel stagnated, fatigued with the wanderings of the corporate maze.

The fetish for emails amused him, the illogical allocation of resources on the basis of persona over economic opportunities fascinated him. He was disgusted with the obsession with designations, but had seen himself slowly sinking into the same quagmire that he resented. It seemed to have extended its clutches to all aspects of his life.

His assistant walked into his sprawling room, decorated with imposing wooden furniture that he loathed but had been too lazy to renovate.

'Sailesh. Not feeling well? Can I get you something?'

He turned around and noticed a look of genuine concern on her face. *'A rare emotion to encounter these days,'* he thought.

'No, Radhika, I'm fine but thanks for asking.' She smiled and turned around to close the door behind her as she left, but stopped halfway and walked back in.

Radhika had been his life support for several months now, balancing his work load and even covering for him as his personal life fell into shambles, all the while maintaining discretion and a professional distance.

'I forgot. This came in for you earlier today. Was hand delivered at the reception.'

It was an A4-sized brown envelope which had been stapled on its side. It had his name scribbled on the cover.

'Thanks... Who is it from?'

'It's not marked, sir, and even the guard at the reception couldn't tell me much.'

He waited for her to leave his room, carefully removed the staple pins from the envelope and opened the flap. There was a slim white folder with four pages. Numbers, tables, dates, names—all packed into those pages.

He browsed through the contents. He was familiar with some of the details, but the new revelations astounded him. He was not one to display emotion and least of all show surprise, even in private. The last six months had impacted him even more, making him a quieter and more reflective person. He had become wary of people and their motives. He had distanced himself from most of his family and friends, receeding into his cocoon—one which he had pulled himself out of several years earlier. Back in its confines now, he felt it was a place which protected him.

He was also wearing two hats. The first was of a shrewd marketing strategist, creating magic with almost everything that he touched but the second was that of a reclusive alcoholic, experimenting with substances and experiences that had been beyond his vocabulary till a few months earlier. It had been a quest to figure out what had gone wrong, how it had gone wrong, what mistakes he may have made and a journey in his attempt at understanding others.

The Machiavellian iconoclast had been beaten down to the ground, and he was struggling to pick up the pieces. He hadn't had a good night's sleep for several months, and the situations had just worsened over the last one week.

He attached the scanned documents and marked the email to ajay.anand@newstimes.com.

He pressed the "send" button and noticed beads of sweat dripping from his eyebrows on the table. His back was soaking with perspiration. He searched for the blood pressure tablets in his table drawer, popped in two, and gulped them down with a glass of water.

BCL Office, Mumbai

The advertising agency director walked back into Agastya's room.

'News Time is not willing to let go of the Stark front page advertising spots, Agastya. They're one of their biggest clients. They wouldn't risk it.'

'But those were our front page slots. And we are no small fry as far as they are concerned either!' Agastya barked, thumping the table.

'I know... but you know how slippery these guys are.'

Sebastian stormed into the room with a bunch of folders tucked under his arms.

'Sebastian, run some permutations with the pricing analyst. I need to know how much it would cost us to run a promotional 20 per cent off for the next three months on Sparkle.'

'In which cities, sir?'

'Across India, Sebastian.'

'But, would we have the profit margins to sustain that kind of a discount?'

Sebastian was right. Sparkle was yielding BCL a gross profit margin of about 35 per cent which was much lower than their other products. They had planned to invest heavily in promotion and marketing as well, which would have meant that the product line would possibly make money only from the third or fourth year till it picked up and sustained a significant market share. It was going to be a bleeder, but BCL needed this to get back into the game or they'd miss out on the upper end of the market.

'Speak with the finance team and get the latest cost sheets as well. I need to see them as soon as possible. They were working on some cost reductions on the packaging. Need to see if those have kicked in.'

'They haven't been implemented yet. It's not going to happen for another three months at least.'

'How is Stark doing it at this price point? It just doesn't make any sense. Plus they are importing the damn thing. They would be bleeding on every single packet they sell!'

Nitin Chandra walked in. 'It's going to be a bloodbath, Agastya. There's no doubt about it. You've just given birth to a stillborn. You need to do something quickly.'

'Where have you been?'

'Was with Vikram. He has gone back to his room. Mark is coming over from the hotel.'

'Who told you about this, Nitin?'

'I've been hearing rumours about this for quite some time, but you know how these things are ... they just come ...'

'I need to run, Agastya. I need to have a debriefing with my team; they're out there in the market. I'm really in a tight spot here. You'll need to tell us what to do with the 50 crores of stock I've already billed and pumped into the market!'

BCL followed a classical FMCG distribution model, with stocks being dispatched from their manufacturing locations to Carrying & Forwarding Agents (C&F Agents) which were storage facilities located in each of the states. The BCL sales teams would collect orders from the distributors and the C&F agents would dispatch the goods to the distributors on basis of the orders. The distributors would in turn sell the stock to the retailers. The sales teams were responsible for managing the distributors, ensuring that sufficient stocks were ordered by the retailers. They also supervised the display of the product and monitored the sales from the retailers to the end consumers.

The distributors and retailers earned commissions on the goods sold by them, and it was common practice to roll out additional incentives and contests over and above the specified commissions to increase sales and counter competition and increase share of sales.

The sales teams held a wealth of market reconnaissance and information on competition, their promotional offers and stock movements.

BCL had wanted to ensure that Sparkle was available across India in good quantities, to ensure that the demand would be met when the advertising and promotional blitzkrieg was launched. Over 50 lakh packets of Sparkle had been dispatched across the country.

Agastya nodded. Nitin must have been relishing this.

He needed to work closely with Nitin. They needed to help each other, but Agastya knew that Nitin would take advantage of this situation.

'Nitin, I need to discuss some options with you …'

'We could carry a promotional offer for customers …'

'How much?'

'Match whatever they are offering on Velvet!'

'But, how would you execute it?'

Agastya hadn't thought it through, but needed to come up with something. He looked at Sebastian, who seemed too petrified to even utter a word in this crossfire. Sebastian had just purchased a house in Bandra and was wondering about his next month's EMI on the mortgage payment with the current state of affairs.

There was no time to lose. Ideas raced in Agastya's head.

'We could offer a coupon in tomorrow's edition for the next several days. In the meanwhile we could have stickers on the stocks in the market.'

'And do you know the nightmare that would ensue in picking up the vouchers, the reconciliation issues, the abuse that happens? Do you know how much effort goes into putting stickers on stocks on retail shelves? You think it's all that simple, don't you? We sales guys are just here to cover up for marketing goof-ups. Seriously!'

Nitin didn't even consider the fact that Sebastian and the agency director were in the room and went on with his unforgiving assault. He wasn't about to let go of this opportunity and was pulling out all stops, but what surprised Agastya was his own silence.

Nitin strode out of the room in a huff.

'Sir, he's just stressed out,' Sebastian piped up after a few seconds.

Agastya glanced at a text message from Vikram.

'Why didn't you know about this earlier?'

Maithili emerged from her corner as Sebastian left the room.

'Did you miss me in Goa?'

Agastya pushed his chair behind, without letting his eyes off the screen. He quickly shifted to thinking about his situation with Maithili. His head was instantly working on several permutations and combinations in handling the matter. He needed to make some big bets and quickly. He was considering selling all his stocks and then assessing the opportunities. At least then he wouldn't have to worry about the sliding market or his rapidly depleting equity portfolio value. The current value of his portfolio was already lower than the amount which Maithili was demanding, but at least then he would have time and the mental calm needed to think the situation through. It always made sense to have funds in hand. A shortfall could be recouped or covered by a last minute quick trade or maneuver, with some inside information. There was still some time to make those moves.

Should he sell the whole lot, lock, stock and barrel, and create some leverage for a larger move when the opportunity arose? What recourse did he have really? Protecting his capital was possibly a smarter move to make, but his instincts were drawing him to making some large bets.

He needed to get into the zone to think, where he couldn't be touched, couldn't be disturbed or distracted. He took three deep breaths, closed his eyes and immediately felt much calmer. It was clear; he would just sell the whole damn stuff and then take a call. It was final.

He called up his broker.

'Mukund bhai! I'm going to be in meetings. I'll be sending you some trades from my messenger.'

'Haan, Agastya bhai! All ok?'

'You will also need to transfer the funds today itself.'

'But why? All ok?'

'Yes. I'll send you the account number.'

'Which bank?'

'Our bank. That won't change and you'll have to send the money by 3:30.'

'Are you serious? This is very unusual.'

'I know, but we've known each other too long. I trust you can do that?'

There was a pause.

'Yes, Agastya bhai. I understand.'

'So please arrange for the funds in the meanwhile.'

He opened his eyes, took one more look at the screen before the mobile rang again. It was Nitin.

He looked towards Maithili, who smiled and closed the door before she retreated into the conference room.

He connected the call, balancing the mobile between his chin and shoulder.

'Hi, Nitin …'

'Agastya, come over to my office,' Nitin disconnected.

Agastya tossed his mobile to the side. He didn't have time for this nonsense. Nitin would consume his brain on one of his several innovative strategies and break through approaches to every situation known to mankind. He needed to get himself out of this situation.

The screen refreshed and the current prices appeared. The Sensex continued to slide. He began making mental notes of the stocks to be sold and the quantities. He believed in maintaining a compact portfolio and that it was the leaner and smarter approach to follow when holding stocks for a longer term. He couldn't believe that he was actually going ahead with this. Within a few moments it would all vanish. All his babies would be liquidated. He hated her. He despised her. He loathed her.

Rebecca walked in with the coffee, her eyes moving around the room, searching for Maithili.

'She's in the conference room,' Agastya said agitatedly .

'The boss is looking for you,' she whispered as she set down his mug of coffee.

'Ok.'

Agastya knew he needed to come up with something, and quickly. It had to be genuine and credible, without causing too much suspicion. He also needed to ensure his privacy.

Rebecca left the room.

'Damn!' he yelped in anger, as he dropped the scalding coffee on the table and his trousers. Unfortunately, his keyboard also bore the brunt of the accident.

Maithili rushed across from the conference room towards him, wrapping his hand with her handkerchief.

'Does it hurt?' she enquired. The concern in her eyes seemed to be genuine, and for a moment he felt that she still cared for him. Maybe she wouldn't go through with this audacious plan after all? They looked into each other's eyes and remained silent for a few seconds. It seemed like an eternity, in contrast to the rush of the last several minutes.

She let go of his hand and walked back towards her chair and stood beside it. There seemed to be a moment of hesitation or doubt, possibly even concern. The intensity of the moment and their feelings were apparent to both, but they both resisted the natural temptation of expression. The struggle was clear.

'I still care for you, Maithili. You do know that, right?'

She smiled and sat down on the chair opposite him, and continued looking into his eyes. She felt vulnerable and desperately wanted to regain her composure and not lose sight of her purpose for being there. It was becoming a struggle for her to remain objective and shear her emotions from the moment. It struck her that he possibly did genuinely care for her, but she couldn't let go of the pain or the suffering he had caused her.

'I don't think I doubted it, Agastya.'

Agastya realized that he possibly had a brief window of opportunity. He needed to calm down, suppress his rage and reach out to her. He also knew that he had to be genuine, else she would see through the charade. He took a deep breath and slowly walked towards her. He tried not to lose eye contact, but his anxiety drew his eyes towards the laptop screen and the iPad that were flashing updates and stock prices. In a flash of a second he noticed that there was some turbulence in the markets again and some of his stocks seemed to have stopped in their slide. They seemed to be holding steady or was he reading too much into it? He quickly turned his eyes back towards hers and was relieved that her gaze was still fixed on him; his momentary distraction hadn't affected her. He wasn't able to make a trade. He didn't have the pulse for the market, and his gut told him to stay away. It was too turbulent out there and he wasn't getting any tips or insights from the players.

'Please leave this room, M!'

She remained seated for several moments, testing his patience and hoping to incite a response. He ignored her, staring at his laptop screen, till she withdrew back into the conference room.

He called up his broker again.

'Mukund bhai … what's happening?'

Mukund bhai alias Mukund Patel, was an Oxford–educated, third generation broker. He had had stints with Morgan Stanley and Lehman Brothers, before returning to India and managing the family broking business, but in a quaint manner, had stuck onto the traditional format of addressing everyone with the appendage of "bhai" against their names.

'Nothing's certain. As usual, the bears are moving in, but I can't make too much of it. Very low volumes with the FIIs. There seems to be some action on the home front!'

The home front referred to the BCL stock. Agastya had been tempted on several occasions to have a feel of the stock and play it, but his company guidelines prohibited any form of trading in the BCL script.

'Anything hot?'

Agastya could hear the furious commotion in the background in Mukund's office.

'I wouldn't do anything hasty. It could turn anytime. It's very fickle there today. I would stay away.'

'Some action?'

'Let me get back to you?'

'Sure, Mukund, but make it fast!'

He was restless and finding it difficult to focus and think clearly. He walked across to her room and noticed her sitting on the sofa. There was an eerie calm about her that disturbed him. He wanted to hold her hand and give her a hug but wondered if he should. He considered taking the risk. After all, a little indiscretion was worth the risk when weighed against his life savings and his marriage. As he neared her, he held out his hand towards her and waited for her to reciprocate. He was encouraged to see her eyes moisten.

Was he getting through to her? She seemed to hesitate and then she raised her hand and opened out her palm. Her long fingers met his and he clasped her hand but realized that she was holding back.

'Why today, Maithili? What happened?'

'You need to introspect on that one, Agastya!'

'Then allow me some time for introspection?'

'Nice try but you will have to try harder than that!'

'I know we haven't been able to spend too much time, but I will make it up, Nandita!'

Maithili smiled before he could correct himself.

'I think you wanted to say Maithili? But then, you've just answered my question, haven't you? I'm just not on your radar, darling.'

'It's not like that, M. You know that!'

'You didn't wish me on my birthday!'

'Is that what this is about?'

She shook her head.

'Agastya, my dear. Let me make this easier for you.'

'What do you mean?'

'Just tell me when my birthday is. I'll let this pass. No money. No pestering calls. Nothing. I'll just walk out of here, right now. You have my word on that one!'

Agastya smiled.

'As easy as that?'

'Yes, my dear. As easy as that!'

His mobile rang, disrupting the moment. *'Damn!'* he thought to himself.

'Yes, Sebastian?'

'Boss. There are some rumours going around about Vikram being fired!'

'Just ignore it! This stuff always comes up when we have a crisis.'

'It doesn't sound like that though.'

He hung up on Sebastian.

'So, where were we, my dear?'

'You were asking me to state your birthday, and this entire thing would disappear!'

She nodded.

Agastya smiled. 'What's the catch?'

'How could there be any catch in such a simple question?'

Agastya smirked and shook his head. He was about to tell her what he thought of her puerile games when it struck him. He didn't remember her birthday. Try as he might he could just not recall it.

He thumped the door with his clenched fist.

She smiled.

Chapter Seven

ONE YEAR EARLIER

scars of touch sowed seeds...
now I relish torture and
moments of passionate insanity

Maithili sipped the scotch. She stared at the glass, held herself back and took a large swig. She placed the glass on the wooden floor panel, pulled off her blouse and flung it on the floor. The guitar rested gently against her naked body as she placed her fingers on the strings above the sound hole and then gently slid them towards the saddle. The smell of the guitar evoked several memories; of the band, her friends and her compositions that had faded away with time. She could still feel the beats of the percussionist and the cheers from the audience. The whiff of marijuana, rum and heavy smoke, the applause of the audience, the pulsating stage floor with the reverberations from the Marshall sound system—memories floated across her mind. She smiled briefly as she recollected brandishing a tattoo on her lower back and the beating that she had received at home when her father saw the skull for the first time.

The fingers of her left hand pressed the strings, feeling the frets on the fingerboard and slid towards the neck of the instrument. She tapped her feet gently as she tuned the guitar and was pleasantly surprised that she hadn't lost the knack for it. She could feel the guitar settling into its zone as the strings tuned into synchronous harmony. The chords were coming back to her as she gently moved the pick across the strings with her right hand. The notes were finding their way back, tearing through the ravines of her memories… and then it all suddenly burst out.

Music exploded from the guitar and her feet progressed from gentle tapping to rhythmic stomps in her dark tan leather shoes. The pick in her hand was moving rapidly, up and down, as her thumb slid smoothly on the rear of the fingerboard. Her eyes were now closed as her face assumed a meditative poise quite in contrast to the rapid movement of her hands and feet. The notes consumed her and she embraced the feeling of being overpowered by them. She was now deftly and effortlessly gliding between chords, and as she struck the first crescendo in the composition, her head began to swing wildly and the guitar was raised towards the ceiling. The strings were soon being dealt severe blows as the composition reached the third portion.

She was perspiring heavily, biting her lower lip, eyes clenched tightly together. Her wrists and fingers were in pain and yet she persisted on increasing the pace of the music as she entered the fourth segment of the composition. She could feel the gentle bruises on the fingertips of her left hand brutally evolving into cuts as the strings pressed deeper through her skin. Not that she cared; the writhing pain had been overcome by the joy of having found the rhythm and rediscovering her groove.

Her head was now swinging wildly again and the beads of perspiration were now dropping on the wooden floor planks and on the guitar. It almost seemed like she wasn't conscious anymore of the wild and inexplicable expressions that were transforming her otherwise stoic poise. The final chord was struck with one wild swing of her right hand as the tears flowed down her cheeks. She was overcome by emotions and a muted joy.

She felt the cuts on her fingers and smiled. She then raised her head and looked towards him. Agastya had sat in the same position throughout her rendition of the Bert Weedon number. There had been no emotions expressed, no movement to indicate that he was enjoying the music. He seemed almost frozen in awe of her.

The fatigue was evident on her face and she was breathing deeply to gain composure and slow down her heartbeat.

She forced a smile.

He placed his glass on the floor and moved towards her. Her hands continued to hold onto the guitar. She didn't want to let go, afraid that the loss of touch would dissipate the magic of the moment. He knelt down and pushed her sweat-drenched hair back, revealing her soaked and distinctly splendid forehead. He tilted his head and kissed her gently on her lips. Her breathing was still heavy. She kissed him back and clasped him in her arms, in an awkward tight embrace. She tilted her head back, and he tightened his grip even further as they kissed each other passionately.

He pulled himself back, snatched the guitar from the tight grip of her hands and flung it on the rug. He then pulled her up from the chair and clasped her tightly around her waist, while steadily looking into her eyes. She pushed him away and unbuttoned his shirt. They were both perspiring heavily. He kissed her on her neck and as she pulled off his shirt, he thrust himself on her till they both collapsed on the floor. She ripped his clothes apart in a fit of passionate rage and clutched him fiercely as their sweating bodies slid against each other. She pulled his hair as he bit her repeatedly across her body, pushed her to the ground, and made love on the hard wooden floor, causing mild bruises on her back. She countered him with fierce blows as she clawed into his body with her long nails. Their lovemaking was as ferocious as it was passionate and they consumed each other with the assumption that there would not be another time. A heady cocktail of angst, hate and lust steered them as they explored, ravaged and hurt each other.

Their relationship was based on the principle that every meeting, conversation and act of love could be their last. They didn't inhibit their spontaneity, maintaining a forthright brashness in their words and actions each time. It had taken a toll on both of them, but they relished the fierce and brutally passionate summits that were attained by the unceasing uncertainty and ambiguity that fuelled the mystique of their relationship. Their disagreements resulted in unabated bouts of fury, animosity, vicious verbal duels and stark violent episodes.

She placed her palms behind her, supporting her upper torso, and looked up towards him as she spread her legs on the floor. He was staring at her breasts unapologetically. He revelled in the fact that he could stare at her body without any inhibitions. She felt more in sync with him when he was close to her without even touching her.

'Why are you with me, Agastya?'

'Why do you ask?'

'Just…'

He leaned forward .

'Because I can, M!'

She detested his audacity and also knew that she found it irresistible. His insane arrogance almost verged towards megalomania but she couldn't let go of the simple fact that she found deep comfort within the shelter that these traits provided. She allowed him to just effortlessly sweep, and even ravage her without providing an ounce of resistance. The fear that every time they met could be their last meeting was a poison that had consumed her and eroded her confidence in the relationship and herself. But the instinct of holding on to any semblance of a relationship and the rare and splendid moments of feeling wanted by a man were too precious for her to let go. She had wanted to explore the fragility and futility of her liaisons with him, and her constant search for companionship. Beneath her bold and unflinching demeanour was concealed a being with rapidly eroding self-confidence and identity.

The moments with him transposed her into realms of frenzied ecstasy which were instantly followed by a deep sense of despondency and futility. The unpredictability and inevitability of the emotional journey of each interaction, and the voyage in the relationship had stumped the rationality that she exhibited at work. She had evolved to draw strength and strains of purpose from the memories of their passionate and over indulgent experiences with each other. It had settled into a parasitical mesh of intertwined emotions, cravings and addictions, which powered her drive for professional success and recognition and yet constantly gnawed away at her emotional strength. Every professional accomplishment further battered and eroded her, as she realized that it was reliant on her affair with him. She yearned to find a balance but succumbed to the reality that it was a path to oblivion in which she was slowly losing her identity. She had wanted to hurt him for his increasingly indignant behaviour and attitude towards her, but she also recognized the fact that she had been the one who had taken him on that path. Her audacity and irreverence had been the basis for his obsession and purpose in the relationship and the transition to a softer, compassionate plane would have been incomprehensible to him.

'And what if we never meet again, Agastya?'

'I don't think too much about later…'

'Don't bluff yourself. We all do…'

'I'm sure you'll miss me, M!' Agastya laughed.

Maithili was dejected by his response but was more upset for allowing herself to be upset by him. The fragility of their relationship had always been evident but an aspect that she hadn't felt comfortable dwelling upon.

She picked up the guitar and rested it on her legs, running her fingers across the strings.

'Will you ever let go?' he smiled.

'Of the guitar, or you?' she laughed. 'I know the answer for one of us … I'm not sure about the other though.'

'You're very sure?'

'A woman's instinct, Agastya, never goes wrong!'

'You're not one for stereotypes, M!'

'It's not about stereotypes, Agastya. It's about experience.'

'Not very pleasant ones?'

'Pleasant exists because of the not so pleasant … right?'

'Touché!' Agastya grinned, pulled out a cigarette from his jacket, and lit it. He took a few deep puffs and handed it over to her.

'I think I need men … it's not necessary that I like them ….'

'Is it a primal instinct, this dependence and need for protection?'

'Hmmm … I just think it's the need for physical touch.'

'So, when did this journey with the touch begin?' Agastya grinned.

'I was barely eighteen when I eloped.'

'But I thought you were with your parents when you finished your graduation in Delhi?'

She shook her head and signalled his silence.

'He was my senior in college. A college union leader actually. We had a long affair, then the usual jazz happened. Our families found out and our instinctive rebellious streak set in. We ran away and got married in some damn temple on the outskirts of Delhi.'

'Quite filmy!'

She laughed. There was a glint in her eyes when she laughed, a desperate attempt at concealing the pain.

'I know! We were on the road for several weeks. We borrowed money from our friends, switching between cheap hotel rooms and guest houses making sure to change rooms every night. We just couldn't risk it.

'His family was involved in politics. It got messy. Our friends got dragged into it. The police even interrogated some of them ... and you know what I mean by interrogation.'

'How bad?'

'One of them landed up in a hospital with severe wounds. The poor guy walks with a limp till this day. Don't have the guts to even speak with him.'

'How long were you on the run?'

'For over two months.'

'Then?'

'I think he just got tired of the whole thing. We kept having arguments ... it wasn't as romantic as we had thought it to be.'

'And?'

'Let's just say, I was found in a cheap hotel in Paharganj with multiple fractures and a bruised ego.'

'He hit you?'

She laughed.

'Hey! We were a feisty couple. He just got the better of me on that day. Poor bugger thought he had killed me and ran like hell.'

'He just left you there?'

'In my undergarments, and with a broken nose and jaw. In fact ... anyways ... you get the picture, right?'

'You went back home?'

'They picked me up from a government hospital. It became a police case, and was then squashed. Both the families

100

wanted to extricate themselves. Nobody wanted the media to get a hang of this.'

'Where is he?'

'He went off to Wharton after a year. He's a country manager with an MNC. Works in Europe. Has done quite well for himself.'

'You guys are in touch?'

'Of course'

'I don't get you!'

'We catch up whenever he's passing through Mumbai, or when I'm in Europe.'

'As in?'

'Do I need to spell out the fact that we sleep with each other whenever we meet? Isn't that what you wanted to know?'

'I didn't say that. Is he married?'

'Yes. You know the funny part?'

'There's more to this?'

'He married my first cousin.'

'What?!'

'He had managed to get her pregnant. Just doesn't get the concept of rubber.'

She smiled.

'Are you sure you want to talk more about this?'

'Yes! Quite sure. So that you know what a glorious mess I am!'

'I already knew that.'

She kicked him on his shin.

'Now shut up.'

'There's more?'

'Yup, they're happily married. They've got two children.'

'That's good to hear. So is one of the kids named after you?'

'The sick bastard that he is, he did contemplate it. But thankfully they didn't.'

'What did you do after you got back home?'

'It took me three to four months to be able to get out again. Therapy, medication…the works. I had lost a year in my academics. So I switched colleges just to get a fresh start.'

'Then?'

There were tears in her eyes.

'I couldn't take it anymore…'

'Take what, M?'

He stood up and sat beside her. She clutched his arm in a tight grip and didn't let go. He could sense her breathing heavily and the tears kept streaming down her face. She hadn't ever cried earlier and he hadn't imagined that she was capable of crying in front of another person. She had always come across as a very private person and he was slightly taken aback by her revealing her personal details with such abandon in this conversation.

He didn't look towards her but stared at the Monet print that was hanging on the wall opposite them.

'He just wouldn't let go. He kept coming again and again and again and again…' She was getting breathless and was taking even deeper breaths to rein in her emotions.

'Who, M?'

She looked towards him. It was a cold stare. He could see the fear and disgust in her eyes and felt her trembling body against his.

'I'm going to burn you alive if you ever mention this to anyone else!' she snapped and then began to sob softly.

'I get it…take it easy…'

She didn't speak for several minutes and waited till the trembling stopped.

'My uncle.'

'What about your uncle?'

'Does everything need to be spelt out for you?'

Agastya looked at her and wasn't sure if he should hold her tight or give her space. This was a side of her that he hadn't seen earlier.

He hesitated, not knowing if she wanted to hear the words.

'He abused you?'

She nodded.

'He just kept coming and coming…'

'You didn't tell your parents?'

'I finally told my father.'

'And then?'

'Dad couldn't do much about it. My uncle is a very powerful man. '

'And that's why you left Delhi?'

'And then last month I found out that he had been abusing Priyanka as well.'

'And that's why you got Priyanka to Bombay?'

'She didn't know that he had abused me too. We were both trapped in our own silos…'

'You didn't deserve what happened to you, M!'

'He called me a slut the last time he pounced on me. That was when I had just come back home from the hospital…'

'Have you spoken to anyone else about this?'

She shook her head.

'You know, Agastya, my sister and my relationship with her is the only one thing in my life that is sane and feels right. It's not screwed up like everything else. But she's not like me. She's still hurting.'

'So are you, M…'

'I've moved on, Agastya. Now it's just Priyanka I need to look out for.'

Maithili paused. She seemed distracted, and was about to utter something and then withdrew again. He could sense that she was retreating into her shell again.

'Hey, M, what happened?'

'Nothing...just thinking about Ismail...'

'How're you guys doing?'

'He's going through a rough patch in his business. He's quite stressed out really.'

'You planning on converting your live-in status with him into something else?'

Maithili smiled.

'Neither of us is made for marriage. You know that he's gone through a torrential divorce. His wife left him with the baby.'

'How's Roshan doing?'

'Not too bad. Ismail's mother is staying with us and helping out right now. But she's leaving in a few days.'

'And Priyanka?'

'She stays at my apartment most days, but then she has a colleague from the college where she teaches. She stays with her as well, sometimes.'

'And you think you'll be able to cope with all this going on in your life?'

She placed the guitar on the floor, crawled across towards him, perched herself on his body and pecked him on his cheek.

'I've got some plans.'

He kissed her on her lips.

'I've got to go...' she whispered into his ear.

'What's the hurry?'

'Ismail has planned a birthday celebration for me today!'

'It's your birthday today?!'

She smiled and kissed him again.

Chapter Eight

2:45 pm
Today

adversaries in a serpentine twist
neither spewing venom yet
soon this knot will reach their necks

'Agastya, what have you thought of? I'm waiting for you.' Vikram's voice was anxious on the phone.

Sebastian's words about Vikram's firing were still echoing in Agastya's mind. Strange things happened in corporates and Vikram had been on shaky ground for quite some time. Was this going to be his downfall? Surely, the senior brass at BCL wouldn't just fire him over this? It didn't seem logical.

'Working on a promotional 20 per cent off for a short period…'

'How much is it going to cost us?'

'I should have that out in the next couple of minutes.'

They all knew the math. It was quite well known that they were planning a ₹300-crore-sale with Sparkle in the first year itself, but the impact of a sales promotion on the MRP meant something different altogether. They also knew that a discount was not something that could be withdrawn within a few months, especially if Stark was planning to maintain the low price even when they manufactured their product in India. This product would be a bleeder for its entire life unless they could have a dialogue with Stark, which was unlikely to happen now. The daggers were drawn.

That single move by Stark could potentially have been the death knell for Vikram, Agastya and perhaps even Mark, with his presence in India for the launch and his close association with its strategy. Stark might just take them to the cleaners for the pure thrill of seeing three very important heads on the block.

'Mark will be walking in any moment now. Agastya, is this confirmed news?'

'Which news, sir?'

'About Stark? How do we know for sure that they will be launching tomorrow?'

Agastya hesitated, but it got him thinking. Vikram did sound very stressed.

'Cause they've booked all the front page slots on News Times and HT...'

He knew he would take a drubbing on this one. And then it struck him that he didn't know if those were indeed for Velvet, or if that was also a move to confuse them. Or perhaps Nitin was playing him?

'But why hadn't we taken the front page in the first place?'

'We had, Vikram, but Stark has played dirty and the newspapers have been paid crazy money.'

'Well, at least that's one thing that you can manage?'

They had a larger issue at hand. It then struck him. If Stark had stocks in the market, then Nitin's team would definitely have known about this in advance. The stocks would have been with the distributors at least two to three days earlier. Nitin must have sat in on this. His team was too smart to have missed this out altogether. But Nitin would have been smart enough to conceal that fact. It was also unlike Vikram to be as direct as that. He had always been subtle in his interactions. It had taken Agastya a while to understand the difference between a compliment and an admonishment since Vikram only used a singular composed tone in all his interactions. He had worked with Vikram in several high pressure situations but hadn't seen him losing his cool as he had in the last few minutes.

'Let me work it out. I'll come back to you shortly.' Vikram disconnected just as Sebastian walked in with his laptop.

'I heard that Nitin just fired one of the state sales heads for not discovering the Velvet news earlier.'

'Hmmm...' Agastya seemed neither convinced nor shocked. The state sales head could have been but a pawn in the game.

Sebastian continued. 'On initial estimates, we would need to shell out at least 18 to 20 crores in the next few months if we meet our sales projections.

That was a colossal number and this was straight cash out! It wasn't a call that could be taken this quickly, and considering that the MRP had already been printed on huge quantities of stocks which had been cleared past excise, they couldn't send it back to the factory easily, or could they?

'Check with the production team what it would take to recall stocks to the factory and repackage or place new stickers with the new pricing.'

'That's a nightmare. The stock returns, the billing reversals, credit notes, reconciliation…there would be tremendous confusion. The whole sales team would be doing only that for the next couple of weeks. We would also lose credibility with our distributors.'

Sebastian was right and Agastya knew that would be the collateral damage they would have to suffer.

'Please check with the production chaps first and get back to me?'

Sebastian rushed out and then turned around at the door.

'I've asked the agency to work out some design options announcing the 20 per cent off promotional offer. They want to know the terms and conditions. We would also need to give the trade some incentive to pick up the coupons and reimburse the customers.'

'We'll cross that bridge. Ask them to pick the terms and conditions from one of our earlier campaigns, and get the legal guys on it as well. Speak directly with that new legal head who joined yesterday. We need the department heads to be directly involved.'

Sebastian nodded and disappeared.

Agastya needed to confirm that Stark wasn't bluffing on the price point. For all he knew, that could have been a one-off promotion they were planning to undertake at the mall for the promotional exercise. Or maybe it wasn't an all-India campaign at all?

He dialled Nitin. 'Can your team pick up some stocks from the distributors? We need to understand if the 20 per cent off is a one-off or a nationwide pricing.'

'I'm too busy managing trade queries and issues right now, Agastya. I don't have the time for this mess that you've created!' Nitin hung up.

Was Stark playing them? Agastya just couldn't get the pulse of the situation.

He called up the western zonal sales head. His line was busy. He then dialled the northern zonal sales head.

'Hi, Agastya.'

'I need your boys to pick up some stocks from the distributors and check the price on the pack.'

'But the stocks are yet to hit the shelves.'

'But how would Stark be placing front page ads in the papers without the stocks being on the shelves? That's not possible!'

'I get what you're saying. Let me see what I can do. Let me check with Nitin as well.'

That was going to be a brick wall. Agastya decided to bluff.

'Nitin is with Mark. I don't think you want to be disturbing him right now.'

'Let me give it a shot, Agastya.'

'I need this in the next ten minutes.'

He hung up.

Agastya walked out of the room and looked for the agency

director. He was around the corner at a workstation, in a team huddle. He ran across and tapped him on the shoulder.

'Listen. Can you confirm if Stark has blocked front page ads in all cities for tomorrow, or only Mumbai?'

'But I told you...'

Agastya cut him, 'Just check for me once again. Don't get some flunkey to make the call. You call up the sales head at News Times directly. Also, I need to see the final advertisement copy that Stark would have shared with News Times.'

'How do I get my hands on that?'

'Use your channels, I don't know, leave no stone unturned.'

****

Maithili walked back into his office.

'I think you're taking your eye off the ball again, Agastya.'

Agastya glanced at the BCL stock flashing on the tablet. It had begun to take a heavy beating and had lost over 3 per cent in a little under ten minutes. The trading volumes were also increasing rapidly and forces seemed to be colluding to bludgeon both BCL and the BCL – Metrics JV stocks.

'Maithili. Please be realistic. You can see what I'm going through. Don't you get it? Seriously, just let me finish this press conference, and then let's talk about it. This is insane!'

'I've gone through quite a few insane things myself, Agastya, and I have a meeting with Nandita as well.'

'Listen... I know I've hurt you, but this is neither the time nor the place for this. You need to understand that.'

'I do understand, Agastya. And in the last four minutes, you've lost over 5 lakhs and counting. I know that's small change, but what can I say?'

Agastya veered towards the tablet. The numbers and graphs were brutal. All indicators were against him. He realized that every moment of indecision was compromising his position. He had to take a stand. He had to either stay in the market and take some tough calls on going short or long on some of the scrips, or he had to cash out and fast.

Stock traders adopt two approaches in trading. They go short on a stock when they expect its price to fall and go long when they expect the price to increase. Hence, when going long, a trader would purchase stocks in anticipation of the price to increase and then sell the stocks to make a profit. Similarly when going short, a trader would sell stocks expecting the price to fall and then actually purchase them when the price does fall. These are called positions, and all positions are required to be squared off before the settlement date. One could also take leverage on some stocks, wherein some scrips may be picked up at a fraction of the actual price, and the ratios are defined by the stock exchanges, but the stocks would require to be either purchased with the entire amount at the time of settlement or sold.

On a normal day, he would have placed stop loss positions and recouped the following day if he were uncertain, which was clearly the case for the day. However, Maithili's constant presence and the myriad events around him were crushing his confidence and shrouding his judgement. His instincts were blunted. His gut had eluded him. He was in the precarious territory of indecision.

He needed a smoke to calm his nerves. He needed to get out of the office, breathe in some fresh air and clear his head, but he didn't have the time. Time. It was now proving to be his nemesis. His fingers were frozen And his brain wasn't transmitting anything.

'I need you to get back into the conference room!'

She shot back. 'That's very considerate and thoughtful of you. Two of your more admirable qualities, I am sure.' The overbearing sarcasm stabbed at his conscience.

He thought to himself, *'If rationale doesn't work, the approach has got to be emotional.'*

'How's Ismail doing?'

She scrutinized him. 'Don't you even dare attempt to project empathy. You're absolutely pathetic at it. It reeks of contempt. So give yourself a break and get back to giving me my money!'

Agastya toggled the screen and noted the moves by Sailesh Rao on the virtual chess game that they had been playing for several weeks now. He made a move and then toggled back to the mailbox.

His mobile beeped. A message.

Sailesh: We should catch up some time. It's been quite a while. ☺

Agastya was tempted to fling the mobile across the room, but realized that he was allowing the situation to get to him. He took a deep breath, scanned the ever falling value of his stocks in despair and decided to take his eyes away from Maithili and type a response.

Agastya: You're paying!

Sailesh: Sure. This one's on me. ☺

He wanted to beat his nemesis to a pulp. He visualized knocking him down in the boxing ring and punching his face repeatedly, but as his eyes met Maithili's, he descended quickly to reality.

Alliance had dropped over 4 per cent and he could see a downward trend, but knowing the frivolous nature of the stock, he also knew that it could bounce back within a few seconds. It was a true-blooded blue chip and a "thoroughbred". It was for the long haul and it had been one of the few scrips that he had held on to for several months now. It also constituted almost half his portfolio holdings.

He believed that it did have a long term story and could have safely generated returns in excess of over 20 per cent, if only he could hold onto it. However, he also knew that when it fell, it didn't hesitate. It plunged without a care in the world. His gut insisted that this was going to be one of those days when it would dive into an inebriated free fall. He was however, worried that he had caught the downswing a little late.

He messaged Mukund.

'Dump Alliance asap. Short one million… let's connect @ 4.32'

He knew that it was a risky move, but he felt comfortable manoeuvring Alliance. He had already lost over ₹18 lakhs on Alliance in his portfolio, holding in barely under 15 minutes. One million Alliance with a drop of ten rupees would have given him a gross yield of a crore and a net yield of ₹80 lakhs, but he wasn't sure if it would drop to those levels. He was also nervous with the loss that he had yielded on his existing holding of Alliance, but realized that he had to make a move. There was a rush of adrenaline. He was back in the game.

'Four to go!' He muttered to himself.

The BCL scrip continued in its downward spiral. It would have been a sure shot under the circumstances, but he realized that he needed to steer clear of it.

Sailesh Rao's Office at Stark, Mumbai

The CEO had scheduled another meeting for 5 pm, later in the evening, before the official function, and had wanted to see some more data and charts. He wasn't sure what he would accomplish by seeing all these numbers and data points, given the ball had already been set in motion. It had taken him months of perseverance to make Prem understand the ramifications and strategic impact of thwarting Sparkle with their product, Velvet. Sailesh believed that loss leaders were equally crucial in a marketing portfolio and Velvet was that critical piece in the puzzle.

He was browsing through an email that the BCL team was reading at this point of time. He imagined their reactions as they read the words that would change their lives. It was a landmark moment in the titanic tussle between two of India's most reputed marketing companies, and he would be remembered for seeding this. This would be the turnaround for Stark in India and the information that he had just shared with the journalist at The Times of India would be the nail in the coffin. It would blow their entire top management into smithereens and would take them several months to recover and regain their reputation in the market. And that would set the ball in motion for the new and stronger Stark to emerge as the market leader in India—only the second country after North America to hold that distinction in the Stark conglomerate.

He was the architect and he meant to ensure that the senior management team in North America knew that this had been his grand design. The CEO was but a rubber stamp in this slew of initiatives that he was rolling out. He was the heir in waiting. It was just a matter of time.

He moved towards the chess set and admired his increasing appreciation of the Smyslov Defense and its nuances. The game had begun and he was playing black. He replicated his move on the chessboard, on the laptop as well, eagerly anticipating his opponent's next salvo.

He could hear the commotion around the office. Only seven people had been made privy to the stealth launch of Velvet in India, till 48 hours earlier, when the customs had cleared the consignment at Nhava Sheva port outside Mumbai. The stocks had been transported overnight in large Volvo trucks to major metro locations into their warehouses. Even the promotional materials had been printed in Thailand under his supervision.

The idea of reducing the price had struck him while he was having a drink with the CEO of Stark, Asia, who was enamoured with the idea of annihilating BCL. They had both emerged from statistical backgrounds and their common fascination for game theory was now infectious across the organization, quickly becoming an aspect of reckoning in most strategic decisions.

Sailesh scanned through the final media plans and sent the final budgetary approval for the campaign. The agency had been given a one month notice to block the newspaper spots for a social campaign that the company had been promoting. He had even managed to get some discounts with the newspapers wanting to be a part of this large "social good" campaign that he was unleashing. The worksheet in front of him had the new advertising rates with the goodwill having been withdrawn with an additional premium that had been built in for the last minute change. As the manager of one of India's largest newspaper advertising budgets, he had access to the managing director of News Times and a brief call had helped him pare down the premium. The fact that he was a classmate of the MD's wife came in handy as well.

He called Radhika in.

'Can you get me the final agenda for the evening? And tell them to reduce the commotion outside…sounds like a fish market.'

Radhika nodded, sensing his irritability.

Sailesh picked up the mobile and pressed six on his speed dial.

He uttered the word, 'Now,' and then disconnected.

Next, he opened his trading screen and smiled. He was going short on the BCL and the BCL Metrics JV stocks for 10 million shares. He had been tempted to go long on Stark, to make a killing on a potential upside, but had decided to steer clear of his company stocks. The probabilities were now stacked heavily in his favour.

The trading volumes on the BCL and the BCL Metrics JV stocks were picking up. The market had already accounted for the fact that BCL was making a big foray into the premium detergents market and with a slew of new product introductions having been announced, the stocks had already gained momentum. There was no significant spurt in prices expected after the press launch later today, but it was also normal for some retail investors to join the bandwagon over the next couple of days. The FIIs had been skeptical of the BCL turnaround story, but in an otherwise lacklustre economic environment, any ray of good news was met with a slight upswing. BCL was a blue chip stock that had been consistently giving dividends for decades now, and it was a stock which had lost its sheen in comparison to the new age Telecom & IT stocks, but most fund managers believed in the long term value of parking some of their investments in this sector and in this company.

Radhika dialled him on the intercom. 'Sir, Nikhil is here to see you.'

Nikhil Mathur was the head of strategy for Stark India. It was a new position that had been created to assist Sailesh in formulating the growth plans for Stark over the following three years, to design and execute the ambitious three-time turnover and double profit blueprint that had been chartered by the Stark board. It was a blueprint that was privy to only select senior management team members in Stark India.

Nikhil had worked with a leading global management consulting firm for over twelve years and had even been invovled in some senior engagements with BCL operations in Asia. He was one of the few people who had a bird's eye view of BCL's financials and the finer intricacies of their operating framework. He understood their DNA and more importantly, he knew their numbers. His passion for numbers and unquestionable memory were his key traits, which offered tremendous value to Sailesh.

He looked at the monitor and could see that trading volumes in both stocks had already gained momentum. The market had started selling them down. He switched on the large 52" LCD panel across the room with a remote. The news had already rolled out.

'There are unconfirmed reports about turmoil at BCL, which seems to be creating havoc on its stock and its logistics Joint Venture company BCL–Metrics.'

Nikhil walked into his room and handed over a printout.

'Sailesh. These are the numbers that you had asked for.'

Sailesh scanned the page quickly and read the four bullet points on the bottom right hand corner. He admired Nikhil for the accuracy of his summaries in each of his reports and preliminary documents. It was a skill unlike any other.

'Looking good?'

'I would think so. I've been on this for a while now and have examined each and every dimension. I don't think we've missed out on anything. It's watertight as far as I'm concerned.'

Sailesh finished reading the summary and looked up at him.

'This is quite radical. You do know that, right?'

'That's what you pay me for, Sailesh. You're not going to grow threefold by adopting conventional strategies. Those have already been tried. You have to think big and play big.'

'Let's meet in the morning tomorrow. Please ask Radhika to block some time.'

'Sure, and by the way, all the best for today.'

Sailesh smiled.

His eyes were on the trading screen again. The slide was now even more evident than when Nikhil had walked in.

He picked up his mobile and searched for Vikram's contact and sent him a text message.

'Many happy returns of the day. Have a great year ahead!'

He scrolled down his messages inbox and opened one that he had been waiting for.

'Good to go…'

He deleted the text message. He didn't like clutter in life. He then switched on iTunes on his laptop and played Summertime by Miles Davis.

He toggled to the live chess game , admiring Agastya's move, who appeared to have brushed up on his chess. Agastya had read into the Smyslov Defense that he had set up. As ever, Agastya had been willing to sacrifice his pieces for the lethal win. Agastya's game had been more about quick, brutal and bloody attacking moves, whereas Sailesh was the more subtle and defensive practitioner of the two. Sailesh always believed in suffocating the enemy in chess, but had been inspired by Agastya's bold and often brash moves. He was learning much from his adversary. There was merit in surprise and swiftness after all.

He thought for a few moments about his next move, and about Agastya's predicament. Should he give him a hint, throw him a lifeline perhaps? It was Agastya after all. Surely he could do that much for his adversarial ally.

He smiled as he imagined Agastya fretting and realized that the events that were to unfold during the day would paralyze both Agastya and BCL. The impact would be devastating. Sailesh took a deep breath and tried to make sure that his rage towards Agastya wasn't shrouding his moves in the chess game or in his frontal attack on BCL. He knew that it was now personal with Agastya, and had realized that he had possibly adopted the wrong battlefield to wage war, but Agastya hadn't left him any choice. Agastya's actions had hurt him and shattered his life. The pact had been forfeited and he was feeling free.

The noise outside his room was now muted. Radhika had done her job, yet again.

Chapter Nine

Two Years Earlier

perhaps together
they'll down their poison
do survivors
always taste freedom?

Strobe lights, smoke, loud 80's pop music on a dilapidated sound system, cheap beer, and waitresses dressed in miniskirts and sleeveless T shirts. The bar was extremely crowded and running surprisingly full for a Thursday night.

Agastya settled down at a table on the far right of the room, which, in all this chaos, appeared to be vacant. There was a circular stage in the centre of the room with girls dancing and flirting with the patrons on its periphery.

This was the first time for him in Bangkok. He had arrived via a flight from Kolkata three hours earlier, checked into a hotel room and picked up a cab that dropped him about a hundred feet from the bar. He had navigated himself to the bar after taking directions from several inebriated tourists and was wondering if he had indeed come to the right place after all.

A waitress in her mid-twenties, with stained teeth and extremely large breasts, struggling to confine themselves in a pink T, walked up to him, and placed a local beer on his table. She smiled, turned around and then walked away. He sipped the beer and absorbed the sights and sounds reminding him of his college days when he and his friends would scrounge money to visit the local delights and taste the local delicacies.

The skirmishes between BCL and Stark had reached maniacal proportions, orchestrated by overzealous managers to gain visibility at the Head Office or to find justifiable reasons for not meeting their targets. There were now various incidents ranging from stock dumping, negative advertising and price cutting to a plethora of other manoeuvres. It had become a symphony of acceptable anarchy. Battle lines had now breached media debates, retail storefronts, price wars, and consumer discounts that had reached delirious proportions.

When they did go at each other, they didn't hesitate in pulling out all punches. There were periods of deliberate silence punctuated with bouts of brutal assaults in which they pushed each other and their teams to the hilt. Their teams and agencies were confounded with the excruciating spells of restraint followed by over-the-top phases of attacks which assumed unheralded dimensions of viciousness.

They emerged in those combative zones brandishing their intellect, acumen and the vast resources at their disposal. They relished each adversarial situation and thrived on determining newer and even more spiteful methods of inflicting pain and damage on the opponent.

It was a tenuous web of deceit and unrestrained hostility that had been woven by them, which hung in a nervous balance when they both reluctantly agreed on control, non-aggression and even inaction in events of mutual truce. They were in uninhibited awe of each other's capabilities, and had earmarked the moments of ceasefire as a mark of reverence and not a submission of fear.

Sailesh and Agastya were evolved pugilists who relished every opportunity to assault each other in particular. In those periods, they forsook everything else in their lives, the stocks, the women, the budgets, their families and even alcohol. Nothing else mattered. It was the battle that defined them. Their conflict, which had originally been bred and fuelled by the organizational rivalry, had soon evolved to being but a pretext for them to exchange blows in any given opportunity. It had offered them a legitimate canvas to constantly be at each other.

Agastya resented the rumours and gossip that crept around BCL, and within corporate marketing circles, fuelled by Vikram, that Sailesh would have in fact made a better CMO.

Millions of dollars had been expended in random and maniacal manoeuvres often throttling profitability, sales and even careers of professionals in both organizations. Any signs of remorse had been wiped out of their vocabulary and even the slightest victory was overshadowed by the quest for the next opportunity for a conquest.

Both Sailesh and Agastya had been officially reprimanded by their respective managements for crossing the line on several occasions, but then the congratulatory messages in the privacy of text messages and washroom huddles, followed by drinking binges all but endorsed the true spirit that prevailed. They were the heroes who gained, both, maniacal followings and undaunted admiration from their seniors, peers and subordinates. Emotion overwhelmed profitability and rationale when they were at the helm.

When it went wrong, it was deftly attributed to unreasonable and arbitrary actions of the other organization which could not have been foreseen, or a revered member of one of the other departments was blatantly exposed for ineptitude in managing the situation.

They didn't want the other to be slain, as that would have been a cruelly abrupt end to the pain that they wanted to inflict. The opponent needed to feel the sting, but not succumb. The opponent needed to bleed, but not die. They needed each other.

The DJ was playing "Janie's got a gun". Agastya was tapping his feet, appreciating the rich, layered notes of the local beer. He looked at his watch and realized that his guest was running late.

'Agastya?'

The deep voice of Sailesh Rao emerged from behind him. Agastya, who was facing the entrance, wondered how he missed him coming in through the door.

'Hi, Sailesh.'

At five-feet-four-inches, and with a stout, round frame, Sailesh perched himself on the chair with some difficulty. His receding hairline, dark eyes and the heavy moustache highlighting his rather thick nose, made him out to be quite the unlikely adversary, but Agastya knew well that the unassuming PhD could pack quite a punch in any corporate boardroom.

There were going to be a few cold moments between the two adversaries as they sized each other up.

Sailesh sat down to Agastya's right and nodded at one of the waitresses. He seemed to be well-acquainted with the staff and had an air of confident comfort about him.

'Unique place, right?'

'Interesting, actually…'

Sailesh was fiddling with his mobile on the table and seemed to be distracted and restless. Agastya knew that Sailesh had been peeved with him for snatching the BCL position from him. Sailesh had flown into India to join Gillette as their India CEO, but within a few months Gillette was taken over by Stark. The Stark management team had retained him and urged him to take on the CMO position as they transitioned Prem Mehra, the Indian CEO of Stark, to another role within six months. But Prem's stranglehold on Stark had been greater than he had anticipated. It had frustrated Sailesh, knowing that many peers had already secured country head positions across the world, and the "genius" had remained behind in the race.

He was now seated opposite a man who had out-maneuvred him and was holding a CMO slot that had rightfully been his. He knew that Agastya's appointment was a more secure one for Vikram, giving him a longer lease of life within BCL, as Agastya was clearly too young and brash for the top spot. It had been a complex web of convenience and subterfuge, and it had taken Sailesh several months to reconcile to his undermined position. It had also been a demanding sequence of events that had forced him to be seated at this table, seek reconciliation and broker a truce.

This was going to be one of the more humbling moments of his career as he sat with this professional, several years his junior, but quite clearly the one who held the upper hand in terms of scale and influence. Their skirmishes and conflicts, from their days at Pepsi also played on Sailesh's mind.

He considered Agastya to be brash, and was at loggerheads with his personal work philosophy, but he also respected the brilliance in the anarchy and chaos that his adversary could unleash in the market. Agastya's instincts and speed were a lethal combination when poised against Sailesh's shrewd, subtle yet dramatic plays.

He also realized, much to his disgust, that he possibly needed this truce more than Agastya. It was often important to hold one's position and retreat in war, before an assault. Agastya and BCL had struck several blows to Stark's products and distribution network in India. Sailesh had attempted to reach out to Nitin at BCL, as well, but their egos had made it an attempt in futility. Nitin had viewed it to be an indicator of his enormous power and strength and Sailesh's weakness, and had ended up letting go of an opportunity that would've worked to their mutual convenience.

Agastya however was in a hurry to cement his position at BCL and needed some big wins without distractions from

Stark. As events played themselves out, they both realized that they held in their hands the road and formula for their respective CEO aspirations at BCL and Stark. This was going to be an affair of nervous co-existence for mutual gain. Even attempting to infuse trust into this pact would have been foolish, at the least for both of them. They would have to take calculated and subtle steps of reconciliation and sometimes make moves that would be mutually beneficial, ensuring at the same time that the market didn't get a whiff of this pact.

'So, first time in Bangkok, Agastya?'

'Yes, actually…'

'It's a great place to just lay back and let your hair down.'

'You come here often?'

'Once in a while.'

The same waitress with the rotten teeth appeared again and placed Sailesh's beer on the table along with a bowl of wafers.

Sailesh raised his bottle.

'Cheers, Agastya. I'm sure you'll enjoy your first trip to Bangkok.'

'Cheers, Sailesh.'

They sipped their beers and looked awkwardly in different directions.

'So, how's Vikram doing? Under a lot of heat I hear.'

'The usual. You know how it is…'

'And Nitin still yanking your chain?'

Agastya wasn't surprised by the high-handed tone.

'He's got a fascination for chains.'

'He's quite a player. He'll chew you and Vikram and spit you out. He's street smart and one hell of a fighter. You need to give him that. '

'What's he upto?'

'I wonder why he's been to Hong Kong twice in the last five months.'

'HK?'

'He's going to take you guys down hook, line and sinker.'

Sailesh excused himself to go to the men's room. It was a deliberate pause in the conversation. Agastya reflected on the conversation and wasn't sure what to make of his "archrival", as termed in the business press.

Sailesh returned and sat down opposite Agastya.

The meeting had been set up by Sanjeev Prakash, a PR consultant and an influential government lobbyist. Sanjeev was a mutual acquaintance and it had been suggested by both parties that a conversation in person was crucial.

Their bickering was now getting played in the media with allegations of malpractice and corruption by both parties against each other. It was time for a truce and Sanjeev had been selected as a mediator.

Agastya decided to take him on. 'Your old man being packed off to the US?'

'Who? Prem? Nope, those rumours have been doing the rounds for several months now, but it's just wishful thinking. He's been in India for so many years already, he won't be able to work anywhere else. Stark doesn't know what to do with him.'

'But I thought he was in the good books of the global board.'

'He is. But they also know that he's too rigid and stubborn. He just doesn't have it in him, so they are stuck with each other. He's been doing a damn good job in growing the business and getting it to where it is right now, but we need someone to come in with some fresh thinking. We are just doing a rehash of everything we've done earlier.'

'Why don't you find him a job somewhere then?'

Sailesh laughed. 'Trust me! I have already tried that one. The deal fell through at the last moment. The old man got the jitters. He's too comfortable at Stark.'

They were both evading the main purpose of their meeting, with each one waiting for the other to bring it up. Agastya was already feeling tired and the ambience was really wearing him out.

'They could make you the joint CEO!'

Sailesh smirked. It was common knowledge that he was the restless, and now even tired, king in waiting.

'Sure! The old man would absolutely love that. What keeps you at BCL? You should be on a global posting. Don't know why you're in India really.'

'A man's got to earn a living!'

'Agastya. Let's get down to it. Sanjeev said that you wanted to meet.'

Agastya laughed.

'He insisted that you were the one that was pressing for this meeting.'

Sailesh shook his head.

'Anyway. Let's move forward. You've started hitting under the belt. It wasn't like this earlier.'

'You're the one that planted the cockroach in the detergent story to the press.'

'That was quite a neat one, right?' Sailesh winked.

'But that was after you guys picked up the entire sales team in Uttaranchal. And then that mysterious fire in the warehouse in Patna,' Agastya retorted.

'Hey, that's not even up for discussion. Seriously.'

'Your distributor is the main accused in that case.'

'And your distributor is on the run from the cops in a case of attempted murder, so let's…'

Sailesh was about to blurt out some statistics, but then held himself back. The dirty laundry was mutually known.

'Listen, Agastya. You need to get a message across. This can only get uglier for you. Your folks haven't held back in taking shots at us. I'm not going to take this sitting down.'

This hadn't seemed to have got off to the start that Agastya had envisaged. He had believed that he would have the upper hand in this dialogue and truce formulation, but was taken aback by Sailesh's approach to the situation. He wondered if this was in fact his nervousness or desperation that had triggered this tirade.

Agastya lowered his tone but continued.

'You've increased retailer commissions across the board. What triggered that generosity? Even you should know that you can't drop commissions once you've increased them. Retailers just won't bite.'

'You didn't leave us a choice after the 10 per cent discount on the shampoo range.'

'But that was a consumer promotion. And that was after you started doling out free shampoo sachets with your soaps.'

They paused again and took a few seconds to reflect. They had both wanted to call for a truce, but neither was willing to say the words.

'Agastya. We're just salaried guys with our companies. You need to stop taking this personally.'

'Personally?! Of course not, Sailesh. By the way thanks for the compliment on my gambling streak!'

Sailesh laughed. 'Oh that! It was just a joke. They just got it the wrong way. By the way, you must give me the name of your broker.'

They were both finding it difficult to take off their duelling hats.

'The journalists always get it the wrong way, Sailesh.'

They both laughed.

'We need to start somewhere, Agastya. There's too much bad blood, but you and I will have to steer this one through. Our current assignments are not the end of the road for us. We need to look ahead and not get consumed with this stuff. We've been scoring brownie points with our escapades, but it's really not helping either of our causes.'

Agastya was taken aback by the blunt reality of it. They had been in the midst of this war, and had lost sight of their individual goals. The insanity had consumed both of them, and it had stopped making sense. They were gladiators playing to the audience and it was going to take them both down one day. Some wise-ass from the respective head offices would emerge and knock them off on seeing the impact that all this was having on their balance sheets.

'And you're willing to cool off, Sailesh?'

'Let's put it this way. We both need to come out winners, and time our wins.'

'And?'

'We either do this for ourselves or the situation will do us in. I don't know about you, but being CMO at Stark India is not the end of the road for me. My old man is playing along for now, but he's going to lynch me the day he gets a chance. I've got NY backing me at the moment, but that won't last me forever. And in your case, Vikram and Nitin are not going to be lying low much longer. You've been getting too much of the spotlight. You're not the classical low profile CMO that they're used to. You're too hot to handle for them, and I might say, too much of a direct threat. And may I add something?'

It was a surprising but possibly sarcastic attempt at politeness. He would have said it anyway, but just wanted to temper the discussion with a shade of supposed empathy.

'Don't hold back, Sailesh. You're in the flow,' Agastya laughed, hoping to ease the tension in the conversation.

'You're too in-your-face and inflexible. You need to bend once in a while. You can't play out to be this hotshot, "I know it all" son of a gun forever you know. It was bound to upset everyone around you, and it has. I'm just surprised that you've even lasted this long.'

Agastya was amused listening to this discourse on the need for humility from a man who had taken confrontationist stands with his CEO in most public forums. He also admired the senior statesman and almost big brotherly mantle that Sailesh had adopted in this dialogue. It was possibly a deliberate attempt to enervate and even agitate him, but Agastya now knew his rival well enough to expect any of a vast array of games.

'I am flattered by this infatuation that you have with me, but let's stick to our original discussion. What do you have in mind?

'I've got a new soap being launched next quarter.'

'Everyone knows that.'

'Yes. But you need to steer clear of it.'

'In the sense?'

'Don't do the usual stuff…you know…blocking display spots in stores, hiking the customer discounts…   Come on, you know what I'm talking about.'

'I am not sure why I would do what you're proposing, but a lot of that is under Nitin's purview.'

'Well, you will have to influence the situation.'

'And?'

'I don't have the full script worked out. We'll have to play this out by ear.'

'Interesting, and you've been mulling on this for a while?'

'Just as much as you!'

'What's in it for me?'

Sailesh laughed. 'First blood, eh?'

'I wouldn't put it that way.'

'I'm going to ease off on the Patna issue. Let's work together on that one. Your guys are taking it much more seriously than mine. Your PR team could do with a save as well.'

'I've got that covered, Sailesh, and that's nothing compared to your new launch.'

Saliesh smiled.

'I'll be withdrawing the additional retailer pay-outs in a few days. That good enough for you?'

Agastya was uncomfortable with the ease of the conversation. It was all flowing too smoothly. Sailesh was too smart to give in so easily, and so quickly. He must have needed a save very quickly or had been cornered. It wasn't adding up.

They didn't speak for a few minutes as they both got busy with their emails and messages.

Agastya broke the silence.

'Why now?'

Sailesh looked at him blankly for several seconds.

'The big bosses from the US are going to be here for the launch. I just want it to go smoother than usual.'

Agastya smiled. He figured that Sailesh was keeping something very close to his chest. He wasn't going to let on so easily.

'Nielsen has been giving you a tough time on your market share numbers?'

Sailesh laughed. 'Those numbers are doctored and everyone knows that.'

The international conglomerates followed Nielsen market audit reports like religion. These were numbers shared globally and Stark had been taking a hit in some of the markets, as per Nielsen. It was also a deep secret that their audit sample had been compromised by one of their senior executives, and Agastya had discreetly piled up the stocks at those retail outlets which were being tracked by Nielsen. He even concentrated his promotional and advertising investments in those specific areas in which the retailers were situated, to influence the customer off-take as well. This was something that he had steered along with Sebastian, who had been sworn and bludgeoned into secrecy.

'Well, you know BCL … Nielsen is like the bible in there.'

He could sense that he had touched a raw nerve as Sailesh started fidgeting with the ashtray on the table. He had expected a counter question from Sailesh, but was relieved when he didn't get one.

'How're you doing on your gross margins? Don't you think we could do with some boost there?' Agastya continued.

Pricing was one of the most crucial factors in consumer marketing. Most of their products were purchased by women, including extremely budget-conscious housewives. Brand shifting happened for as little as ₹2 on an item priced at ₹120. It was crucial to get it right and that in turn determined the profits that each of the players could make.

BCL and Stark led the pack and had always led the market in price increases, but with the entry of several Indian brands leading to greater competition, both companies had faltered by continuing to charge a premium to their customers. Discounts and special offers had become an all year affair, constantly pulling down their profitability.

'Chief, that's the 800-pound gorilla for both of us.'

'Let's crack that one?'

'That's going to take some doing, and we have a long way to go on that one, Agastya. Let's cross some smaller bridges first?'

'I need to understand the full intent and course of this conversation.'

'Let's not push our luck. You do know the trouble we'd be in if this conversation or meeting ever got out?'

'It has struck me.'

'We'd be castrated and hung out to dry for the vultures.'

Sailesh handed over a piece of paper to Agastya with a series of numbers and alphabets.

'What's this?'

'That's my BBM messenger pin.'

'I thought it was a code to some hotline in Bangkok.'

'I could arrange that for you as well!'

They both raised their bottles and clinked them together.

'How long do you plan to be in this rat race?'

Sailesh mulled on this for a while. 'Why? You feeling fatigued?'

'I've just about started, Sailesh. I'm worried about you, old man!'

'I can complete a marathon in under three hours. What's your time?'

'If it's women, I can last longer than you!'

They both laughed.

'What's your thing with Nitin? Do both of you have a history?'

'Why do you ask?'

'Just sensed something. Nothing specific. It's just that he's in an awkward position between you and Vikram. An angry tiger can do some crazy stuff that he will regret later…'

'Is he onto something?'

'He's swimming in some rather dangerous waters…'

'That's a load of crap. What is it really?'

'All I can say is, you need to watch your back there.'

Agastya scribbled a name and number on a paper napkin and handed it over to Sailesh.

'What's this?'

'That's my broker's number, Sailesh. He'll look after you,' Agastya smiled.

Chapter Ten

2:50 pm
TODAY

the luxury of thought
a script, a plot
while in the wings
waiting...

Agastya looked at Sailesh's contact details on his mobile. He was hesitating to make the call. He didn't know what to expect. Why would Sailesh open up to him? Would he even take his call? After all, Sailesh would surely get a promotion and a bonus purely for making a joke of Richard and Mark's India visit. There were accolades waiting for him the following morning.

He couldn't understand the motive or the rationale behind this grandiose scheme that Sailesh had unleashed. He scanned through the incidents and moves made by both of them in the recent past and wondered if he had breached the norms that they had set for themselves. He couldn't recollect any surprises or manoeuvres that may have set Sailesh on this path. He wasn't sure anymore if Sailesh had played him all along and set him up for this day. There was possibly a leak within his team or within BCL, as Sailesh appeared to have orchestrated this with deliberate and calculated poise. It also didn't seem to be in line with Sailesh's normal pattern of doing business.

The occasional tactical assault was quite different. He realized that there was something else that had driven Sailesh and Stark on this path. He also knew that this couldn't have been decided by Sailesh alone, and he would have had to gain the confidence and trust of his CEO, Prem Mehra, and possibly the Asia Pacific senior management team as well. There were significant funds that would have been allocated for this operation.

Agastya fidgeted with the phone. He pressed the dial button and then quickly disconnected. 'Sebastian!' Agastya screamed.

Sebastian had been hurtling around the office and rushed into the room.

'Yes, boss?' The disgust each time Agastya yelled his name was apparent, and Sebastian had stopped pretending that it didn't offend him, while Agastya remained apathetic.

The commotion outside his cabin had reached cacophonic proportions. The entire team was in chaos and he realized that he would have to steer them into a coherent direction.

'Get the larger team into the board room. I want to have a chat with them.'

'Agastya, there's too much happening out there. We are running against time. I know we need to settle them down, but every moment is precious as of now. Really can't afford to get them away from what they're doing.'

There was a strained pause.

'Make sure to speak with each of them as you meet them, and settle them down.'

'Will do!'

'Who do you know at Stark?'

It was sacrilege even to be seen seated next to a Stark employee on a flight, if you worked at BCL. And to declare an acquaintance with one, leave alone a friendship, at these senior levels would have been blasphemy.

'No one!' Sebastian quickly countered, and looked towards Maithili, thankful that he had a witness for this adversarial and potentially career ending, conversation. Was Agastya suspecting him of sabotage? Was he out on a witch hunt? He could make out that Vikram was going to pass the buck to both Agastya and Nitin. Was Agastya looking to corner him on this one? He needed to steer clear.

'We need to know what's going on there, right now. We're running out of time. I need to know the facts, and fast. I can't play such a huge hand blind!'

Sebastian didn't even pause. 'I don't know anyone there, chief!'

Agastya knew that Sebastian was bluffing but sensed his apprehension.

Sebastian rushed out faster than ever.

Agastya looked at the tablet again. He needed some help, and fast.

He dialled his compatriot in arms and stocks.

'Manish! Drop whatever you're doing. This is urgent. No jokes here.'

'What happened to you?'

'Got a situation. You need to be with me on this one.'

'Shoot!'

'I need some liquidity, and I need it fast!'

'Sounds intense.'

'I'm messaging you some stock scrips. I need to know how they're going to be looking before closing today.'

Manish laughed. 'Sure! If I had that, my dear friend, I would have been in the Bahamas right now.'

'Just get whatever you can. Check with your FII friends as well!'

Agastya disconnected and noticed that Vikram's call was waiting.

'Agastya, what do you suggest we do? I'm going to follow your lead on this one. Mark is getting frantic. He's just realized that the head office made some announcements in an analyst's meeting at Wall Street earlier yesterday. They've already announced that we're launching Sparkle in India today, and it will be launched in other countries soon.'

Agastya got the message. This wasn't something that could be managed and quelled in this outpost called India. This was now a global incident. He had also heard that the global CEO had already written a note to Mark enquiring about this "rumour" that he had just heard.

It took Agastya a couple of seconds to switch from his stock escapades back to the current saga at work.

'I think we should call this off for today and see what Stark comes out with tomorrow. That would be a safer option!'

'The press would lynch us. We'll be the laughing stock for the next three decades! Do you know the magnitude of what you've suggested?'

Agastya was hoping that Vikram would bite the bullet and give him some breathing time, allowing him to manage Maithili and Nandita.

'Think of it this way, Vikram. Our stocks have already hit the shelves...it's out there. Our cards are on the table for everyone to see. Stark already has the upper hand if what we've heard is at all true. It just doesn't make any sense to make any major announcement today. Just let's wait it out for a few more days, that's it. We would have a more coherent strategy. We can come up with something for the press. Don't worry about that one. We'll manage something.' Agastya emphasized with conviction, but knew he was up against a brick wall.

'That's not an option. We've never backed down and we're not going to start today, definitely not with Mark here. Think harder.'

'But, Vikram, we need to be calm.'

'You don't have Mark sitting six feet away from you!' Vikram disconnected.

Sebastian called, 'Sir!'

'What happened?'

'The hoardings...what do we do with them?'

'What do you mean?'

'We were supposed to unveil them at 5 pm. I need to give them a two hour heads up. It just can't happen instantly.'

'You've got all the information that I have Sebastian... hold!' He disconnected and flung the mobile on the carpet.

Nitin walked in.

'Any word from the market?'

'I'm just a sales guy, Agastya. I've pumped the stocks into the market. It's for you to now sell it and move it from the shelves!'

'Cut the bull, Nitin. What do you have for me?'

'I've just come back from Vikram's room. Mark is there with him. He's mighty upset with the situation. In fact he's livid. You've put him in a sticky situation. I'm glad I'm not in your shoes right now!'

'It's not me, Nitin. We are all in this situation. If you had the information earlier we wouldn't have been in this mess in the first place.'

'Don't drag me into this one, Agastya. This is your baby. I've done everything at my end.'

'You're the one with an army of guys out there, Nitin, not me. You would have this information much earlier if your team had just done their job!'

'Well, that's your point of view and it seems to be different from the general view! And if it wasn't for my information that came in today, this would have been an even bigger disaster!'

'Come on, Nitin!'

Nitin winked and left the room.

The stock markets remained in the red. Alliance had moved down by another six rupees and didn't seem to have any support either. He was restless to hear from either Manish or Mukund, but neither had reached out. The charts looked weak and all the trends pointed towards a potentially bloody last hour of trading for the day.

He realized that he was damaging himself more by holding onto his other stocks, DSQ and Infitel. He should have liquidated them along with Alliance.

He messaged Mukund.

'Sell all DSQ, Alliance.'

Agastya searched his table for a piece of blank paper and found a notepad lying below a large heap of files. He pulled it out and started scribbling, noting down all the assets that he had.

He received a text message from Nitin.

'You're clearly distracted today!'

Maithili walked back into his office.

'I asked you to sit there so that you could be away from my office, M!'

'I know, darling, but I miss you!' she winked.

'Go to hell, M!' Agastya snapped at her.

'My, my… aren't we short-tempered today?'

'What do you want, M?'

'I may know Sailesh.'

Agastya shot her a look. 'You know him?'

'We met on a couple of occasions. I'm doing some business with his brother.'

'Why didn't you tell me?'

'I thought you were upset with me,' she winked at him.

He wasn't upset with her. He just felt like throwing her from the top of the frigging building.

'Can you reach out to him?'

Was he asking Maithili for help after everything that they had been through, and that she was putting him through right now?

'I can try.'

'So dial that frigging number!' he snapped at her again.

'Let me think about it. It's not that I know him that well either.'

Maithili's eyes glistened.

'You know, Agastya. I can do something else to help you out here.' It was a tone of feigned concern.

Agastya felt a rush of disgust. He resented her calm demeanour and control that she had over him and her last statement both bruised his ego and fuelled his animosity towards her. He just couldn't submit to her. He then realized that he couldn't allow his ego to interfere with the situation. He needed to objectively assess and evaluate each opportunity that presented itself. Each conversation with her was an opportunity to penetrate her armour and sabotage her defense system.

It took him a while to look her in the eyes.

'What do you have in mind?'

'I've got a potential buyer for your properties. I know you've got mortgages on most of them, but he would be willing to make you a handsome profit, under the circumstances.'

He knew that he was going to regret it, but decided to ask her anyway.

'Show me the numbers.'

She smiled and pulled out a small piece of paper from her purse and slid it towards him on the table.

He read it and flung it back at her.

'Those numbers are crap. These properties have appreciated by over 30 per cent since I bought them, and you want me to sell them for a song.'

'Think of it this way, Agastya. This would at least give you a leeway for another two crores right now. Just sign these documents and I will give you credit for that amount! You really don't have all that much time, you know! I could even toss in a kiss as a goodwill gesture. This offer will hold for the next two minutes!' She smiled and walked back to the conference room.

His BlackBerry was vibrating ferociously and he finally picked it up.

'Yes, Nitin?'

'Vikram's job is on the line.'

'What the hell?'

'Mark asked him to put in his papers.'

'He doesn't report to Mark!'

'Well, even Richard seems to be in on this one. He's cornered.'

Agastya hesitated. 'Because of this incident?'

'No, Agastya. There's some major share scam he's involved in. It's going to be on the news soon.'

'With the BCL Metrics JV?'

'Looks like it. The mess is out in the open. It had to happen one day. The press seems to have gotten hold of some internal documents.'

Agastya toggled the screen and noticed that Sailesh had made a move in the chess game. He was moving faster than usual. Sailesh had just made an assault on his queen in a rather aggressive move. The move had its merits but he also noticed that he had left a glaring option for him to take his queen. Was he tempting him, or possibly even distracting him? Was Sailesh playing him, or was he actually giving him a hint? He surely couldn't have missed the chink in the armour. Was he actually willing to let go of his queen at this stage of the game? They would have both lost their queens, but Agastya knew that it wasn't Sailesh's style to let go of his queen in the game.

If Sailesh had a discernible and unashamed weakness, it was his penchant for the queen. He just couldn't think of a game without the queen, and now he was presenting an opportunity for them to kill each other's queens. It puzzled him.

'Are you sure you don't want to sell these properties? No change of mind?'

'No thanks, Maithili. I could do with some tips though.'

All three of his stocks—DSQ, Infitel and Alliance—continued on their downward spiral, at different speeds. But Alliance seemed to be in a much greater hurry to hit the circuit breaker limits for the day.

Alliance had crossed the target, the ₹432 mark he had set for himself—and was now at ₹431. He had made his first crore. It was a rush.

He messaged Mukund.

Three million short—Alliance.

He realized that if he managed to get at least another five crores, if it continued to slide further down, it would have made him another ₹2 crores. He had a feeling Alliance may stabilize at ₹425, at which it had settled a couple of weeks earlier when he had picked it up.

He looked at the time on the laptop. He desperately needed more action.

Sailesh Rao's Office, Stark, Mumbai

His mobile rang. It was a landline number.

'Where did you get those documents that you sent me?'

'Hi, Ajay, how've you been? How's life at News Times?'

'Get on with it, Sailesh…'

'From a reliable source, my restless friend.'

'I can't use those documents to prove anything. They're just dates, names and numbers. I need a source or something that I can use. How do I corroborate this?'

'This will be your loss, not mine. I do have more, if it's ever required though.'

'This is going to take some time.'

'If it's too hot to handle for you, let me know right away. There are others who would be interested.'

There was a long pause.

'What's your play?'

'That shouldn't concern you, Ajay. You come out the winner. I know you're not a gambling man. But this is what they call a sure shot thing.'

'But some of this news is already out.'

'Those are just rumours, my friend. Dalal Street breeds millions of rumours every minute. Even you should know that. You've got the meat with you, but it can go stale very soon in this weather.'

'I could lose my job over this.'

'This could make your career as well, don't you think?'

'Let me think about it.'

'Sure! I understand. You've got two minutes.'

'Is this personal?'

'Why does it matter?'

'You're going to ruin them. Corporate guys don't get away easy with this stuff. They're not like politicians.'

'It can be tough.'

'You know what surprises me?'

'What?'

'Why do they do this?'

'This is not the time for philosophy, Ajay. You in?'

There was a long pause again. Sailesh was getting restless.

'I'm pushing the buttons as we speak.'

'And, Ajay, have a word with your sales guys. Hope they don't budge on the front page slots for this month?'

He disconnected.

Sailesh got up from his chair and briskly walked across to the conference room adjacent to his cabin. His team had been assembled there by Radhika.

There was a murmur when he entered the room which soon dissipated to pin-drop silence.

'The next seventy-two hours are going to be crucial. We have lots to do. Please call your families and tell them you won't be seeing them for some time. You got that?'

He looked at the faces of the fourteen people who had been assembled and acknowledged their hesitant nods with a smile.

'That's the spirit. Radhika has made arrangements for those of you remaining in Mumbai to stay at the Trident. Freshen up and catch a few hours' of sleep if you can afford it. We've got the press meet at 6 pm and the live CEO interview scheduled on the news channels 6:30 pm onwards. You know the drill. None of you are going to speak with the media or offer any comments. Is that clear?'

He waited for their nod before he continued.

'As you know, the consignments are hitting the stores in the next few hours. The visibility materials need to be up as well. Most of you are going to be taking flights out tonight to Delhi, Chennai, Bangalore, Kolkata, Ahmedabad and Hyderabad. The sales training programmes have been scheduled for 7 am sharp tomorrow morning in each of those cities. Then you're going to fan out to Jaipur,

Mysore, Pune, Rajkot and some other towns for afternoon training sessions.'

'Boss, how much stock has been despatched to each of these locations?'

'The numbers are being emailed to you as we speak. It's going to be just about sufficient to stack up at the large supermarkets and some of your key outlets in main areas. The sales team is going to have its hands full with achieving even that in the next 24 hours.'

One of the new product managers emerged with the obvious question.

'Why this rush?'

He received angry looks from his nervous colleagues seated around him.

'Welcome to Stark.' Sailesh smiled. He had admired the young man's guts, or innocent ignorance of the culture and norms.

Sailesh paused and then asked, 'Any other questions?'

He could see on their faces that they had a million. A product launch of this nature usually took months of planning and analysis. Some of them had received a 48 hours heads up and most of them had got under 24 hours. It was a veritable blitzkrieg and several of them hadn't even worked in the detergents business.

Stark couldn't fail. It wasn't an option, not under Sailesh's reign.

'And I would like to share something else with you …'

The team wasn't prepared to handle any more surprises.

The same product manager spoke again, figuring out that he was the spokesperson for the group.

'What's that, sir?'

'We are fast tracking the new product pipeline. We're going to be rolling out six new products in the next sixteen weeks!'

Silence pervaded. It was that of anguish, despair, horror. Memories of sleepless nights, red eyes, airline meals, late night check-ins and early morning check-outs, tussles with the advertising agencies and squabbles with the sales teams—this, six times over. The nervous enthusiasm and vigour of a few minutes earlier was now replaced with trepidation.

Chapter Eleven

TWO 6 A HALF YEARS EARLIER...

hardened minds in armoured suits
around their necks a silken noose

The markets had been choppy for several weeks. Most analysts had been suggesting that the BCL – Metrics Joint Venture should postpone the IPO in India, but Vikram stuck to his guns. This was one feather in the cap he wasn't willing to let go off that easily.

The new CEO of the joint venture had arrived in the midst of the IPO planning. The earlier CEO had been tainted in rumours of a corruption scandal and had been asked to leave overnight. Vikram, a director on the board for BCL, had been asked by the board to take on this project and make it a success.

Metrics was an Indian logistics player with interests in trucking and warehousing and had commenced setting up a nationwide cold chain. They needed the capital and BCL was keen on being a part of the India growth story. That was the official version, of course.

Metrics was founded by Madhavji Patil, the dynamic nephew of the Union Finance Minister, Keshav Deshpande. The company had access to a vast amount of capital, but mismanagement and nepotism had withered its balance sheet and left most of its projects incomplete and in tatters. The Honourable Union Minister had been troubled and aggravated by the high decibel negative coverage received by his nephew's company and needed to resuscitate the venture.

Vikram had been seeking approvals from the government to expand his facilities and had been facing tremendous challenges in acquiring the land for his new projects. Red tape and conflicting views of several departments had delayed the projects by over eighteen months and frustration had been setting in. A chance encounter with the Finance Minister at a CII summit and several meetings later, it was suggested that

BCL would find an investment in Metrics to be viewed as a commitment of the global BCL organization in the India story.

It was to be a small investment for BCL, not exceeding 20 million USD, for a 40 per cent stake with an option of taking it upto 51 per cent which had seemed a fair enough valuation for the real estate and contracts that the company had. The joint venture would now serve the purpose of managing the entire logistics and supply chain for BCL in India. The idea and approach did have merits and would have provided a scalable platform for BCL's aspirations in diversifying its business lines and in introducing some of its global brands in India including a frozen foods line of products like ice cream, frozen desserts and possibly even dairy products.

The approval for the joint venture had been received in record time and Madhavji was appointed non-executive director, a polite way of asking him to come into office once a quarter to attend the board meeting and nod his head. His uncle reviewed the operations on a monthly basis and with the appointment of a senior team of professionals comprising both BCL and other executives, the company had been set on an assured trajectory of growth.

The clearances and approvals for all proposals had been fast tracked. BCL had received the land clearance certificates and the joint venture was well on its path to setting up a network of state-of-the art warehouses across the country. It also leased a large fleet of trucks and was set to change the economics and efficiencies of freight and goods transport in India. It had been a win-win for all concerned.

The BCL – Metrics Joint Venture registered a 230 per cent growth in turnover in its very first year of operation and had been set to clock another stupendous year with over 160 per cent growth. BCL had not been keen for an IPO and had been of the belief that the organization had yet to realize its true potential. However, both organizations soon realized that the need for capital was immense for a company in this line of business. As the Metrics JV expanded, it soon realized that its leverage was crossing dangerous lines. The BCL management was wary of growing and taking on debt at this rapid pace, and had wanted the revenues to settle in on some of the existing investments, however the Minister's enthusiasm couldn't be curbed as banks and financial institutions continued to lend money to the Metrics JV with unprecedented ease.

However the meteoric growth in its turnover had been attributed to the access that the Metrics JV had to BCL's logistical needs across India. It had originally been allocated the Maharashtra and Goa regions but had soon penetrated the entire Western and Southern regions to transport goods from its factories to the warehouses and C&F agents. The existing suite of transport service providers had been swiftly replaced by a state-of-the art fleet from the Metrics JV.

The BCL Metrics management teams, as also the Minister, were thrilled with the progress and success of the joint venture and its operations. The Metrics JV was quickly gaining traction in receiving high value contracts from leading government and private sector companies across India. Its comprehensive and modern suite of logistics and storage services, though considered to be a premium, had made a significant impact within board rooms with access to real time tracking systems and state-of-the art facilities.

The finance minister had been convinced that it was all going right and the time had come for the common man of India to participate in the success story. He believed that an IPO was the route to tap the true and hidden value of this company.

Vikram had been summoned to New Delhi over a 3 am text message from the Minister's assistant, suggesting a 9 am breakfast meeting with the Minister at his residence on the same day. The meeting commenced promptly at 2 pm and lasted for about four minutes post which Vikram found himself in a cab, back to the airport with explicit instructions for speaking with the BCL management and informing them of the need to have an IPO for the joint venture within the following three months. He was also handed over the portfolio of a girl in her early twenties.

'I'm sure she would be great in one of your advertising campaigns,' had been the Minister's departing words before he headed out for his next important engagement.

Vikram was aware that the national elections were rumoured to be held within another six months, and the position of the current coalition didn't appear to be too strong for a re-election. The finance minister had completed a long run in the current ministry, and rumours were rife that some fresh thinking would be in order soon.

Vikram smiled to himself, and knew that he would be the one holding the ship together when the crap descended. He had been the arbiter and the forced matchmaker for this unlikely and unnecessary marriage. He noticed that he had been provided an escort to the airport and the car was now speeding on its way to Terminal 3. As the car sped past the Taj Mahal hotel, he reflected on the real state of affairs of the BCL-Metrics Joint Venture and shuddered to think the listing of risk factors and declarations that they would have to make in the red herring prospectus.

He flipped through the presentation that had an update on the performance of the Metrics JV, that he had carried with him, knowing quite well that the Minister wouldn't be inclined to view or even discuss a colourful and complex set of pages with graphs and statistics. This had been a cultural bridge that Vikram had found difficult to traverse in the journey of establishing the Metrics JV, but he was now more at ease in dealing with the idiosyncracies and ways of the bureaucracy and melee of politicians. As he flipped through the pages, he shook his head as he read between the lines.

Hidden within this stellar performance was a flood of over-billing, issues with damaged and lost goods and cases of stock being cleared without excise clearance. The Metrics JV had resulted in a nexus between the employees of the Metrics JV company and those in sales and production, leading to a rampant collusion in misappropriation of funds and goods. The situation had got out of hand and Vikram soon realized that key senior management team members had been engulfed in this.

He pondered and wondered if the minister was even familiar with the term Red Herring Propsectus. He had pleaded and appealed to the Minister, but he soon received a counter threat that the BCL factories across India may just come under the investigation of the Environment Ministry. It had been a futile but necessary attempt; at least he was in a position to tell his global team that he had tried to urge the minister against this preposterous move.

The car had reached the airport in under twenty-five minutes and Vikram decided to stretch his legs and refresh himself with a pint of beer in the lounge. It had been a frenetic rush to New Delhi and the excruciating five-hour wait for the minister had only accentuated his ulcers. He picked up a few sandwiches from the buffet counter and settled himself on a recliner. The lounge was sparsely populated at this early hour and

Vikram relished the silence. As he sipped the beer and nibbled on his sandwich, his moment of calm was abruptly interrupted.

'Vikram?'

'Yes…' he politely replied, though he felt like saying bugger off! 'Hi!' The gentleman in the suit extended his hand and Vikram was forced to reciprocate.

Nirmesh Sindhwani was the man who made things happen and move in the corporate circles. He was the matchmaker, the artful arbiter and a ruthless but indispensable deal-maker. He moved around with a badge of investment banker and managing director of NS Financials, which seemed to be the respectable title for a business card and an acceptable and honourable channel for corporate social interaction.

'A pleasant surprise, Nirmesh…'

'Yes I know.'

He sat on the recliner beside Vikram and folded his legs.

'You heading back to Mumbai?'

Nirmesh fiddled with his watch and then settled down.

'Yes, Vikram. How about you?'

'On the 4 pm flight.'

'Good. But I'm on a later flight.'

'We haven't met for quite some time.'

'I know, but you know how it can be. It's been a crazy couple of months.'

Vikram sipped his beer, sure that Nirmesh wasn't one to beat around the bush.

'What brings you to Delhi?'

Nirmesh smiled. 'Had a meeting with a Ministry.'

His tone indicated that this wasn't a chance meeting.

'Some PSU coming up on the market?'

'Wouldn't say a PSU, but something quite interesting.'

'Well, I'm sure that would be a cinch for you!' Vikram laughed.

These chaps at UBS, Morgan Stanley and Merrill are breathing down our necks these days. They have all dropped their fees and there's not much money to be made. It's just not like the old days, Vikram.'

'I can understand,' Vikram nodded.

'But, you know, this is a business where loyalties and relationships make the difference between a good IPO and a great one.'

He paused, awaiting a reaction from Vikram but then continued.

'I hear your Metrics JV is exploring some opportunities as well?'

Vikram's calm and poise was shattered instantly.

'We're just focusing on growing the business right now, Nirmesh.'

Nirmesh nodded. 'I can understand where you're coming from, but there are some opportunities that just come knocking on your door. Anyway, Vikram, it was a pleasure meeting you, as always. Let's catch up soon in Mumbai. How about breakfast day after tomorrow morning?'

'Would love to, Nirmesh. But it's quite a hectic schedule this week … but we should meet soon.'

'I'm meeting the minister again next Monday, Vikram.' Nirmesh got up and patted Vikram on his back and left.

Vikram realized that NM Investments was to be the merchant banker for the IPO that was yet to be discussed with the BCL management. The Minister had sought it fit to move quickly in the matter.

The BCL board strongly presented its resentment and disapproval for the IPO, but it soon receded as the

Environment Ministry launched an investigation into BCL's Nasik plant.

The IPO was lead managed by NM Investments and two other players. It was a runaway success, with both the institutional and retail quotas being oversubscribed handsomely. The script opened at a remarkable 123 per cent premium on opening day and it soon settled at the ₹370 mark. The minister's family had disinvested over 40 per cent of its stake in the company, requiring BCL to retain most of its shareholding in the now publicly listed company. The minister's nephew Madhavji Patil was relieved of his executive responsibilities shortly after the IPO and was replaced by a seasoned logistics professional.

There had been a preliminary enquiry into the rapid rise of the BCL-Metrics JV stock by SEBI, but had been squashed and brushed off hastily after the SEBI officials received a call from New Delhi.

A few months later, as the elections were announced, Vikram was summoned again to Delhi by the minister. As he anxiously waited, in the waiting lounge, Vikram wondered what was in store for him and his joint venture. He was called into the Minister's office for a seven-minute interaction after waiting through the day. At 7 pm Vikram left the Minister's office and noticed a police escort waiting for him to take him to the airport.

He managed to get a ticket for the 9 pm flight out of Delhi and reached the airport well in time despite the heavy traffic on NH8, as the convoy guided itself seamlessly through the congestion and chaos.

As Vikram boarded the flight and sat down on his preferred window seat in the second row in Business class, a gentleman dressed in a white linen shirt and khaki trousers came up from behind and sat beside Vikram.

'Hi, Vikram. I believe this is the first time we're meeting.'

Vikram nodded and had a feeling of immense déjà vu.

'Yes, Paresh bhai.'

Paresh bhai was a stockbroker based in Kolkata and was the prima facto mover and shaker on the bourses. The Metrics JV and Nirmesh had employed his services, with Paresh bhai's firm having picked up a sizable portion of the Metrics JV stock in a pre-listing closed door offer. Paresh bhai and his coterie had ramped up the stock price and had made a healthy packet for Vikram and his senior team members via a slew of shadow accounts that had been set up in the names of their relatives and friends. The senior management team had been prohibited by compliance norms from investing in the IPO but Paresh bhai had been kind enough to facilitate the same via a slew of complicated transactions that had been seeded to ensure that there was no linkage directly with the employees.

'Has your wife finished furnishing your home in Alibaug?'

The beach house in Alibaug had been gifted to Vikram's wife by her uncle, a few months after the IPO.

'It's been quite hectic, we haven't been able to spend as much time there as we had hoped.'

Paresh bhai laughed. 'I know. Life doesn't make any sense when we can't even find the time to enjoy the fruits of our labour.'

Vikram was uncomfortable with the discussion and the proximity of his neighbour. The business class section was the more high profile and visible section of the aircraft and he didn't want to be noticed or seen having a long discussion with Paresh bhai. The consequences could be damaging.

'You travel to Mumbai quite often?' Vikram wanted to deflect the conversation and quickly.

'Not too often really. I prefer my little office in Kolkata. But before I take your leave, I just thought that I should mention to you that the minister was keen on picking up a stake in BCL.'

'I'm sure that would be a sound investment, Paresh bhai.'

'Yes, I know. The outlook has been quite good for them. I'm sure your seniors in the UK would be able to assist …'

Paresh bhai shook Vikram's hesitant hand and left.

Vikram looked out of the window and was relieved to see the aircraft doors being closed and the seat adjacent to his lying vacant.

He reflected on his earlier conversation with the minister and the brief interlude with Paresh bhai. This was getting all too messy for his liking. The Alibaug house was not something that he had favoured or endorsed. It had just happened and it was now irreversible.

The minister had gradually diluted most of his holdings in the company and now wanted to sell off its balance stake. BCL had expressed its keenness to pick up his stake, but with the elections around the corner, they wanted to wait it out, but the minister was keen on closing the transaction before the upcoming elections. The conversation with Paresh bhai had discomforted him further.

The global BCL team didn't have a whiff of the degree of involvement of the India BCL team in the IPO listing of the Metrics JV company nor the misdealings. It was getting murky. The minister was unable to offload any further stock in the market and Paresh bhai too wanted to exit from his holding in the Metrics JV. There weren't enough buyers out there for this large block of shares, without the risk of the stock price going into a downward spiral.

Vikram quenched his thirst with a bottle of water and opened his laptop and searched for a document. He found it after searching extensively within sub folders he had created during the formation of the Metrics JV. The document contained the shareholding of the various entities which included some companies based in Mauritius, legitimate investment vehicles used by several corporates and high net worth individuals. He leaned on the head rest and closed his eyes.

He could still remember the opening session of the IPO at the BSE. He and Mark, both members on the board of the new company had celebrated with champagne and a special event organized for the head office at the Taj Mahal hotel. The stock had surged within a few minutes of its opening. It had been listed at ₹ 225 after book closing, but it had soon touched ₹ 400. Paresh bhai had pumped in enough euphoria for the stock, and retail investors moved in by the thousands to get a piece of the action. Word had already been out that the minister was a part of the action and this was a sure-shot winner. Even the BCL senior management had been overwhelmed by the response and patted themselves on the back for the sound but hesitant decision that had been thrust upon them. It was a great story.

Vikram and his direct reports had been given proxy access to shares that had been dispensed in the pre-IPO stage. And this was off the record for obvious reasons. He and the finance head had a piece of the action and the situation had gotten sticky.

Chapter Twelve

2:55 PM
TODAY

great kings nurse respect
for their falling equal

Maithili strolled back into his office examining some of the curios in the glass cabinet placed behind him.

Agastya called the advertising agency director.

'Any word from your media folks?'

'The News Times guys are not budging. Same goes for the guys at HT.'

'They're not willing to give in for a premium? They've done that in the past.'

'They've got into a huddle as we speak. Let's see what happens.'

'But didn't your media buying team confirm the front page ads with them?'

'They had! But they were just negotiating and playing for some better rates. Stark just barged in.'

Agastya didn't have the time to wait.

'Make some calls. Push some buttons,' he said but in a calm, resolute voice. He realized that he needed to exercise some emotional restraint.

'I am on it, Agastya! Let me assure you, I've briefed my CEO. Even he's trying to pull some strings. We're all at it.'

'How about the new advertisement layouts?'

'It's just been a few minutes, Agastya. I have to give them some more time.'

'Have you managed to at least get the Stark ad layout? I need to see what they're going to be announcing. I don't want any more surprises.'

'Don't use that word.'

'What?'

Agastya could hear a door being closed before he responded in a hushed tone.

'I just got off the phone with Stark's advertising agency

creative head. We had both started our careers together in Victor & Bennett...'

'And?'

'They seemed to have signed up some major film celebrity.'

'Shit!'

The ship was sinking, even faster than he had imagined. Stark was gunning straight for him. They were coming with all guns blazing. The whole damn armada was out to get him. It was all crumbling around him. How could he have missed out on all this information? How could his team have been so out of sync! Had he lost his touch? Had he lost that finesse he was known for? Was one of "India's savviest marketers" getting knocked out? This was unreal. Something was amiss and he couldn't put his finger on it.

Agastya looked at his inbox. There was an email from Nitin, in which he had been marked a copy.

Hi Vikram ,

Please find attached a photograph of the new Sparkle *packet which has hit the shelves at Q Mart in Mumbai. It's been priced at ₹115.*

He opened the attachment and saw the price for himself. It was ₹115. This wasn't a 20 per cent discount as they had originally anticipated, but a 15 per cent discount.

Agastya glanced at the tablet. The Alliance scrip had taken a U turn! It had moved up to ₹433. He had gone 3 million short at ₹431. He wasn't sure if it was teasing him or lashing back at him.

He messaged Manish and Mukund.

'Alliance?'

Manish sent back a response. *'Weak.'*

Mukund messaged back. *'Can't say. Take cover.'*

Sebastian called. He had been marked on the email from Nitin.

'Agastya, we'll need to rework the business impact numbers with a 15 per cent discount.'

'Keep both options open. We may need to present both options for Mark and Vikram to take a call.'

Sebastian nodded and dialled out to the finance team, urging them to come down to his desk.

Agastya reflected on the situation and the facts. It was clear that Stark was indeed launching Velvet at a lower price. That had been established. It was also clear that they would have the upper hand right from the day of the launch, and if they retained the price difference, consumers would surely resist picking up Sparkle. It was a premium product offering, but housewives would remain housewives. Every rupee counted, and it wasn't as if they were offering anything spectacularly superior to Sparkle.

They were seeking to upgrade some of their existing consumers from their lower priced brands to Sparkle. There didn't seem to be any other option other than to take the price cut and hit the market. They would have to work out some methods of cost cutting and reduction in the months to come, though it didn't look quite plausible. They had done enough work on this over the last two years. It was a dead end. He had no way out.

He wanted to believe Nitin, but also wanted to connect with Vikram personally. He dialled Vikram's extension, but it was engaged. He was unable to get through his mobile either. If there was something in the offing, it would impact much more than the press conference. It would alter the DNA and the power structure within BCL.

He had been aware of irregularities within the BCL Metrics JV as had most of the senior management. He however had limited interaction and involvement with its operations and was relieved that he was at a safe distance. Agastya had been careful to not invest in any BCL or associated stocks. He did have employee options, but had parked them in a separate account.

'Vikram on the firing line?' Maithili piped up.

'You overheard?'

'You must learn to speak in a lower tone if you don't want people to overhear.'

Agastya hadn't heard from Manish for several minutes now. He needed to get the juices flowing and feel his pulse quicken again. He quickly scanned the graphs and the overall trading volumes. The market was still in the red, but some sanity seemed to have prevailed. However he sensed this to be a nervous calm. The mobile rang.

'Manish. Where have you been?'

'Listen. Just hold on for some time. Don't offload just as yet, but it may not be a bad idea to go short on Nectar.'

'I've already sold DSQ and Infitel and gone short on Alliance!'

'No worries. I've got you covered, but look at Nectar…long.'

'What's the story?'

'The FIIs are pumping money into it.'

Agastya looked up the Nectar stock, a large pharmaceutical company that had a great run in the markets three months earlier, but had taken a fall in recent weeks. The results had been good and a stake sale to one of the world's leading pharmaceutical conglomerates had given this company a large potential upside play. But he wasn't sure if there was an opportunity for the scrip to make a significant upward movement in the brief time left in this trading session.

It had been one of the few scrips that had held its ground during the day and had in fact gained over 2 per cent from its opening for the day and was hovering near ₹735.

He messaged his broker. *'Long 500k Nectar…'*

Maithili moved closer to him, stroked his hair and sighed. 'Finally I get to see some money?'

'Let's see.'

It was a terse response. He was getting back in the game. He could feel the adrenaline again. His heart was racing and his fingers were furiously slamming the keys as he tried to discover any opportunities and trends in the market. He wasn't going to let go so easily.

'Now, Agastya, how about I make you a proposition?'

'What now, M?'

'Let's make this worth your while?'

'I'm not letting go of my property.'

'I know. But let's make it interesting.'

'What is it?' he snapped.

'If you make 20 crores by 3:30, then you can just pay me 5 crores!'

'Are you out of your mind?!'

'It's just an option. No need for you to be upset with me!'

'Stop these mind games!'

'Not mind games, Agastya. Just an option!'

He received a message from his broker. *₹200-crore exposure… no more!*

He replied *'Not today.'*

Mukund wrote, *'Can't go further.'*

'Damn!' he muttered to himself. Alliance was heading

towards ₹434 a couple of rupees higher than the level at which he had gone short.

Agastya had over leveraged himself. He currently had equity trades whose principal value was over ₹200 crores and had barely under ₹11 crores with him. If the tides did turn strongly against him, his money would be wiped out in a few minutes.

His mobile beeped.

Sailesh: Vikram under heat?

Agastya: ?

Sailesh: Having a nice day?

Agastya: Thrilling!

Sailesh: Impressive packaging.

Agastya: So is yours.

Sailesh: ☺

Manish called again. 'Keep a distance from Alliance. It can go either way. Quite possible that they were just rumours.'

'You sure?'

'For the next couple of minutes at least. And check out Pulse, the FIIs seem to be flirting with it.' He disconnected.

'Has it occurred to you that you seriously haven't thought of why I'm doing this?' said Maithili.

Agastya looked up at her. Her simple statement had shaken him again. He had just presumed that a vengeful streak had consumed her. But now, he realized that it wasn't as simple.

'What was Dubai about?'

'It was much more than Dubai, Agastya. Something you would never understand. I don't feel like talking about it now. Just get back to your mess.' She looked past him.

'Come on, Maithili. I am trying. Tell me. You need to understand that I'm under a lot of stress.'

She laughed.

'The great Agastya succumbing to stress? That's a first!'

'Come off it, M! It's not like that.'

'You're cold, manipulative and self-centred. That's you, Agastya. The main problem is that you don't even know why that's bad.'

Agastya smiled. 'That's why we've been together so long. Right?'

'Yes, Agastya! You know better than anyone else how good my taste in men is!'

'How can I make it up to you, M?'

She grinned. 'Want to make love to me?'

Agastya smiled. Had he sensed a crack?

'How about the suite at The Trident? For old time's sake?'

'Champagne and lots of it?'

'You forgot the strawberries.'

'How about some whipped cream as well?'

'To go along with the strawberries?'

'For that too.' She was beaming. the innocent effervescent vigour had emerged again. Was she finally opening up?

'We did have fun with the cream, right?'

She sat on his desk, folded her legs, kneeled forward, folded her hands together and placed them below her chin supporting her elbows on her legs.

'Yes, Agastya. By the way…' she paused.

'Yes?'

'Have you ever loved me?'

Agastya froze.

'Is that what all this is about?'

She gave him a peck on the head and resumed her walk around his office.

'Can you excuse me, darling? I need to go to the restroom.'

He glared at her. 'Button up your blouse!'

She turned around and glared at him.

'Please…' he pleaded.

She opened the door, buttoned up her blouse and left his room.

The mobile was vibrating again. It was Vikram.

'Yes, Vikram?'

'Agastya, I am making this call personally to my direct team. It's going to be a quick call though, under the circumstances.'

'Yes, Vikram.'

'There are some developments, and I wanted to tell you myself. Or rather Mark asked me to tell you. I may not be attending the press conference today.'

Agastya clenched his fist. He had hoped for the press conference to be called off, but that now clearly seemed unlikely. He was finding it difficult to have this conversation.

'Yes, Vikram.' He bit his lips as he realized that he had repeated the same words for the third time.

'The press are going to be asking some questions which are not related to the Sparkle launch, and I'm sure you would have heard about some of these things. We are told that it may just hit the news soon.'

Agastya was surprised that Vikram was making this call himself. If he indeed had put in his papers, Richard would have been the one having this conversation with him. Maybe it was untrue after all?

'What can I do, Vikram?'

'I just wanted to inform you.' Vikram disconnected abruptly.

He placed the phone on the table and saw an email from Nitin, marked highly important.

Vikram,

My sales managers have received calls from over sixty distributors across the country in the last ten minutes. They are suspending business with BCL with immediate effect. Stark seems to have hijacked them. Will update you with more details shortly.

'What?!' Agastya shrieked.

The distributors were responsible for buying stocks from BCL and then selling them to retailers across the country. BCL had over 1200 distributors across the country, but knowing Stark, they would have swooped in on the bigger ones. It wasn't easy for a distributor to switch allegiance, and certainly not overnight. Stark would have been planning this for months. It was quite uncommon for distributors to give up their association easily, and the leading ones had been reputed to have a bond with BCL across multiple generations in their families. The Stark deal must have been exceptionally sweet for them to bite the bait.

It was sheer chaos that was unfolding at BCL. Their CEO was being blown to smithereens. Their new product launch had been sabotaged and now their distribution system was crippled.

'Why, Sailesh…Why?' Agastya whispered to himself.

Agastya was restless. He wanted to pick up the phone and speak with Sailesh. The messages being exchanged on messenger disturbed him. There was an urge of disgust and revenge that swept his body. He wanted to reach out to him, look him in his eyes and understand what had triggered it all.

The commotion and the buzz outside the office was evident. The teams were grouped into huddles and the chatter was clearly about Vikram's resignation. The text messages were rife with speculations, enquiries and theories. The news appeared to have hit the outside world as well and the marketing and financial circles of Mumbai all seemed to be talking about it.

He toggled to the screen with the chess game and made a move. He took out Sailesh's queen in a rage of fury.

He reflected briefly on their journeys and their personal rapports. It then occurred to him that he infact respected Sailesh. He may have tricked him out of the BCL CMO spot, but it didn't take away from the fact that Sailesh was a far better strategist than he could ever be. Sailesh's pulse for the customer and markets was impeccable and the work he had undertaken at Stark had been remarkable and instrumental in the turnaround of the company. Beneath the exterior of hate and resentment, lay a deep sense of awe and respect for his foe. It occurred to him that he had to counter Sailesh, but more importantly he needed to understand what had triggered the breakdown of the pact.

Inspite of their daily rivalries, there had been trust when he had shaken hands with him. It had to mean something. What had he missed? Had his team or the organization done something? If only he could have a frank chat. They could have resolved this. But he also realized that it was too late in the day. The wheels had been set in motion. The cause didn't matter anymore. It was now irreversible.

Agastya suddenly felt a sense of despondence and helplessness. He also realized, Nitin would have been too occupied with handling the collapse of his distribution system. He couldn't sit down with Nitin and work things out.

Agastya figured that he would have to strike a blow. That would have been the only way for him to gauge Sailesh and get a sense of where he was coming from. Maybe this was beyond Sailesh as well? But then Sailesh could have given him a heads up. It didn't add up. Had Sailesh concocted the bridge of trust? Had this been his master plan? Had he been outmanoeuvred by Sailesh after all? The despondence was soon replaced by a sense of indignation. He was now bearing the pain of a wounded soldier. He needed to be either meticulous and sharp, or he had to be just brutal and thrust everything he had on Sailesh, back at him. He had to make Sailesh blink.

He called Nitin.

'Yes, Agastya? What is it?'

He could sense the dejection and frustration in his voice.

'We need to do something.'

There was a deliberate pause.

'What do you suggest?'

'Take them down. Use everything that you've got.'

'We need to manage our ship first, Agastya. Don't have the time to do this right now.'

'Think about it, Nitin. We don't know what else they may have in store. We can't just sit and take cover.'

'What do you have in mind?'

'Some of the usual stuff and then we'll see.'

'Too messy. And you don't have too much time, Agastya.'

'Let's give it a shot at least.'

Nitin remained silent for several seconds.

Agastya's eyes moved towards the tablet again. The stock markets continued taking a bludgeoning. Some of the mid caps seemed to be holding steady, but the blue chips were taking a pounding. It was senseless. There appeared to be no clear reason or rationale for the sudden pounding. Not that there was ever any. He realized that he had made a fair amount of money on Nectar, but his indecision on his stock holdings had cost him dearly. He should have sold ten minutes earlier.

A bead of sweat rolled down his forehead and traced its way down to his nose. He wanted to wipe it off with his hand, but sensed that his eyes and hands were both frozen.

He realized that as he had spoken those words to Nitin, he too had crossed the line. There would be no looking back with Sailesh and all that they had done to back and flank each other would just disappear. It would be demolished. The last twenty minutes had already cast a spectre of doubt across their bond and pact. The next few minutes would thrust him down a path of no return.

He grappled with the recent events and was desperat to give Sailesh the benefit of the doubt, but realized that he didn't have it anymore within him to give him that latitude. He reached out deep within to seek out and trace the last few drops of empathy and perhaps even sympathy for Sailesh. 'Agastya, let's go for it.' Nitin disconnected.

Agastya sent an SMS. *'Use the worm.'*

He opened his messenger service and shook his head as he typed.

Agastya : Don't...

Sailesh : Enjoy.

Agastya understood that Sailesh had been deliberate in his words and actions. He also knew that Sailesh was well aware of anticipating his reactions in this situation.

Agastya quickly looked for a contact and pressed the dial button. It rang twice and was fortunately picked up. Agastya hesitated and thought of disconnecting, but then the voice spoke.

'What's happening over there, Agastya?'

'Will give you the dope later. You need to look after my friend, Ajay.'

'I had a feeling you'd call.'

'Just do it!'

'What's in it for me?'

'Just speak with your ad sales team. They'll tell you!'

'Ha!'

'What was that for?'

'Journalistic integrity, my friend.'

'Of course...'

Agastya disconnected.

Sailesh Rao's Office at Stark, Mumbai.

Sailesh was back at his seat and fidgeting with his pen. He realized that the entire team at BCL would be on to him, and they would retaliate with everything that they had in their arsenal.

He needed to review the questions and answers that had been prepared for Prem Mehra for the evening function, but wasn't able to focus.

He looked at the photograph of his wife and their two children. It had been taken on a recent visit to Disneyland. Theirs had been an arranged marriage and he knew well that she wouldn't have been with him if it hadn't been "arranged". She was vivacious, fun-loving and yet focused on her career. She had made several sacrifices on her professional front to keep the family together and look after the children.

Sailesh had left Singapore to join Gillette in India, and then the transition to Stark as their CMO after the takeover had given him a new lease of life. On this occasion however his wife had decided to stay back in Singapore along with their children. It had been a tough stretch in their married lives and the distance appeared to have amplified the fissures in their relationship that had remained hidden when they lived together. He also realized that he had grown intensely dependent on her and that he wasn't as independent and strong as he had often perceived himself to be.

He had planned to visit his family in Singapore on a fortnightly basis, but initially their schedules and then their differences made the visits and interactions infrequent. He maintained a four bedroom apartment in South Bombay, but stayed in a single bedroom service apartment closer to office. He had found it convenient to manage and the compact space helped stay the loneliness he had often felt in the larger apartment.

He had often found himself lost in thought, introspecting on his marriage and what had gone wrong. He was wary of the flaws and mistakes that they often revealed. And then the obsession with obliterating Agastya had but provided further fuel to distract him.

He opened the drawer in the desk and searched for an analegesic, and was frustrated with himself for being unable to locate one. Radhika walked in.

'Sailesh. May I ask you something?'

'Yes, Radhika.'

Radhika's BA degree in psychology and two years of teaching had proven to be a boon for Sailesh. She had moved from Hyderabad after her marriage and had taken up the assignment at Stark as an interim measure in making ends meet in the hyper-expensive city, as she termed it. Referred by a neighbour, Sailesh had been impressed by her candour and found her lack of corporate experience to be an added bonus. It had taken her but a few months to settle into her assignment and he had even prodded her to take up a role in marketing.

'I know I may be out of turn, but I have to ask this.'

'Don't hesitate, Radhika.'

'You need to take a break.'

Sailesh smiled as he watched his nervous assistant stammering.

'That's not a question.'

'You do know that you're taking on quite a bit with all this you've planned. Don't you think you're losing the plot? There is a difference between professional rivalry and hatred. Don't you think you should focus on what's really important to you? And more importantly, don't lose sight of who you are! I've seen you change and I've seen you lose yourself. Are you really sure that this is how you want to do this?'

Sailesh nodded and smiled.

'It's not just simple rivalry, Radhika.'

'Revenge perhaps? I thought both of you had worked things out.'

'We had, but that's changed. He did something that I wouldn't have done.'

'And you haven't?'

'It's now personal. He crossed the line.'

Sailesh paused and took a deep breath. She noticed his eyes moistening.

'What happened, Sailesh? What is it? You don't think this has affected your marriage?'

Radhika continued, 'May I be candid?'

Sailesh laughed. 'I would be offended otherwise.'

'You've become obsessed with Agastya. I know he played you for the BCL position, but this has affected you more than you seem to acknowledge. You're so distracted with these tricks that you play with each other. Why is it bothering you so much? Just let it go.'

'You worry too much, Radhika.'

'You seem to have forgotten how many friends you have here. Your age seems to be eroding your memory.'

Sailesh laughed.

Chapter Thirteen

FOUR MONTHS EARLIER

history trusts turmoil and suspects stability

Sailesh Rao's office at Stark, Mumbai

Sailesh was in the midst of the quarterly review meeting and refused to be distracted by the vibrating mobile, as he amused himself with complaints about BCL.

He finally picked up the phone and was about to put it on silent mode when he scanned the first few words that appeared on the screen. He opened the text message and read it twice. He rushed out of the conference room, towards his cabin on the same floor.

He had not been able to access emails on his phone and the technology support team had been resolving the connectivity issue. He ran towards the laptop, typed in the password and searched for an email from the Bangalore branch head.

He read the email twice and scanned the persons to whom it had been marked in the organization. The branch head had used his discretion and had kept the mailing list to a limited number, but all those who mattered had been covered including the CEO, legal head and some of the other senior management team members. The email had however, been addressed to him.

'This is not a darling situation I guess,' Sailesh muttered to himself and smiled.

The situation had predictably catalyzed an avalanche of messages.

Sailesh opened the emails and read them carefully.

To Rao, Sailesh
Subject : Reports of insects in Stark *detergents*
Sir,
Two local language papers have reported that consumers have seen insects in Stark *detergent packets. Many retailers have*

stopped taking new stocks and don't even want to display the product on the shelves.

This is a serious matter and we would need your help in addressing the same with the press urgently.

Nalin Mehta
Branch Head, West Bengal

To Rao, Sailesh
Subject : Incorrect Details on Detergent Packets
Sir,

We have found several detergent packets which have incorrect declarations on them. The local inspectors have already picked up some samples and sent us a notice to meet them. I have attached the images of the packaging and also the notice received.

I would need your help in resolving the matter.

Bhaskar Naidu
Branch Head, Ludhiana

To Rao, Sailesh
Subject : Protests outside the Bangalore Depot
Sir,

We have about fifty protestors outside the Bangalore Depot demanding that we remove the hoardings with the advertising campaign for the new children's toothpaste. They are protesting against the lewd portrayal of a housewife being displayed outside schools.

They have even torn off posters from nearby shops.

I didn't want to bring the police in, but may have to if it turns violent.

Naveen Chadha
Zonal Head - Karnataka

Sailesh was amused by the barrage of issues. He searched

within his emails for the new hoardings that had been put up in Bangalore and other cities in Karnataka. They portrayed the hackneyed images of a lady with two children in a bathroom, flooding their faces with obnoxious amounts of toothpaste. The new fruit flavour range of toothpastes had been quite a hit, and he had been contemplating introducing some flavours for adults, subsequently.

He didn't notice anything amiss in the visuals at the time, but, when he opened the email again and scrolled down he noticed that a deep cleavage was now distinctly visible on the mother. To make matters worse, she was now wearing a saffron saree with a bindi shaped as an Om. The image had been doctored to the extent of making her lip curl suggestively. Although entertained, he was disgusted by the poor execution.

He forwarded the email to his team and the advertising agency with the necessary expletives, insisting on an urgent correction. He smiled as he pressed the enter button, knowing quite well that it was a missile targeted at innocent bystanders, but he had to set the wheels in motion. He wasn't sure if he should throw one of his team members into the firing ring right away or wait for some more time.

Sailesh picked up the mobile and called up the local agency director based in the Bangalore office.

'Hi, Sailesh. I'm sorry about this mess. I just can't figure out what happened. Those were not the creatives or designs that I had sent out, I assure you.'

'Listen, Ramki. This is a real mess and we need to clean this up quickly. I want those hoardings down in the next thirty minutes.'

It was quite unusual for the chief marketing officer of Stark to call a regional agency director and he could sense the anxiety and nervousness in Ramki's tone.

'Yes, Sailesh. I'm working on it right away.'

'And how the hell did this happen?'

'I can assure you that it wasn't anything at our end, Sailesh. I can vouch for the integrity of my team.'

'Are you sure? You've had several people leaving your agency of late, and many new employees...'

There was a pause and he could sense the restlessness of the agency director.

'I can...'

'Listen, Ramki. Just figure this out right away. Trust me. You're on a bad wicket right now. If I were in your place, I would be at the printer where this stuff got printed.'

'Will do.'

He disconnected the call. He would have, usually, asked one of his team members to do this for him, but he had wanted to get a pulse of the situation himself. He was convinced that Ramki didn't have a role to play in the matter.

It was also unlikely that a printer down the value chain would doctor images and risk losing his reputation and a large business opportunity with Stark.

He stood up and walked up to the large window in his room to reflect on the situation. He had quit smoking for over six years now, but had the urge to light one up.

He opened the messenger services, clicked on Agastya and typed a message.

Enjoying yourself?

Agastya: I love saffron!

His team started streaming into his office, justifying that they had followed the due processes and the designs that they had signed off were the same on which his concurrence had been sought. The Public Relations head was now seated, holding his head and warding off calls from the media with this sudden outbreak of juicy gossip for their publications and channels.

Some of the incidents had also broken into the online media and there was information that the news channels would be broadcasting some of the visuals from Bangalore in the next hour. The situation was worsening and the incorrect packaging and the insects were now crawling across the grapevine at Stark. A heads-up had already been given to the Asia-Pacific communications team in Singapore and North America as a precautionary measure by the PR head. Sailesh scoffed him for it, but also knew that he was following protocol while correctly covering his backside.

He resented the complex matrix of reporting structures, with the Singapore department heads having a dotted line relationship with some of their team members. But that was something that he would have to address later.

He needed to contain the situation quickly, with the global compliance head scheduled to arrive in Mumbai the following day from New York. He was sure that the set of antics would have been to commemorate his grand arrival on Indian shores.

He called the Bangalore advertising agency director again.

'Ramki. Please send me the details of the printer where these got printed.'

'I have it with me right now. It's Venkateshwara Printers in Koramangala. Why do you ask?'

'Just curious. Also, when was the hoarding put up?'

'It was put up late night early morning…'

'And what time did the protesters start off?'

'They were there first thing in the morning.'

'Don't you find it unusual?'

'The convenient timing?'

'Everything about it, actually...'

'Let me look into it. I'll call you back.'

Sailesh's phone rang again.

It was a call from his HR Head.

'Sailesh, is this a good time?' The tone was tense and quite in contrast to the jovial and loud exchange that he had been used to for years.

'Yes, Shankar. Sure.'

'I believe there's a situation in Bangalore?'

'Yes.' He wasn't surprised at the speed at which news travelled in Stark.

'I was speaking with Prem, and this situation seems to be getting quite serious.'

'Serious? Yes, it is a serious matter, but we need to work towards resolving it quickly.'

'I understand. But this seems to have some political implications as well.'

'I know. There are some protestors out there.'

'Prem just received a call from New Delhi.'

'And? Shankar, we know each other quite well. So, please don't beat around the bush!'

'Let's just say we need to take a sense of ownership on the matter.'

Sailesh paused.

'Sailesh, are you there?'

'You're looking for a scapegoat, Shankar?'

'I wouldn't put it like that. But in a situation such as this, it is important to address the requirements of the business in a professional manner. And, there is an increasing apprehension that these skirmishes we keep running into are because of your feud with Agastya.'

'And since when has this become a situation that is not quite tolerable? We've seen dozens of other such instances. What's new in this case?'

'There comes a time, Sailesh. I'm sure you would understand.'

Sailesh hung up and clenched the mobile in his hand.

Shankar and Prem had wanted his neck on the block. It hadn't even been an hour since the crisis broke out, and they had already decided to axe him. It appeared too smooth and convenient. The daggers had been drawn in unanimous spontaneity, quite in contradiction to the spirit of acceptable rivalry that existed between the two organizations.

His exceptional career flashed by him and it amused him that a saffron saree and a gorgeous cleavage were going to be his death knell at Stark. It seemed almost banal. The general had overshadowed the king for quite some time, and he needed to now appease the him.

The mobile rang again. It was Shankar.

'Yes, Shankar. Was there more?'

'Prem needs to get back to New Delhi quickly.'

'Really? What's the rush?'

'You know how these matters can take a turn rapidly. It's not just about the hoarding, Sailesh.'

Sailesh was now puzzled.

'As in?'

'The audit team has been conducting an investigation for a while now on misappropriation of funds within the marketing budget. It's estimated to be over 6.5 crores over the last one year and most of it in the Bangalore region.'

'And why wasn't I informed about it? Since when has this been on?'

'A couple of weeks now. But that's not important. They will be submitting their final report shortly, but this whole situation is now quite grave.'

Sailesh realized that there was more to it than what Shankar was letting on.

'Shankar, you need to let me in on the details.'

Shankar paused and took a deep breath.

'All I can say is that it's a situation that has been going on for some months now. There are documents that implicate your department. The audit report is being presented within the hour.'

'Is that the time available?'

'I would imagine...'

'Thanks, Shankar.'

Sailesh was tempted to check with his team members, but didn't know where or with whom to start, nor did he have the luxury of time.

Karnataka had an annual budget in excess of 60 crores across the product ranges, and this didn't include television and press advertising. It was one of the larger and more important markets for Stark and one region in which they had usurped the number one spot from BCL in recent months. The sales and marketing teams had worked together in creating an optimal mix of distribution reach, trade commissions and consumer promotion backed by high decibel promotions, advertising, sampling drives and consumer offers. It was now the jewel in the crown for Stark and this scandal would rock the boat for Sailesh, as well as his company.

He called his assistant on the intercom.

'Radhika, can you get my promotional budget file for the last two quarters?'

Sailesh had insisted on maintaining hard copies for all key budget sign-offs for ready access.

Radhika walked in within a minute with a large box file and placed it in front of him on his table.

'Anything else, Sailesh?'

'Just give me a minute.'

He opened the section which had Karnataka marked on the file separator. His eye for detail and an enormous memory had trained him to quickly identify gaps and loopholes. He skimmed through the budgets and the reports and realized that everything was in order. It had to be deeper and well outside the simple purview of invoices and budget documents.

'Thanks, Radhika!'

As she left the room he dialled another number from his mobile.

When the line connected, he spoke abruptly.

'Why are you derailing me?'

There were no words exchanged for several seconds as he could hear the person on the other end getting up to close the door in his room and retreating to a quieter corner of the room.

'You shouldn't be calling me, Sailesh!'

'Listen, Mandy, we've known each other too long. I've known you from your days as a wet-behind-the-ears management trainee. Now, don't give me bullshit. What's going on?'

Mandar Kelkar, was the general manager, Internal Audit, at Stark and a colleague from Gillette.

'I've not had this conversation with you, Sailesh. Is that clear?'

'Yes, Mandy, now don't waste my time. I clearly don't have enough of it. What's going on?'

'Make sure to delete this call from your records on the mobile.'

Sailesh decided to pull his seniority in the conversation.

'You are irritating me, Mandy. Out with it!'

Mandar spoke in a hushed tone.

'It's in Bangalore and the rest of Karnataka as well.'

'What's happening there, Mandy? Out with it quickly!'

Sailesh was reputed for his ability in persuading and pressurizing individuals even in situations of severe adversity. His ability to keep calm and stay focused had haunted and diligently frustrated everyone he had interacted with in his professional career, and to his chagrin he seemed to have let it flow into his personal interactions as well.

'It's very dirty, Sailesh. You've paid for hoardings when they really weren't there. For millions of free customer sampling drives, where the free samples didn't reach housewives, but in fact reached the wholesalers at deeply discounted prices. Payments have been made to promotional agencies for work that wasn't done by them. There have been event sponsorships at inflated prices. The list goes on, Sailesh. In fact there are instances when agencies have been paid for work that they've done for BCL!

The deeper we get into it, we just find more. It's a vermin that's crept into the system.'

'What was that? Work done for BCL?'

'Yes, Sailesh. In some of the events where the agency was appointed to distribute free samples in Koramangala and Jayanagar, they were in fact distributing free samples of BCL's products!'

'You're joking!'

'I wish I were, Sailesh.'

'And what makes you think I would be involved in this?'

'All I can say is that it's not only you. But with the sequence and multitude of events, you're the one common link. You would've known about it for sure. In some cases it was too blatant and even foolishly obvious. We know that you're too sharp to have missed out on it, unless you were involved!'

'Wonderful, Mandy! I'm good at what I do, so that makes me guilty?'

'It's not as simple as that, Sailesh. This has been happening for quite some time, across business lines, agencies, different product managers and executives and even sales teams. Hundreds of violations and flaws. It's a damn pandemic.'

'Why didn't you let me know earlier? I could have stopped it, right? I could have helped you with this.'

'My hands were tied, Sailesh. You know how it is. I just couldn't! I have to go now, Sailesh.'

Mandar hung up abruptly.

Sailesh looked at the time on the laptop and opened the box file again.

He flipped to some of the pages in which photographs of hoardings had been attached as supporting documents for some of the outdoor advertising invoices. He then compared the visuals across photographs and matched the lighting conditions with the backgrounds of each site. It didn't take him too long to understand that the photographs had been manipulated.

Sailesh took a deep breath, stood up and stretched his arms. He pushed the yellow suspenders away from his belly and massaged his tummy vigorously. He realized that he had been accosted and played by several people within his organization. His antics, craving for the spotlight and infatuation with the destruction of Agastya had made him miss the fundamentals. He had taken his eye off the ball. He wasn't the master practitioner of marketing that he had touted himself to be. He had fallen prey to the obvious and foul machinations of corporate greed.

He was attuned to dealing with external adversarial situations, but this had proven itself to be a state in which he seemed to be under siege internally.

He was tempted to call the sales head, but then realized that it would have only compromised his situation. The sequence of emails, the Bangalore saffron clad saree incident and now the Internal Audit enquiry appeared to be too conveniently timed.

Radhika walked in again with some packaging designs and placed them on the table.

'These are the samples that you had wanted to see. One of the product managers dropped them at my table.'

'Thanks, Radhika.'

'Sailesh?'

'Yes, Radhika?'

'I was speaking with Mandar's assistant. There is a high level meeting with Prem in a few minutes. They're expecting some heads to roll. Any idea what it's about?'

'What else did she tell you?'

'Not much. Just that Aditya met up with Mandar in the morning today. It was kind of official and I believe he too is going to be in that afternoon meeting.'

'Which Aditya?'

'The sales head Aditya, Sailesh...'

Sailesh was thankful for not making the call to Aditya a few moments earlier.

'That must be routine.'

'They're going to fire you, Sailesh! You do know that, right?'

Sailesh was pleasantly surprised that his calm demeanour had rubbed off in the period that she had been working with him.

'That's quite a confident statement to make! When did you find out about this?'

'I heard about it last evening, but I thought you would do something to overturn it.'

'So, why are you mentioning it to me now?'

'Because you don't seem to be doing anything about it!'

'Really?'

'Don't give me that look, Sailesh.'

Sailesh smiled. 'And what look is that, Radhika?'

'Like I'm a kid!'

'You are one, Radhika. Don't get yourself into this mess. It's not worth it!'

'I can take my own decisions, Sailesh.' Radhika asserted.

She handed him a file that she had been carrying, opened it and placed it on his table.

'What's this?'

'That's your chargesheet, Sailesh. They're going to hang you out to dry with that!'

He browsed through the document which had billing advices, statements of payments and interviews with several of his team members and agency personnel as well.

The findings were brutal.

He ran his fingers through his hair and scanned the documents again. Radhika stepped out and returned with a mug of coffee.

'Is there anyone that you can speak to?'

'It's too sensitive, Radhika.'

He received an email from Mandar, inviting him for a meeting with Internal Audit within the hour. He looked at the time and began perspiring. He wondered if Agastya had played a role in the spate of events.

'You don't have too much time.'

He picked up his mobile and called up the CEO, Prem Mehra.

'Prem.'

'Hi, Sailesh.'

'Good time to speak?'

'I believe Shankar had a word with you?' It was a measured and polite delivery of words.

'Yes, about that …'

'This is really not a good time, Sailesh. But I do hope you've given it some thought?'

'This is rather sudden, Prem. It's not that we've not had incidents like this before.'

'I understand, Sailesh, but there have been a few other incidents as well. We're meeting in some time.'

Prem Mehra disconnected.

He looked towards Radhika and beamed.

'I think Agatsya has been up to some mischief!

'You find this amusing?'

'Yes!' He was now clenching his fists.

****

Sailesh returned from the Internal Audit meeting, looking characteristically amused.

Radhika walked into Sailesh's room with a mug of hot lemon tea.

'What happened? I hope I didn't offend you with what I said earlier?'

'No. You were being honest. Don't think too much about it.'

'What happened in the meeting?'

'It was strange. They came at me with all guns blazing and then they received some documents and went into a huddle.'

'And?'

'Quite a turn of events. Ashish Bedekar is being relieved of his duties.'

'Ashish?! The detergents marketing head?'

'Yes. He had been complicit with the promotional agencies for false billing and even in working with BCL representatives for the situational anarchy in Bangalore'.

'What do you make of it?'

'It's just strange. This whole thing has just been very strange.'

Chapter Fourteen

3:00 PM
TODAY

gladiators come to life
in fresh warm pools of blood
their breath survives
till they quench their thirst

Sailesh Rao's Office at Stark, Mumbai

Radhika finished her call and noticed Sailesh standing beside the window.

'Do you remember a few months back when you were in a spot?'

'You mean when they almost fired me?'

'Yes.'

'What about it?'

'How did you get out if it?'

'As in, Radhika?'

'It was a very tight spot you were in. What really happened?'

'You know what happened?'

'Yes. They got to Ashish.'

'That was quite convenient. Don't you think?'

'I don't follow.'

'Do you know how they arrived at that decision?'

'They had proof.'

Radhika shook her head. She handed him a set of papers.

Sailesh browsed through details of wire transfers and account details of a company that had been set up by Ashish.

'What are these?'

'Ashish had set up a company into which funds were getting routed from the hoarding and promotional agencies that he was doing business with. He was taking a share of all contracts being awarded to them and signing off on activities that had never really taken place.'

'I didn't know about this. How did you get hold of these papers, Radhika?'

'Do you know why the whole matter went away so smoothly?'

'There was enough evidence in the matter. We couldn't go public with it. It would have been a huge PR fiasco! That's obvious.'

'You think it was that simple?'

'Out with it, Radhika!'

'It was a company that Ashish had set up with Prem's nephew.'

'What?!'

'AK Enterprises.'

'And, how did you get hold of these papers?'

'Nitin sent them across to Internal Audit.'

'Nitin Chandra?'

'Yes. Nitin Chandra from BCL.'

Sailesh was livid and confused, but remained silent for several seconds.

'When did they receive the documents?'

'A few moments after you walked into that Internal Audit meeting.'

'How did you get them?'

'I go home with one of the secretaries at Internal Audit. She had misplaced a set of copies she had made before sending them into the board room,' she winked.

'Why do you think Nitin sent these documents?'

'I don't know, Sailesh. I guess he was trying to reach out to you?'

Sailesh browsed through the documents once again and smiled.

'What happened?'

'This couldn't have happened without Agastya knowing about it.'

'Why do you say that?'

'I just realized. It's all coming together.'

'What?'

'Ashish joined us from Pepsi, right?'

'Yes, around the same time you joined,' Radhika paused.

'Ashish used to report to Agastya. For several years ...'

'So you think Agastya would have known about it?'

Sailesh smiled. 'That's for sure.'

'And he would have known that this was building up against you?'

Sailesh kept smiling.

'This just got very interesting, Radhika. '

Agastya's office, BCL

Maithili walked back into his room and closed the door behind her.

'Don't get personal, Agastya,' Maithili was smiling.

'I don't think you're in a position to talk to me about getting personal.'

Agastya was clearly agitated.

'What's between you and Sailesh should be professional. Think about it!'

'What gave you the impression I was getting personal?'

'Because I know you, Agastya. When you get ticked off, it all starts getting blurred for you. '

'What do you know?'

'That doesn't matter really. Does it?'

He realized that she wasn't going to be forthcoming and decided it would be energy better conserved to back off from enquiring about what she was referring to.

'Why does it even matter to you?'

'It doesn't.' She smiled again.

Sebastian walked in with the numbers and two members of the finance team and instantly looked towards Maithili.

She stood for a few seconds and then walked towards Rebecca's desk to make some calls. As Rebecca closed the door, Sebastian spoke.

'Sir, got the two scenarios worked out with six and twelve month projections. We have taken most of the cost elements into account.'

Agastya raised his hand and quickly scanned all the items. It was astounding. The number of aspects that would be impacted and the logistics involved in this was mind boggling. Agastya knew that their work was comprehensive but now also realized that some of the factors and assumptions were possibly off by substantial margins. He did a quick mental calculation, with his eyes on the time at the bottom right hand corner of the laptop. He just wished it had a measure for seconds as well.

They would have been off for sure, and only time would tell clearly what the true impact of this was going to be.

'Good to go. Let's take this up.'

And then it struck him. He wasn't sure to whom the numbers should be taken. Was Vikram at the helm? If he wasn't going to be at the press conference, then it would clearly imply that he was not going to be taking any calls. He could have spoken with Mark directly, but that would upset Richard. He needed to get all three of them together, which under the circumstances was a herculean task.

'Boss, please speak with Mr Sharma.'

Abhishek Sharma was the chief financial officer and an arrogant but talented finance professional. He had been credited with the financial performance of BCL as he turned around distributor credit terms, put in tight controls on all leakages and squeezed suppliers by not releasing their payments to the last day. He was the blue-eyed boy of the investor community and was ruthless when it came to wasteful expenditure, the definition of which was wide ranging and varied with each quarter and business cycle.

Abhishek was vacationing in Goa and didn't seem to care much for the launch or the arrival of Richard and Mark. It was rumoured however, that he was to cut short his vacation and return to Mumbai the following day, so that he could be around for an executive committee meeting, on Vikram's request.

Agastya called up Abhishek. 'Hi, Abhishek, we have a bit of a crisis here.'

'I heard you guys have buggered this up!'

Abhishek wasn't known to mince words and Agastya knew that he was going to be ground and beaten in this very short conversation. He had no financially sound agreements to place in the call, neither could he financially justify the move. Abhishek had been one of the biggest opponents to the grand launch of Sparkle, insisting that they needed to raise the gross margins to tolerable levels, else it would never be sustainable. Agastya had taken on Abhishek in several forums, at Vikram's behest. It had finally been Vikram's call to go ahead with the launch and Abhishek hadn't been too pleased on being shot down.

'Agastya, you there?'

'Yes, Abhishek. It's taken us all by surprise.'

'This is one crazy plan you've put in place. My team told me you're planning to introduce a discount. And to top this all off, you actually want to increase your advertising budget. Now, what do you want me to say?'

'Abhishek, the team will take you through the numbers; I need your go ahead…'

Abhishek paused and then finally responded. 'Agastya, I am not in a position to sanction this, especially under the circumstances. You know what I mean?'

Agastya got up from his chair and walked towards the window.

'Abhishek, we just can't freeze down like this. We've got a press conference in under thirty minutes. We don't have time for indecision.'

'Agastya, we don't have the structure to make a decision right now. Let me get back to you.'

'Ok. I'll wait to hear from you.'

'By the way, how bad is it out there? You guys are enjoying all the action when I'm away?'

'What can I say?'

'I just hope it doesn't get too messy. It's unfortunate really.'

'I know. Let's see how it turns out? We've got enough of a mess as it is ...'

Abhishek hung up.

Agastya didn't like the tone, but understood the bind that Abhishek was in.

'What was that?'

'Nothing, Sebastian. Get me some printouts. I need to take this up ...'

'Here,' Sebastian handed him three copies.

He had to make a recommendation to Vikram. He couldn't be seen stuttering in Mark's presence.

The tablet was flashing the stock prices. Alliance was still holding at ₹434 and Nectar had moved up a rupee to ₹736. He just hadn't made any headway. He needed more plays and options. Even with ₹200 crores on the table, he wasn't able to get the needle to move.

He messaged Manish. '*Need leverage...*'

Manish replied instantly. *'How much?'*
Agastya: *'How much you got?'*
Manish: *'About 4 cr. rest in play.'*
Agastya: *'Tell Mukund.'*
Manish: *'Ok.'*

He realized that would have given him another 80 to 100 crores to play with in the market. But now there was a predicament. He didn't know where to use it.

He received a text message from Ajay, the News Times journalist. He scanned the contents and took a deep breath.

Everyone had a weakness, an indulgence, something on the side. There were always skeletons in the closet, one just had to know where to look and how to interpret them. Sailesh seemed to have a few, not too surprising for someone like him. He and Sailesh were both very ambitious and passionate about their work and organizations. They were both considered to be at the top of their game, but Sailesh was considered the more suave and strategic thinker, whereas Agastya had been interpreted by the media as the brash maverick who was driven by the purpose of shocking the establishment. Some thought that it was more the media glare and attention that he derived from his stunts and escapades, others considered it to be an addiction, but few doubted his genius.

Did he want to take Sailesh on this?

He had wanted to reach out to Sailesh. Something had gone wrong, and dramatically so. Something or someone had ticked off Sailesh, and he couldn't put his finger on what that could be. Or was this beyond Sailesh as well? He had to read Sailesh's mind to predict his next steps.

Sebastian called Agastya on the intercom.

'Just a minute, Sebastian…'

Agastya sent a message to his broker to pick up APCL and Wireline. Both the stocks had been his allies in hard times. They had flanked him and given him a cushion in some tough situations. They were his "white knights" that came to his rescue only on certain specific occasions. It was the respect he had for the two mighty blue chips. He had noticed a certain upward pattern in both the scrips that seemed to merge with his times of need. He had been tempted to make long term plays for both of them, but realized that he would bank them for their occasional mood swings and milk the situation.

'Agastya. The lady in your room? Is she helping us with the launch? '

Agastya wasn't used to being accosted by Sebastian, but he realized that his position had now been compromised within the office. The gossip would have hit the grapevine for sure. He decided not to respond.

'How're the preparations for the press conference?'

'The agency will be sending the new price creative in the next few seconds. Will send it across to you.'

'Ok.'

'Nitin is under extreme pressure. The distributors are falling across the country like nine pins. Everything is coming to a standstill. It is insane and our stocks are stuck with them. They will not hit the retail stores.'

'How many distributors?'

'It's crossed seventy is what I hear.'

'Ok. Let me know if you hear anything else.' He disconnected and then opened an email from Richard.

Agastya,
Send me the budgeting for the revised pricing.
Richard

He hadn't mentioned Vikram nor had he marked him on the email. The vultures had started moving in. Vikram seemed to have been cornered. It had been rapid and ruthless. Did they have anything substantive against Vikram, or was there more to it than met the eye? Agastya needed to have the details, and quickly. He needed to assess and play with the changing landscape. It would impact the way things would progress today, and his career.

Agastya and Vikram hadn't been friends, but their relationship had been professional, cordial even. There was a mutual respect and they had worked closely together on several aspects of the business including the Sparkle launch. They had their disagreements, and there was always an undercurrent of tension with Agastya's proximity to Richard. He had learnt and evolved as a professional working with Vikram, a fact that he realized as Vikram was being ousted.

Vikram had always been a warm person at heart and also maintained a discreet yet approachable style about the workplace. Their arguments had been fierce yet objective on most occasions. Agastya also knew that on certain occasions there was a chain of command to be adhered to, and respected Vikram for neither fuelling nor being a proponent of sycophancy.

He also regretted the fact that Sparkle had triggered more flash points in their relationship and had possibly strained their daily interactions. The emails and text messages suggested that Vikram was quite deep in the stock scam with the Metrics JV. The allegations had included insider trading, price fixing and even unethical access to the company's stocks prior to the Metrics JV formation with BCL and the IPO. It had all gone bad for Vikram. There seemed to be too much against him.

However the timing of the revelations appeared too convenient. The chaotic deluge and onslaught of issues almost had a pattern about them. BCL appeared to be under siege. The situation demanded the need for a firm leader at the helm and neither Mark nor Richard could handle the situation and operational complexities in such a short time. They would need someone who knew the intricacies and operational nuances and yet could command respect and trust within the ranks. Corruption, scandals and mayhem offered a poor canvas for anyone wishing to steer at the helm.

It was getting quite clear. This was a coup and the perpetrators seemed to have planned for a rapid and a decisive set of blows to set the wheels in motion and for their moves to be made. The biggest product launch of his career had been chosen as their platform of convenience. It disgusted him. Sparkle would have surely propelled him into serious consideration for the CEO position, especially with Richard's backing. But the recent spate of events would have impacted his performance and cast a shadow on the entire senior management team.

It struck him that he needed to make this an opportunity to impress Mark in this crisis. His had been a market intelligence failure and he couldn't be blamed in totality for the situation. Nitin was now under siege, and perhaps in an even more debilitating manner. He needed to take the situation into his own hands.

He called up Nitin.

'Nitin … hard luck.'

'Tell me about it. And to make matters worse I heard that Vikram has been officially asked to put in his papers. The formal orders have come in from the board. He seems to have made quite a packet in this mess. It just doesn't add up. It's not like Vikram!'

'But we haven't received any intimation yet.'

Agastya knew that Vikram would have called Nitin on his resignation, and noticed that Nitin too chose to remain silent on the matter.

'They're drafting it right now. Mark really came down hard on Vikram. Richard couldn't do much, and now that Abhishek may be involved in this as well...'

'Our CFO Abhishek? I just spoke with him.'

'Yes, Agastya. This is getting really chaotic. I heard he has just emailed his resignation to Richard too.'

'We need to call off the press conference. We are just inviting trouble.'

'Listen, Agastya. I understand what you're saying. But that's beyond me right now.'

'But, Nitin, we need to go up there and have a chat with them. We've got less than half an hour.'

'I've got Armageddon around me. And by the way, there are rumours doing the rounds that you were in the know about the Stark launch and have links with Sailesh. Come across, let's chat, unless you're distracted right now?' Nitin disconnected.

He was hoping that Sebastian hadn't overheard the conversation, but couldn't be sure.

'What's happening out there?'

'At the venue, sir?' It was a coy but tactful retort by Sebastian.

'Yes! Make sure you're on top of it.'

He scanned the charts on his laptop and glanced at the tablet. The pressure was getting to him again. He needed a few minutes away from it all, but realized he didn't have the luxury of even a second. If only he could set some of them aside and then tackle them later. Now even his professional reputation was on the line.

Had Sailesh planted rumours against him?

Agastya rose from his chair and slipped on his jacket. Sebastian left the room and closed the door behind him.

He needed to turn on the ante and fortify his position.

Maithili returned to his office.

'Going somewhere, baby? Aren't you forgetting something?'

Agastya had an exasperated look. 'M. You've seen what's happening here. I seriously can't do this now!'

'I totally understand, Agastya. So, just take it easy, and why don't you meet Nandita and me for coffee once your press conference is over?' She was pressing her left palm with her fingers.

'Come off it, Maithili!' he shouted.

'My, my! Someone's losing their cool!'

'You really think you're going to get away with this, M?'

'It's looking quite good from where I am right now.'

'Where is Ismail, Maithili?'

'None of your business.'

'Does he know you're doing this?'

'None of your business.'

'But, he does know about us, right?'

'Let's not get distracted here, Agastya.'

'Are you still with him?'

'That has no relevance to this situation, Agastya. How's Nandita doing?'

He had hoped to disturb Maithili with the aggressive turn, but she appeared unperturbed.

'I seriously don't care right now, M! Go jump! Cut your wrists for all I care. This is seriously insane. You need some medical help, seriously. I'm not committing to this game anymore. That's it, just get the hell out of here.'

Maithili calmly responded.

'Your portfolio has taken a further hit, Agastya.'

Agastya raised his voice. 'Aren't you listening to me? Read my lips, Maithili. Get the hell out!'

'You know, come to think of it, your lips are not too bad. I didn't really remember them being like that. Did you get some work done on them?' she said, winking at him impishly.

'M, if you do this to me, trust me, I will take you down. You'll have nothing, absolutely nothing. I'll decimate your career, your reputation, your name…every damn thing about you, everything. Even whatever you've got with Ismail. He won't want to breathe the same air that you do. It'll torment you for the rest of your life. You know me, right? What happens today, gets over today. Tomorrow is another day. This will not impact me long term. I will recoup. I will crawl back. I will gnaw my way back; I'll grovel if required, but I will get back. And come out with much more than I've got right now and much more than you'll ever achieve. I guarantee you that.'

Maithili observed his every movement. She noticed that he was now perspiring and his lips were twitching. He was breathing heavily again and his fingers were restless.

'Do you want to hit me?'

He pulled his hair with his hands. 'M, I'm serious. Just get the hell out of here!'

Maithili pressed a button on her mobile as she continued standing beside the closed door to his room.

'Sweetheart, you've got email.'

'I don't want to read anything now, M.'

'I'm sure. But I have a feeling that might just persuade you that little bit. Now, come on.'

He was vexed, but realized that she hadn't been bluffing him for a while now.

He opened the email and clicked on the attachment. He scanned it quickly and then sat down again.

He looked towards the tablet yet again and then at his watch.

'This is seriously below the belt, M!'

'Really?'

'I didn't do those trades on the BCL stock!'

'I know, my dear. But those records clearly reflect that you actually made a fair amount of money on these trades.'

'But these are in Nandita's name.'

'I think your company policy doesn't permit either you or your immediate family from trading in the company's stocks. And you'll notice that she has been trading in the Metrics JV stocks as well. I believe there's some possible heat on that one too?'

'Why are you dragging Nandita into this?'

'I just thought I should be engaging enough for you?'

'But Nandita didn't do these trades.'

'I know, sweetheart!'

'So you've got fudged documents now?'

'I didn't say that.'

'Then?'

'The documents are correct. She didn't do those trades, but her father did … in her name.'

'Come on, Maithili. Don't get my larger family involved in this.'

'Do you like my outfit? I bought it especially for today.'

He shook his head. The mobile was vibrating again.

He picked it up and read the text message. It was from Ajay.

'Will be out in the next five minutes.'

Agastya read it twice. He wasn't sure if he wanted to go ahead with this, but he needed to act. He had to give a blow to Sailesh. He couldn't just be lying around like this. He had the urge and his gut was running quite strong as well.

He then read the message for a third time. It now looked like a question more than a statement. Theirs had been a definitive conversation. Even the journalist seemed to have doubts on the course of action.

And then impulsively he typed back.

'Go for it…'

'Agastya, why did you want to leave me?'

'Isn't it even more obvious now?' he grinned.

'Do you ever think what I would have gone through that day when you left me with Ismail?'

'You need to fight your own battles, M!'

She laughed.

'I didn't want you to fight my battles, Agastya. I just needed you to pick me up that day. I needed you that day, Agastya, to hold me, if not for me, at least for Roshan.'

'I couldn't, M.'

'You couldn't make it or you couldn't care to make it?'

Chapter Fifteen

THREE WEEKS EARLIER

amidst violent cracking of ribs
and piercing cries of pain
I hear a voice of hope...

'I'm scared…'

Agastya was irritated. He wanted to hang up as he could hear Nandita and the children laughing and playing.

'I can't take this now, M! I'm going out with the family. Don't disturb me now.'

'You have to come over!'

'I can't, M!'

'Ismail has been drinking, and he'll be home anytime now. I don't have my car either. He's up to something.'

'But what happened today?'

'It's been rough between the two of us. He's had a few business deals going sour, and he needs to take it all out on something. I guess I'm the lucky one today!'

'But where am I going to take both of you?'

'You need to look out for us, Agastya!'

'You're overreacting. Just don't drink and don't confront him!'

'Damn you, Agastya! Is this all that I mean to you?'

'We've discussed this, M! We need to cool off for some time. I've got too much going on at work right now.'

She yelled. 'You've got too much going on at work?! You bastard! Don't ever forget the times I dropped everything to back you!'

'Don't do this, M! Just take it easy. If it's really that bad, why don't you check into a hotel or go to your place?'

'Check into a hotel? You think I called you to help me check into a hotel? You have any idea what it takes to look after a baby?'

'I've got two of my own, so let's not get into that!'

'You don't know Ismail. You don't know what he is capable of.'

'Then why do you live-in with him?'

She yelled at him again. 'I don't know why I'm with you either! This isn't the time to get into all this.'

'Then it's mutual, M!'

'You should burn in hell, Agastya!'

'I am in hell when I'm with you, Maithili!'

'So that's how it felt all those times we made love?!'

'Cut this nonsense, M!'

There was a long pause.

Maithili walked up towards Roshan and was thankful to see him fast asleep. He had had his evening feed and appeared to be in deep slumber. She closed the bedroom door and cursed the maid who was playing truant.

'M, are you there?'

They had both lowered their voices.

'Was just checking on Roshan.'

'Listen, M...'

'No, *you* listen, Agastya. You are one of the three people who know that I'm living in with Ismail. The other two are out of town. I have no one else here, and you know that. I can look after myself pretty damn well but I called you for Roshan. Even you can't be this thick-skinned?'

'Don't do this, M. You're making a mountain of a molehill. Just calm down.'

'You don't have a 220-pound man about to beat you to death in a few minutes, Agastya!'

'Where's Roshan's mother?'

'I don't know. The last I heard, she was in a clinic in Mussoorie. She's undergoing treatment. I can't tell you anything more than that!'

'What about Ismail's parents?'

'What is this? Some twenty questions game?'

Agastya shook his head.

'Listen, M. If it's as bad as you make out to be it, just call the police.'

'Damn you, Agastya! Damn you for letting me set my eyes on you! Damn your existence! Damn you!'

'Why in god's name did you get involved with him?'

'That's none of your business!'

'I guess it is now,' he taunted. 'Listen to me, M! This is it, this right now, this is it. I wanted it to be smooth but it's not going to work out.'

There was a long pause once again between them. She could now hear Ismail thumping the main door with his fist.

'You're going to do this to me now?'

'There's never a right time for this, M.' He disconnected.

Maithili collapsed on the sofa. Ismail continued thumping on the door. She took a few sips of vodka and placed it on the table beside the sofa.

Her life flashed by her. The men, the relationships, the false promises, her dashed hopes, her quest for meaning and purpose and a pursuit of belonging. She realized that the next few minutes could alter her life forever. She had a sense of despondency and imminent danger. She wasn't in a position to take it any further. She had to end it all.

She rose from the sofa and proceeded to open the door, knowing that she couldn't ward off the inevitable, and she didn't have the emotional energy to deal with the onslaught that she was going to be subjected to.

She could see his bloodshot eyes. They always went red when he drank. There was no exchange of words for several moments as she walked back to the sofa and sat down, raising her legs and folding them to one side. She picked up a cushion and clasped it tight, hoping that it would provide her some comfort.

He flung the car keys on the table beside the sofa and looked across into the bedroom at the sleeping baby.

'Where's the maid?' he shrieked.

'I'm your maid for the day!' she screamed back at him.

'You're not fit to be a whore! I don't even know why I let you be near him!'

She heaved the glass towards Ismail, and it smashed against his forehead.

'You bitch!' Ismail screamed as he covered his head with his left hand. The blood quickly started streaming down his face and trickled on his white linen shirt. He rose and jumped over the sofa towards Maithili who was now standing at the entrance of the kitchen.

Maithili ran inside and picked up the bread knife that was lying beside the sink. She hurtled towards the other end of the kitchen and held her back against the fridge as her hand pointed the knife in the direction of Ismail who now entered the kitchen with a bruised ego and in a volcanic rage. He saw her holding the knife and smiled.

'Where are you going to go, M?' he sniggered, taking small steps towards her. The blood was now leaving a trail on the Italian marble flooring as he continued towards her, covering his forehead with his left hand and the right hand drawn out towards Maithili.

'Leave me alone, you son of a gun! Leave me alone! Get out of here or I will stab you!'

Ismail halted in his steps and looked around the kitchen. He ripped a portion of the paper towel from the roll and held it tight against his bleeding forehead. He then looked up towards Maithili and stood still.

'You can't do anything with that knife! You can't do anything with your life! You can't do jackshit…you hear that, M!' He was in pain but was enjoying cornering Maithili.

Ismail had returned from the project site in Lonavala. He had picked up a bottle of scotch en route and emptied half its contents by the time he reached home.

Now they could hear Roshan screaming in the bedroom, but neither was willing to hold back in this situation. Neither was willing to blink.

'Get the hell out of here, Ismail, or I will stab you for sure today. I've got nothing to lose! You got that?' She was now trembling, words stumbling out of her mouth.

They looked at each other for a few seconds, Roshan's screaming went up a few more decibels. It was now troubling her.

'Listen, M, you can't move forward in your life! Whether it's this relationship, your money, even this child….What the hell are you going to do with that knife?! Nothing. So…'

Maithili was now distracted by the child's screaming. She couldn't take this any longer. Nothing was making sense in her life. She just couldn't connect with Ismail any more. She wasn't even sure if she still loved him, or whether she had ever loved him. Was it just lust and the desperation of having the security of having someone around at home?

His tall frame and dark brown eyes now repulsed her. She hated his arrogance, the over-possessiveness. She also realized that he had sheltered her and given her the emotional support she needed, but she couldn't operate as a slave. She needed her space, she needed some time. She had to find herself.

She had moved in with Ismail two years earlier, when he had still been married. It had been a relationship of convenience with "no strings attached", as Ismail often said.

He had separated from his wife a few months after Roshan's birth. The trauma of discovering Ismail's live-in relationship and the birth of Roshan had resulted in severe depression for his wife, who had to be admitted into a clinic in Mussoorie.

Maithili found herself at a strange crossroad as she juggled her company, a turbulent relationship with Agastya, a live-in arrangement with Ismail that often got passionately violent and the emotional stress of raising Ismail's baby.

'Shut up, you hear me, shut up! You are suffocating me! I just can't take it anymore, I just want to get away from all this. I just want to run.' She was now screaming hysterically, jabbing the knife in his direction.

'Go wherever the hell you want to! But you are not taking my baby anywhere. That child is not leaving this house, you got that?!'

That hit Maithili's weak spot. Enraged, shivering and perspiring heavily, her blouse now soaked in sweat she charged at Ismail.

'How do you know that's even your son? How do you know your wife wasn't sleeping with someone else?!' she screamed.

The doorbell rang. It had to be one of the neighbours.

Maithili got distracted. Ismail lunged towards her and snatched the knife from her hand with his right hand and thrust his left hand towards her neck, clasping it in a tight hold.

Her back was now held back against the refrigerator and her feet were slipping on the smooth floor. She was unable to get a clear foothold, putting even greater pressure on her neck which was being held in his hand as her body weight pulled her down.

Ismail threw the knife on the floor, held her hair and banged her head repeatedly against the fridge. She was soon finding it difficult to breathe.

He kept repeating, 'What did you just say?'

'Get off me, you bastard! You heard what I said!'

The baby's wails could still be heard from the bedroom. The doorbell continued ringing. The neighbours remained persistent.

She had experienced Ismail's grip on her neck earlier as well, and had often planned how she would react or defend herself on the next occasion. Maithili bent her left leg and placed her foot on the fridge, pushing her body upwards. She then made a desperate move and plunged her right knee into his groin. Ismail's lower body was thrust backwards as he winced in pain, and the upper body weight pushed forward, putting further pressure on Maithili's neck.

Maithili was now in immense pain, aware that her neck could break at any moment. She was desperate and all the counter measures that she had thought of and planned were failing her. Her lungs were desperate for fresh air and a persistent cough that was now lingering in her throat worsened her agony.

The doorbell was still ringing furiously.

She mustered the energy to lift her left hand and claw his cheeks with her nails, and managed to get one of her fingers into his left eye. Ismail finally released his grip and fell towards his right, wincing in pain. She collapsed on her trembling knees and held onto the granite kitchen top with her right hand to maintain her balance. She was now breathing heavily and coughing. Her head was spinning, she could still feel his grip on her neck and was immersed in pain at the rear of her head with the wound.

Afraid that she might just faint soon, she pushed herself up, kicked Ismail on his abdomen and ran out of the kitchen, supporting herself against the walls, the microwave and any object she could hold on her way out.

She wasn't sure whether to first open the door or run towards the bedroom and pick up Ismail's baby. As she entered the drawing room, she slammed her foot into a leg of the dining table. Her toe was bruised and the intense pain moved quickly from her head to the foot. She couldn't walk further with the sharp pain. She collapsed on the floor and held her right foot, which was bleeding, with her hands. The pain was excruciating and she cried, 'Goddammit!'

She rolled on the floor and held the foot in a tight grip till the pain was manageable. She could hear Ismail getting up from the floor and cursing her. She had to reconsider her options. The doorbell continued ringing and she could hear the neighbours now banging the door, screaming something she couldn't make out.

Should she head towards the bedroom or towards the door? The bedroom was now about eight feet away but the front door was over fifteen feet away with several obstacles in its path. She could hear Ismail snorting; he had started walking out of the kitchen. Her foot was in incredible pain and the bruised neck wasn't allowing her to raise her body easily from the floor. She released her hand from her foot, and noticed a pool of blood on the floor below her face. She wasn't sure where it was spurting from.

Ismail emerged from the kitchen brandishing the kitchen knife. He seemed to have recovered quickly from the pain in his groin, or perhaps his anger had overpowered the pain. It didn't matter. She had to protect herself.

In a final thrust of force, she pushed herself upwards and stood on her feet, ignoring the pain and the heavily bleeding foot. She made a dash for the front door and picked up the ashtray from the centre table as she passed the sofa. Ismail ran towards his left and decided to hurl his six-foot frame at her, to stop her in her path.

Maithili flung the ashtray towards his chest, but as he had bent his body to lunge at her, the ashtray collided with his face hitting him directly on his nose. Maithili had almost lost her balance as she threw the ashtray but regained it quickly and began to hobble towards the door. She still wasn't sure if she had managed to strike Ismail with the ashtray or even if he was still chasing her. The notions of time and space had dissipated. She didn't know if she would be able to make it to the door, and momentarily wasn't even sure if indeed she did want to make it to the door. Did she even want to continue living this life? Did she want anything? Did anything mean anything at all now? It was all senseless, purposeless.

She could hear the baby screaming and was torn between turning back towards the baby and moving further towards the door. She looked from the corner of her eye, too afraid to look in his direction, afraid of what she might in fact see. Ismail seemed to be recovering from a fall and was now raising his body to get up again and make another dash towards her. She couldn't turn back. She didn't have a choice. She finally managed to reach the door, turned the lock and pulled it with all her might and fell on the floor as the receding door hit her on her forehead. The cut was deep and the wound soon started oozing blood.

A lady was the first to emerge from the entrance and she fell to her knees beside Maithili, raised her head with her hands and rested it on her lap. Her husband moved in with the building security guard and ring fenced Maithili from Ismail.

Maithili whimpered, 'Roshan...'

Ismail was now furious. He continued in his path towards the gathering that had appeared in his home, witnessing his dark, evil and violent side. Now they would never stop talking about this. He would be branded a violent egomaniac and a sociopath. This woman had done this to him! This woman had ruined his life. He hated the moment that he had first set his eyes on her at the Taj Mahal hotel. He hated his first kiss. He hated his first embrace with her. He resented every strand and bone in her body. He despised her. He cursed himself for falling in love with her. He loathed himself for allowing her to enter and exit his life as she pleased. He also realized that he needed her.

Ismail shouted, 'Keep out of this, Mehta! This is a family matter. I will ruin your family. I will feed you to the dogs. You don't know me. I will kill you!'

Mehta extended his arms, quite fearful of Ismail's next moves, and equally concerned for his wife who was holding Maithili on the floor.

'I will call the police, Ismail. This has got out of hand and you know that!'

Ismail picked up pace, maintaining eye contact with Mehta. His shooting red and glaring eyes outmatched the rheumy and indefinite eyes of Mr Mehta. Mehta moved back only to realize that there were two women between him and the door. A quick escape was not possible from this situation in any case. The situation was much worse than he had imagined. But now he was too deep into it. He couldn't get out of it even if he wanted to. Mehta looked around and beckoned the security guard to come into the house quickly.

Ismail noticing that his threats were not having the desired effect on Mehta, decided to take a swing at him. The alert but nervous security guard quickly emerged on the scene and lashed his cane against Ismail's head. Ismail fell to his side with the brute force of the blow.

Maithili had caught her breath and the anxiety about Ismail's baby was now engulfing her. She turned her neck around and saw Ismail lying on the floor holding his head and yelling expletives.

She asked Mr Mehta to go and get the baby for her, but he seemed too nervous to move any further into the house. Maithili forced herself on her feet and headed towards the bedroom, where the baby had been crying for several minutes. Blood was dripping from her forehead on the floor and she noticed that there were already blood-stained foot prints on the floor around her. She ensured that she didn't look towards Ismail and kept resolute in her walk towards the bedroom. Instinctively she picked up the bunch of keys lying on the corner table beside the sofa and proceeded towards the bedroom. She walked alone. 'As ever,' she murmured to herself.

As she approached the bedroom she could hear Ismail being pushed down by the security guard, who was being repeatedly threatened with the loss of job and life. Partially assured, she picked up Roshan and held him tight. He needed a change of diapers and a feed immediately. She noticed a bottle of milk on the bedside table. It had been prepared over three hours earlier, not best for a child, but it would have to work for now.

Roshan's face had turned red and his throat was clearly sore from crying. She managed to calm him down and then started feeding him. She often felt that she hadn't experienced the complete cycle of motherhood possibly as everything else in life.

It took over a minute for the baby to calm down, but the situation outside the bedroom seemed to be simmering again. Knowing Ismail, this could only worsen. She had to act and quickly.

She stepped out into the hall with the baby, now wrapped in his blanket, hoping that the sight of him might just calm Ismail down.

He screamed, 'Leave that child alone, you bitch!'

She was enraged and fearful for Roshan's life as well. She tried to calm down but it actually made her even more vengeful. She wanted to kill him like never before. She wanted to take the kitchen knife and stab him in his chest, and see his eyes when he would be suffering in pain. She wanted to feel that dagger piercing his body and ripping his heart from the inside.

Her mind told her to run, her body told her to collapse, her heart told her to kill Ismail and finish all this once and for all. And then she saw the angel in her arms.

She felt the keys in her pocket. She knew what she had to do.

She ran with the baby in her arms, not wasting any time in thanking the guard or the Mehtas, knowing that every moment would be precious. She ignored the pain in her foot and her quickly collapsing energy levels with her bleeding forehead, or the difficulty in breathing with her bruised neck.

She dashed towards the staircase, not wanting to waste time in waiting for the elevator. The movement and commotion had disturbed the baby who had stopped drinking the milk and resumed crying again.

'I have to be strong…I have to do this for Roshan…I have to do this for him…find the strength, Maithili…find the strength…' she kept mumbling to herself as she struggled to maintain her balance in the downward descent.

As she reached the exit door on the ground floor, she turned back to see if Ismail was in fact following her. She could hear a commotion a few floors above her. It must be Ismail.

The car was parked at the appointed parking slot. She pulled out the keys from her pocket and pressed the button on the electronic key. The car refused to make a noise or offer any vocal acknowledgement. Her head was throbbing and her arm was paining with the weight of the baby. She kept pressing the button and then she finally heard a noise from the car behind her. Hell...these were Ismail's keys! She turned around and noticed a beaming S class welcome her with the cabin lights turned on.

She hadn't driven this beast before. She placed Roshan in the baby seat, buckled the belt and then hobbled towards the front door. As she stepped in, she could see the exit door opening. Ismail!

She started the car and accelerated quickly from neutral and turned right towards the exit. The gate was fortunately open and she wouldn't have to wait for the guard to open it. She looked in the rear view mirror and noticed Ismail running towards the car. She had another thirty feet to go for the exit gate. She pressed further on the accelerator, mindful of the fact that there could be pedestrians in the building or worse still another car moving out of the parking lot. She didn't have a choice. At low speeds Ismail could quite easily catch up with the car. She kept looking in the rear view mirror and noticed that she was increasing the gap between her and Ismail. *'For a change, something's going right,'* she thought to herself. She pressed the accelerator. This beast had an incredible pick up. She flew over the speed breaker and lunged the car out across the exit gate and heaved a sigh of relief as soon as the car hit the road outside the building. She realized that she was driving at too high a speed to take an immediate left turn on the road, but she noticed less traffic on a by-lane of Cumballa Hill.

As the car hit the by-lane, she turned the steering wheel with brute force to the right, resulting in the rear wheels skidding towards the left. She managed to retain control and steadied the car before accelerating it further. She was still another fifty feet away from the main road. She noticed Ismail still pursuing her on foot in the rear view mirror. She turned her eyes towards the road again. The blood from the forehead was now dripping into her eyes and blurring her vision. She needed a second to clear her hair from the blood-stained forehead and her eyes, but she didn't have it. She pressed down on the accelerator , in some concocted way believing that the speed might just dispel her pain.

She took one more look and noticed that she had increased her distance from Ismail who was now waving frantically at her and seemed to be pointing towards the main road. His eyes seemed to express more concern than anger. She read his eyes well. What had happened? It was all a blur. She set her eyes forward again and noticed a child on a bicycle emerging from a gate, two buildings away. She pressed the horn knowing quite well that she didn't have time.

She pressed the brakes and turned the steering sharply to the left. It was a narrow by-lane and there wasn't enough space to manoeuvre away from the child's path. The car was screeching to a halt, but not in time to avoid the speed breaker. The car hurtled above the speed breaker and spun out of control and went crashing into a wall of the building from which the girl was emerging on her bike.

As the car crashed into the building, she could feel its impact on her back, neck and legs. The air bags hadn't ejected and she pulled back her head from the shattered windscreen. She looked to her left and noticed a shocked young girl still seated on her bike. She couldn't feel her legs, they were numb from the crash. She turned around and was relieved to see that Roshan was in his seat, but crying furiously.

She then placed her hand on her abdomen and felt the blood soaking her hands. She knew it … she had lost the child in her womb.

She murmured weakly, 'I'm sorry, Agastya …'

Chapter Sixteen

3:05 PM
TODAY

I love you but loathe you
and yet you fuel my desires

Sebastian barged into the room and realized that he had interrupted an intense conversation, but decided to cut the awkwardness by heading straight into the subject.

'Boss, it's official.'

'What is?'

Agastya noticed tears rolling down Maithili's cheeks. She was looking in another direction, but was unable to hold back. She got up and walked steadily towards the conference room. There was a restless pause in conversation between the chief marketing officer and Sebastian.

Agastya looked towards Sebastian and nodded, urging him to proceed with the conversation.

'Vikram has put in his papers.'

'Sebastian, the press conference is still on. Have no doubts on that.' He wanted to say, *'At least I haven't heard otherwise!'* but restrained himself.

'This is insane, sir. Have you seen the new advertising layouts with the new pricing?'

The decibel levels on the floor were reaching titanic proportions. He had barely had the chance to glance at them, but he had seen the main component wherein the drop in price was being introduced as a special launch offer.

'Looks alright, but we can't give it a go ahead right now.'

'You would need the CEO to sign off?'

They knew the irony of the situation. They now neither had a CEO nor a CFO. He had found it strange that the CFO had decided to go on a holiday at the time of the launch, when most of the senior management team had blocked their calendar for weeks in advance. It would have been sacrilege to not be seen at an event where both Richard and Mark were going to be present and with the biggest product launch in the company's recent history. Had this been in the offing for a while? Had Abhishek and Vikram known about this?

'I'm working on the approvals. Just get some printouts of the new advertisement.'

'I've already handed them over to Rebecca outside. She's got them in a folder.'

'Great. What do we do with the hoardings?'

'The agency has already spoken with the vendor and they are printing back-up overlays that can be pasted on the hoardings once we give the go ahead. They're printing a couple of versions, depending on the final one that gets approved.'

Agastya had always been impressed with Sebastian's efficiency and realized that he had in fact pulled up his socks and had not taken his eye off the ball.

'How long would it take?'

'A few hours, at least. We don't have permissions to work on some hoardings in the night sometimes, but they're pulling out all stops to make it happen.'

'The front page press ads?'t

'We've hit a brick wall on that one. Both News Times and HT are not relenting. They're under too much pressure and have stopped taking our calls. They're claiming to be in some sales conference. Obviously they are fibbing.'

Agastya messaged Ajay.

'Have a word with your bosses… I need front page!'

Agastya had fed the news to the journalist several months earlier when he and Sailesh had hit a flash point, but then a conversation had brought the situation under control. The journalist owed it to him. They had a pact that the news would be released only on Agastya's go ahead.

He received a response almost instantaneously, *'Will give it a shot.'*

Agastya kept looking at the message from the journalist and murmured, 'So?'

'Vikram knows the MD of News Times quite well. It would help if he could make a call.'

'That's unlikely under the current situation. You think it's worth a shot?'

Sebastian nodded. Agastya knew that it would have placed him in an awkward position if he had called Vikram and wasn't sure what Richard may think of the move.

'Give Vikram a call if you want, but Sebastian… make it happen!'

Sebastian raised his eyebrows. He knew that Agastya had put him in an awkward spot, and he didn't have a way out.

'Looks very tough!'

'This is a tough situation, Sebastian. We're all in this together.'

Sebastian shook his head and didn't hesitate in stating his displeasure with the downward delegation of something that was clearly out of his league.

Agastya emailed the revised pricing proposal to Richard. He got a call from Manish.

'Ags, Alliance is going to go down. Don't let go.'

'But?'

'Spectra is in play…'

'Never. Give me some other upsides, and fast.'

The monitor was showing a collage of brutal red, splattered right across. The indecision was costing him dearly. He just didn't have anything against her. He looked at the time and cursed himself.

She stood at the door again once Sebastian left.

Agastya looked towards her and wondered if there was anything that he could do to make her leave his office. Her resolute stares and the determination were evident and he realized that neither his words nor tone would have been sufficient to overcome her.

'Getting into the groove, Agastya?'

Maithili was not displaying any emotions whatsoever. No regret, sympathy, anger, resentment or even hate. She seemed distant, as if she had bagged this and nothing really mattered anymore. She could see that she had tormented her lover and soulmate. The torture was apparent as he fretted with the keyboard and realized that his fortune was being shattered to smithereens. It was all going to disappear in a few minutes from now. The market wasn't supporting him either, and Maithili knew that the stars were in her favour, for a change, today. She also knew that this conquest might seem hollow and without purpose to some. She didn't need the money and didn't even have any idea what to do with it once she did get it. For all she knew it might lie in the bank for years to come or she might even just blow it up in a few seconds in Macau or Las Vegas.

She had dabbled in stocks rather early in her career and had made quite a killing. But the thrill had ceased to excite her any further. She had cashed out and then invested in conventional and safer havens. She didn't get it any more. It didn't seem real. It didn't feel rational. It just didn't add up. It was nothing short of gambling and the technical charts, projections and forecasts were but whitewash with the quantum of insider trading and cartels running the exchanges. She had given it a shot when she first started going around with Agastya, but she realized that she didn't have it in her anymore.

She was also surprised how she had been able to get this whole project executed meticulously down to the last detail. It was all working like clockwork. It had been too easy. His pain, grief, suffering were meaningless to her. She had been hoping to see genuine remorse, but then also realized that she had given him too short a time to resolve the challenges of the situation and be true to himself. His ego and pride were now coming in his way, as they always did. He could be blunt and brutal, but she had also seen his other side. Rare occasions when he did open up to her, and showed glimpses of the man who could care, feel, emote and even touch others. He had been bottling it all up inside, and she had struggled to pare it out of him so that he could even believe in it himself. It had been a demanding, strenuous, and on several occasions, exasperating exercise in infinite futility. She didn't even realize why she did take the effort. It was just another affair after all. It shouldn't have mattered to her. These affairs were never meant to have mattered, but he did and she resented herself for it.

'Just hang around, M, and enjoy the ride.'

'Hmmm. It's taken a while. I'm finally getting to see the Agastya I had fallen in love with.'

Agastya looked up at her and froze. She hadn't uttered those words earlier. They were shunned and almost alien to her vocabulary. He was taken aback by their utterance. A concoction of emotions swept through him. It hadn't struck him that she was capable of love. Marriage, having children, and staying together were terms that had interspersed her conversations, but never love. He had always believed that it was a form of addiction and need for companionship that had led her to stay with him as long as she had. She was living-in with Ismail and then there were all those scars from her past that haunted and shadowed her.

Yet on the other hand it had been years since he had those words uttered to him, though it had now been mentioned in the past tense. It touched him. He wanted to walk across to her and stroke her hair, hold her hand and then sit beside her. In the initial months, he had believed that she may just fall in love with him, but then realized that it wasn't a dimension that he wanted in their relationship. He didn't want a definition to what they had together. He felt that would be a constraint and inhibit them from experiencing and acting on their impulses. It had allowed them to traverse a myriad experiences without restraint or boundaries.

'M, you sure you want to go ahead with this?'

He looked at her from the corner of his eye.

'Don't even bother, Agastya. Just concentrate.'

He took a deep breath, raised his hands towards the ceiling and stretched his arms. Then he shook his head, stretched his fingers and slammed the keyboard.

He logged into the news site and clicked on the corporate section. He smiled.

"Stark *Under the Scanner*

It is rumoured that Stark *has been under investigation for defaults in excise payments for several months now. Their plants in Aurangabad and Nasik have both been raided…* "

The journalist seemed to have kept the story ready. It had struck sooner than he had expected.

He sent Sailesh the web link of the news page via messenger.

It wasn't a massive blow, but he knew quite well that Sailesh would get the drift.

The messenger beeped again.

Sailesh: Loose change…

Agastya messaged the journalist again.

Turn it up.

Richard sent him an email.

Agastya,
Have checked with Mark… Let's go with the 20 per cent off.
Richard

It was a brief and timely email.

Agastya yelled from his cabin.

'Sebastian!'

Maithili remained standing at the door of the conference room. Sebastian came rushing in within a few seconds.

Agastya rose from his chair and drew him out of his office and spoke in a low tone.

'It's final. It's 20 per cent off. Go for it. Just don't ask any more questions. Put them into the press releases, press ads, hoardings…the works. Just go!'

Sebastian disappeared as quickly as he had come into the room. Agastya felt a sense of relief. A decision had to be taken and it had been. It was going to ruin their profits for a long time to come, but then it was a competitive reality. The world was watching. BCL couldn't back down. He noticed that he was subconsciously nodding.

He walked back into his office, closing the door behind him and sat down on the table, turning the laptop around to face him. He refreshed the news web page again.

"Stark *CMO Under the Scanner.*

In yet another breakthrough, there are unconfirmed reports that the Stark CMO is under investigation for a sexual harassment suit from a senior employee.'"

He ran his eyes over the article, but didn't feel good reading it. He realized that he should have listened to Maithili. He also knew that the charges had proven to be false and the case had been closed. He felt petty, but knew that Sailesh would realize that he had even more coming at him.

He called up the journalist.

'Could you have a chat with the ad sales guys, Ajay?'

'It's just been a few minutes.'

'You need to make this happen. Get me on a call with your Managing Director!'

'Goenka?'

'Yes.'

'You think I can pull that off now? I need time.'

'You've been there for decades. He trusts you. Impress upon him, tell him it's important that he take this call.'

'Will give it a shot.'

Agastya disconnected. He realized that Goenka wasn't someone to be ruffled by a CMO. He ran a media conglomerate and was one of the wealthiest persons in media. His family had been in media for over a hundred years and had survived several political regimes; they were rock sturdy. He also knew that they could take BCL down with everything that they had.

The journalist called Agastya back within a few seconds.

'He's at the airport, heading to New York. I've messaged you his number. Mentioned to him that he would be getting a call from the possible future CEO of BCL.'

'That's wild.'

Agastya was nervous. He walked out of the office, wary of Maithili eavesdropping on his conversation with Goenka. He had already compromised several sensitive business aspects with her. He enquired with Rebecca.

'Is Amit's room free today?'

'I'll check right away.'

She made a call and nodded as she put the receiver down. He walked across to the cabin beside his, opened the door and felt energized finding himself in a space without Maithili around.

He took a deep breath and dialled Goenka's number. He had found something that was now giving him an even greater adrenaline rush.

After dialling the number, Agastya realized that he should have composed himself and thought through the situation. The call was picked up within two rings.

'Yes?'

'Mr Goenka. This is Agastya, from BCL. Ajay would have spoken to you.'

'Yes, Agastya. Is this urgent?'

'That would depend upon you.'

Goenka was taken aback and laughed.

'You have my ears. But I won't be able to speak for too long. The flight is about to take off.'

'I understand.'

'And I'm sorry to hear about Vikram.'

'Are your readers going to hear about it as well?'

'That's with my editorial team. I don't get into those aspects.'

'I will be taking a fresh look at our media spends next month. We have decided to consolidate and focus rather than spread ourselves thin.'

'Hmmm.'

Goenka knew that BCL was one of their top ten clients and had been with them for several decades now. He also knew that Stark was one of their top ten advertising clients, and he would have to appease both the players. If he upset either, it would dent his bottom line.

Agastya understood Goenka's predicament.

'We are in the midst of a series of new product roll-outs.'

'I know all this, Agastya. And so are your friends at Stark. We are just a media house.'

Agastya realized that he couldn't do much to protect Vikram's reputation. The news was already out in the open about Vikram's involvement in the BCL – Metrics JV stock scam, and if Goenka didn't, the rest of the media would definitely go for the jugular. He had wanted to put in a word for Vikram, but knew that the damage had already been done. One media house couldn't save him or his job. He felt that if he was to orient his organization and brands with Goenka, the rival newspaper would take it all out against him. But he also knew that the BCL account was too precious and large for either of them to blacklist for too long. Money talked and at most there would be strife for a couple of months and then everything would return to the market dynamics.

He needed to focus. He needed to prove to Richard that he could strike the ball out of the ball park, even under pressure. He needed a sense of comfort that one of the two media houses would back him and give him the front page slots. It also had to be big enough for Goenka to step in and take a call, over riding his team.

Agastya hesitated, closed his eyes and then whispered,

'100 crore additional advertising spends this year with your newspapers, Mr Goenka.'

He hadn't ever spoken with Goenka, neither did he know too much about him. He knew that he was a Yale graduate and had an extremely sharp business acumen. But he had also been reported to have inherited his father's uncouth and candid approach to business and money. He was banking on the fact that below the Yale exterior, the shrewd and manipulative businessman would prevail.

There was a silence for several excruciating seconds. Agastya didn't know if he had just upset the apple cart with

India's most powerful media baron. Was this conversation going to cost him dear? Would the media baron expose the CMO of BCL for bribery? A multitude of thoughts crashed through Agastya's mind.

'We must meet sometime soon.'

Agastya heaved a sigh of relief.

'And, Mr Goenka…'

'Something else?'

Agastya could now hear the jet engines roaring. The flight was already rolling down on the runway and was about to take off. Agastya was running out of time. He also needed to give Goenka enough time to pass on instructions to the team before the flight took off.

'Men make mistakes. Even good men.'

He could sense a restless pause.

'Give my best to Vikram, and wish him on my behalf for his birthday.' The line got terminated.

Agastya looked at the time on his watch. The seconds seemed to be rushing past him and the minutes appeared to be hurtling forward. There was no respite.

Manish called again.

'It's time to put Spectra into play, Agastya. It's a sure shot.'

'Anything but that one, Manish, anything.' Agastya had raised his voice. His trepidation was clear. He loathed it. He hadn't wanted to be anywhere near it.

'I've made some calls. Just dump the damn thing. Just shake out of it, Agastya!'

Chapter Seventeen

EIGHT
MONTHS
EARLIER

your anchor is in the midst
of oceans, at spread out ports
and rarely your own home

Nandita had slept through the entire duration of the flight back from Vienna. It had been two days since they had completed the last rites at the crematorium and had driven to Nasik to immerse the ashes. She had finally cried when they reached home the previous night. He had slept on the couch and she had fallen asleep with the children in their bedroom.

His brother's car crash had been one in a series of setbacks that had hit their families in the last fortnight. His father's demise in Kolkata, followed by her mother's stroke and now his brother's car crash in Vienna had made this one of the darkest periods in their lives.

He hadn't had the time to just sit back and take it all in. The loss of his father had affected him more than he had imagined and all this was turning out to be difficult to handle.

The rage had been pent up and he had been struggling to come to terms with the reality of it all. It had just begun to sink in that his family had been wiped out. He had been distant with his father for several years. He was finding it difficult to come to grips with the situation and he needed something to push him out of it. He needed a rush of adrenaline, something that would jolt him out of this mess and get him back in the game. Something that would fuel his zest and passion for life again. He determined that the market was his only ally. A big win, in fact something with which he would hit the ball out of the park, would get him back in the game. He needed to find his groove and get back on the fast track. He had been bogged down and he didn't have anywhere to turn to.

He was trying to log into some of the news websites to see if he could get any more details. Maybe there were some conditions to the announcements. Maybe the market hadn't read the specifics and had reacted on the headline value. It wasn't unusual for the market to take drastic calls in the initial period of a major announcement, only to correct it when the real changes had been comprehended and the impact calibrated.

Agastya called up the broker.

'One million short on Spectra....' he disconnected.

He could see that Spectra had fallen further in the last minute to ₹ 765. It was sure shot. He felt the need for retribution. It had to be Spectra. The mere act of placing an order had set his testosterone on fire again. He could feel the excitement and thrill. There was a sudden sense of rejuvenation and he noticed that he was even smiling. It had been an impulsive call. He didn't have any insider information on Spectra. It had just felt right when he had seen it, at that very instant. It just had to be right. Something had to be right, and this had to be it for sure. There couldn't be any other way. Emotion was far overpowering the rationale.

'Are you out of your mind?' Nandita yelled.

Agastya was furiously tapping away on his laptop and switching between the multiple tabs that were open on the screen. He was sitting on the dining table and didn't look up towards her.

'What the hell?' he screamed back.

'Look at you! See what you're doing to yourself and to us!'

She hadn't had the inclination to speak the last few days and surely she could have waited till the market had closed.

'Listen, I need to take care of some things, alright?' he barked.

His eyes were locked on the screen again as he felt his pulse racing. He hadn't taken his blood pressure tablets earlier in the morning. He knew he would have done well to take that dosage in time. From the corner of his eye he could see that she was still standing next to him, in visible rage. She was taking deep breaths, and was clearly weighing the options of a frontal assault or muted aggression. In either case he knew that she wasn't going to relent easily. And then he noticed that Spectra was now holding steady. His hands were frozen. The market seemed to be turning around and Spectra appeared to be considering moving along with the market and ride the surf. He didn't want to even blink. Some announcements seemed to have given the market a new lease of life and it was all a bed of roses as the greens suddenly far outnumbered the reds.

'And you don't care for what's happening to your family and children?'

'What the hell? I just want some time for myself. Just pretend that I have gone into office, alright? Now buzz off!'

She was seething with anger at his callous remarks. She had been waiting to have some time with him and attempt a discussion on his obsession. It was taking a toll on him, on her and their relationship.

She took a deep breath and held the chair at the dining table with both her hands, pressing against it very hard. Her hands were perspiring and she was almost trembling.

'Agastya, we need to talk about this. You need to talk about this.'

The market's upward hike into the green continued. He needed to review his selling options and the protection mechanisms he had in place. The graphs had indicated a collapse, but then he had been wrong before as well. There had been rumours the previous night of a calamitous correction around the corner, but the sentiment had indicated that it was still some days away. He had been having a weak streak at the markets, and in life, for several weeks now and none of his moves seemed to be paying off.

He continued looking at the screen as his fingers furiously lashed away at the keyboard. He needed to speak with a few people to figure out what was happening, but she had decided to bring up one of her vicious conversations at this very moment.

She could sense his suffering and he was now taking shelter within the irrational comfort of the bourses. He was running and even trying to escape from reality, hoping that if he ran fast enough and immersed himself in a rush of adrenaline, it would all pass. It had been better not discussing things. It had always been better letting them lie around and resolve themselves. He had believed that details and incisive dialogue more often than not only accentuated the hurt.

'Listen, Nandita, there's nothing to talk about. My father died. That's reality! My brother died, that's reality. Your mother is in the hospital, and even she will die. They will all die. We will all die. So don't get so damn emotional about this crap, got that?'

He was consumed by rage and knew that holding back further was only going to worsen his situation.

'Don't you dare! You're not the only one suffering and in pain. I can feel pain as well, Agastya. You need to understand that!'

The chair was pulled back and then tossed across the floor. She was now in a rage and had decided to let go of her restraint. She flung herself in his direction, picked up the laptop and threw it with both her arms over his head and towards the window that was behind him. The laptop crashed on the wall beside the window and they could hear it crack before it collapsed lifeless on the floor. The screen had broken off from the keyboard unit and was lying dismembered on the floor.

'You're a slime ball, Agastya, and you know that. I am just a trophy for you, and life played a cruel hand to both of us, you bastard. Now deal with it! I know I am! You just can't run away from all this and pretend none of it happened!'

'Just go to hell for all I care!'

'Yes, that's all I mean to you, right?'

'Damn you, Nandita, just damn you!'

Nandita continued. 'You know, Agastya! You hated your father for not approving of our marriage. Did you know he made me promise him that I would look after you? He used to call me every week; every Friday, enquiring about you. Now live with that!'

She had now stepped back and was supporting herself against the wall.

'And you think this is the time for all of this?'

'Don't you dare! You distanced yourself from your father and your brother. You have only yourself to blame, not them. Even you're not screwed up enough to not understand that. Or, is it that you don't want to? Is that it?'

'You're one shrewd creature! You know that?'

'Say whatever you want to, Agastya, but you're no one to judge me! '

'And what does that mean?'

'You've been very distant…'

There was a stunned silence. Agastya was taken aback.

He screamed. 'My father and brother have died and this is what's running in your mind?!'

He jumped from his chair, held her back with both his arms on her shoulders and then pushed her with great force. He tried to hold on to her, but he couldn't get a grip. His brute force made her lose balance and she fell on the floor. She was still looking with rage into his eyes as her head hit the floor and he could see it bounce gently with the magnitude of the impact.

He was standing in stunned silence. He didn't believe that he had actually done that to his wife. He had never raised his hand on her and hadn't intended to, but she had left him little choice.

He wanted to pick her up, but then was swept with a wave of disgust. He needed to escape from this all. He needed to take refuge in a situation that made sense to him; a situation in which he could feel a sense of control. A situation which needed him and was more logical than the irrationality of emotions and relationships. Something that would sweep him away from all this and hurl him into a wave of coherent turbulence and offer him an anchor and take him through the day.

Agastya saw the ticker on the TV screen. The market continued to rise.

His eyes were glued to the screen, even though his arms extended towards Nandita who continued lying on the floor, quite clearly in pain from the fall.

She picked herself up from the floor, pushing his limp hands away and lunged at him once again. He was taken by surprise as his eyes moved momentarily from the TV screen only to see her lunging once again towards him, only this time with her hands clenched and heading straight for his face. He opened his palms and raised his hands to block the attack, but the velocity was tremendous. Her right hand brushed aside his left hand and landed a punch right below his left eye, as he moved his head away. It was a solid knock and the rings on her fingers sharpened the blow even further. A deep gash bared itself from his eye to his cheek as he pulled away and her hand slid down after the impact. She was breathing heavily and there were tears in her eyes.

He fell back with the force and balanced himself with his left hand on the table as his right hand moved back searching for the wall. His fingers had barely touched the wall, when he noticed that she was preparing to assault him again. She wasn't letting go. He pushed himself backwards and moved towards his left, swinging away from her. Her hand was thrust forward again, but this time she missed him completely and fell face down with her trembling knees unable to support her wobbly torso. He could see her fall and his hands reached out to grab her dupatta, but the garment slipped through his fingers and couldn't hold her back from the fall. She fell face down this time, landing on the floor.

He stood still for a few seconds facing her, now crouched, body on the floor. He looked at her head and was relieved to see it moving. He moved towards her, but she pushed him back, and instead rested both her palms on the floor and with her elbows pushed herself up. His fingers felt the cut below his eye and tried to establish the depth and length of it. It hurt when he pressed it and he could feel the moisture of a sticky liquid, which he realized was blood. He pulled out a handkerchief from his trouser pocket and pressed it against the cut. It singed initially and then settled down, but the cloth was soon drenched.

She was now standing on her feet. She moved backwards, turned around and picked up his mobile from the table. She, turned back towards him, raised it high towards the ceiling and then screamed.

'God damn you!'

The mobile fell towards the floor and he could hear the crash of the touchscreen as it contacted the marble floor. The battery had been ejected from its casing and was now lying on the far side of the dining room below the crockery cabinet.

He picked himself up with his left hand, continuing to press the handkerchief against his cheek.

He spoke in a subdued voice.

'You've gone stark raving mad! Are you on drugs, you crazy woman? What's got into you?' The tone may have been subdued but his choice of words hadn't lost their contempt.

'I've gone mad!' she screamed, still breathing heavily.

He wanted to reach out to her and check her head for injuries. He attempted to move towards her but she yelled again.

'You're the one who is throwing away everything, you jerk! You never valued what you had! And you'll never value me either!'

Agastya could see the market rising on the TV screen. He needed to get a grip of the situation and take some corrective actions.

The car keys were lying on the chair beside the main door. He had his running shoes on from the morning jog. He made a dash for the main door, picked up the keys with his left hand as his right hand moved for the door latch. He could hear her screaming behind him, hurling expletives as she ran towards him. He opened the door, jumped out and closed it shut behind him. He noticed that the elevator was on the ground floor and decided to make a run for it down the staircase. He ran towards the staircase and jumped two to three steps at a time. He heard the door open as she charged out into the lobby area.

He had descended four floors when he finally looked back and was relieved to see that she wasn't on his chase. He could however hear her crying and screaming '…coward!'

He reached the basement in well under a minute, ran to the car parked a few feet away from the staircase exit. He fidgeted with the keys and the remote button to open the door. The key was not responding and he pressed it repeatedly with his thumb. It finally opened. He swung the door open, and pushed himself inside it, hitting his shin against the floor of the car as he got in. He switched on the ignition and turned on the radio, scanning for the news on the market.

He raced the BMW out of the main gate, took the right turn, and navigated through small lanes and via roads, slamming the horn repeatedly till he reached Marine Drive. The traffic had calmed down on this otherwise busy stretch.

He searched for the mobile on the dashboard and remembered that it was lying shattered on the floor at home. He needed to contact his broker and cut the losses on his position. He had gone short, and quite clearly the market wasn't in alignment with him.

As he approached Taraporevala Aquarium, the traffic slowed down and he could see the pile up of cars ahead.

'What the hell?' he screamed.

As the car slowed down to a vicious halt, he opened the door, stepped out only to realize that the traffic seemed to have come to a grinding halt for over a kilometre, possibly past the Intercontinental and even up to the turn that led to Churchgate station.

He slammed his right hand on the roof of the car.

'Hell!' he screamed.

The driver to his left gave him a puzzled look, and then looked away from him. Agastya slammed the door shut and stood holding his head on Marine Drive. He took the two steps towards the passenger seated behind the driver, and then looked down to see that there was blood dripping from his track pants.

'Excuse me, madam…'

The woman, dressed in a sari, seemed to be in her mid-fifties, possibly a Gujarati, the way she had draped it. She was startled by this man with a bleeding and swollen cheek, a gash across his face and with blood dripping on the road from his feet.

She impulsively moved away from the window to her left and checked to ensure that her door was locked. She raised her hand and signalled him to move away from her. She seemed too petrified and didn't seem to recognize the man cited as one of India's Top 20 marketing whiz kids as per a recent article in Fortune magazine.

He then walked up to the car ahead of him and tapped on the window where the driver was tapping the steering wheel listening to Stevie Wonder. Agastya wished he had his identity card or at least his business card, but he had left his wallet at home.

The driver gazed into his rear view mirror and noticed that this man had emerged from a BMW and was wearing imported Nikes, a model that hadn't yet been launched in India.

The electric car window slid down.

'Hey,' Agastya spoke in a calm voice. He needed to build a credible story.

'Yes?' The man in his thirties, sporting a French beard responded, though quite hesitantly.

'I'm in a spot of bother. Can I please use your mobile to make one call? It's very important and I would be truly…,' Agastya couldn't recall when he had possibly begged someone in the last few decades!

The man hesitated, and Agastya stood there, with clear, determined eyes.

A smartphone was handed over to him.

'Thank you so much!' Agastya grabbed it, unlocked the touch screen with his blood soaked fingers and then struggled. He couldn't remember the broker's number.

He dialled a number. It rang several times and was then finally picked up.

'Hello, who is this?'

'Rebecca, this is Agastya. I'm calling from another number.'

'What happened? All well?'

The traffic had started moving again and the driver who had lent him the mobile was getting restless as he saw his high-end instrument being dirtied by Agastya's bloody fingers. He was anxious to get it back before the traffic moved any further.

He extended his hand towards the driver and raised his index finger, pleading for some time.

'Can't talk much ... but I need my broker's number ...'

'But, Agastya, I'm on leave today. Remember?'

The cars parked behind his BMW had started honking restlessly as the cars in the other lanes had commenced their slow movement forward. Every inch was precious in a Mumbai traffic jam.

'Damn!' He screeched and handed the mobile back to the driver.

He walked back to his car and then realized that he hadn't thanked the owner of the smartphone for his kind gesture. He surely couldn't head back to him to make another call. The newscast on the radio continued to be grim for him.

His heart was racing. There was a crazy amount of money that he had left in play which would have wiped him out for sure. How could he have been so stupid? This was so unlike him. He was always on top of things. Was he losing his edge?

The traffic moved a few inches and then ground to a halt. Agastya sat restlessly for over a minute and then pushed open the car door, and walked out again. His heart was pounding. Each and every second was precious. The pain in his shin was excruciating and he could feel his sight blurring from the cut. His cheek was stinging with pain and he was unable to think clearly. He was infuriated with the irony of the situation. He had a four bedroom apartment in South Mumbai, three cars, at least five mobiles at home, a couple of laptops and a slew of state-of-the-art gadgets that could have connected him to the markets within nanoseconds, and here he was struggling to get through to his broker. He needed to make a single call, not more than five seconds long, to cut back his losses. Five seconds stood between him and a loss that would take him years to recoup from.

He noticed he was now breaking into a jog, and before he knew it, had graduated to sprinting. As he ran, he wheezed heavily, letting his arms crash wildly around him as he tried to dodge bikes and cars on Marine Drive. Hundreds of drivers, passengers and pedestrians watched a mad man speed down Mumbai's majestic road, in his now blood-drenched clothes. He was gasping for breath as he rested his hands on a black and yellow.

The shocked taxi driver threw his left hand behind to lock the door. Agastya didn't relent and walked up to the passenger seat and stuck his head in through the open window. He was gasping for breath. He looked into the driver's eyes. Agastya realized he could neither go to his office, nor be seen in that state by his broker. To top it all he hated the fact that he still couldn't remember the broker's number.

'Cumballa Hills please.'

The driver paused, and nodded.

It took them over thirty-eight minutes to reach Cumballa Hills.

As the cab drove into the building, he noticed that the lift was engaged on the sixth floor. He took a deep breath and ran up the four flights of stairs and rang the bell furiously.

The door was opened reluctantly.

'Agastya!'

'M!'

He pushed the door open and ran through to the front room and switched on the television. He screamed at her.

'Where's your laptop?'

'On the dining table, over there,' she pointed in the direction of the dining hall.

He ran through the hall towards the dining table.

He clicked on the browser and typed the Moneycontrol URL. The page opened instantly and he keyed in the Spectra scrip.

It was up 3 per cent.

'M! It's over!'

She stood beside him and noticed the blood falling on the floor.

'What happened?'

'I've gone bust on Spectra…'

'How bad?'

'Crazy bad. I know I can make it back, but I need leverage.'

'Have you looked at yourself in the mirror?'

'I have been slightly preoccupied, as you can notice!' he winked before wincing in pain.

'Can I ask what happened?'

'Long story. But for now I need funds, and quickly.'

Upendra Namburi

'How much?'

He turned the laptop towards her.

'I went one million short on Spectra. Now you can do the math.'

'Are you insane? I need to get you to the hospital first!'

He steadied himself, holding the table, feeling dizzy from the frenetic activity.

'Have you lost your head? That's over two crores and rising each minute, Agastya!'

'Just give me the damn money, M!' he screamed and collapsed on the floor.

Chapter Eighteen

3:10 pm
Today

erase the past...
its resurrection
threatens the present

Agastya walked back to his room and noticed Maithili seated on the chair next to his table again.

Spectra had taken a drubbing in the last fifteen minutes. Bizarre rallies of upswings and downswings were quite common with Spectra and it had evolved into a fairly predictable pattern for several quarters.

Spectra had fallen from ₹ 921 to ₹ 897 in a brief span of fifteen minutes, a fall of over 2.5 per cent. The haunting memories and fears all rushed back to him. His fingers froze. He needed to overcome it quickly. Spectra had been both his downfall and his ally. But it lay there in front of him, teasing him. He had vowed not to be within its proximity and had not looked even at its charts or price swings for several months. But the first sight of the scrip and the charts on the laptop gave him a sense of ease with this animal that fascinated him, but he was also in fear of. He knew everything about it and believed that it couldn't hurt him again. He believed he had a connection with Spectra that couldn't be rationally explained.

Maithili spoke. 'Don't allow fear to shroud your judgement, Agastya!'

'Don't preach to me, M!'

'I'm not.' She looked away from him.

He could feel the taunts and was disappointed with himself for allowing her to still affect him.

Alliance had moved back down to ₹ 431. Manish had backed Alliance to go down, but Mukund hadn't given any indication. He needed to follow his gut. He looked at the time, closed his eyes and then typed a message to Mukund.

'One million short Spectra.'

He hesitated before sending the message, looked towards Maithili and then the tablet. Spectra flickered at ₹ 896.89. It had fallen below ₹ 897!

Mukund replied instantly. *'Sure?'*

Was this a signal? Was he really sure? Should he have backed Alliance even further? Did he really want to get anywhere close to Spectra?

'Yes.'

He had exhausted the leverage he had received from Manish. Now he had nothing else to play with.

He needed Alliance to hit ₹ 420 and Spectra to hit ₹ 880, and then he would have crossed the 15 crore mark!

Beads of perspiration reappeared on his forehead.

The flurry of activity had hit a crescendo outside his room. The shrieking and shouting had hit deafening proportions. He just sat there and tried to take it all in.

The mobile rang. It was Nandita.

'Hi, Nandita...' he spoke in a mellow voice.

'Agastya, where have you been?'

'Have the press conference in a few minutes...'

'Who's Maithili? She has been insisting on meeting me today. What's all this about? Who is she?'

He realized that his silence would unnerve her and might even make her suspicious. He needed to calm her down.

'She may want to discuss some investment options with you.'

'But then why does she want to meet me? What's so urgent?'

'I don't know, Nandita! Check with her. I need to go now.'

'Are you sure there's nothing else to it?'

'I will speak with you later, Nandita.' Agastya disconnected and wondered if that was the last civil conversation he would be able to have with her. In the best case scenario, she would have a husband who had driven their life savings to the ground, and in the worst case scenario she would realize that her husband was also a treacherous, deceitful man. He realized that this wasn't the time to be overwhelmed.

'Why don't you just tell her everything, Agastya?'

'But then you wouldn't get the money, M!'

'Hmm, I hadn't really thought about that!' The sarcasm in the room could be cut with a knife.

Agastya didn't respond.

'But seriously, Agastya, knowing you quite well, what's holding you back?'

'I just don't want to mess things up, M!'

'Come on, Agastya. Now you mock me!'

'What do you mean?'

'I think I know.'

'Do tell!'

'I think it's because you haven't told her about your first marriage!'

Agastya was stunned and struggled to conceal his horror. His poker skills were now being tested to the hilt.

'Bullshit!'

'What's bullshit, Agastya? That her name is Vaidehi?'

He didn't want to respond but realized that it would be better to know the extent of details that she had with her.

'What about Vaidehi?'

'I know it didn't last too long. But you should have told Nandita, don't you think?'

'That's a load of crap!'

'I was expecting that response, but marriage certificates don't lie. And I'm sure that the DNA tests will prove that she had your child! And then both of you decided to part ways. So I guess that puts you in a spot?'

Agastya and Vaidehi had both joined Pepsi as management graduates. They had met at a training programme and had soon found themselves involved in an intense, passionate relationship. They remained in touch across their various postings in Pepsi for several years and started living together when they had both secured postings in Bangalore.

They were both driven, ambitious professionals who always placed their careers above everything else. It had been a tempestuous relationship, as they explored each other with gay abandon in a city that was new to both of them. Away from relatives or any close friends, they both plunged themselves into their work and each other.

However, they found themselves at crossroads, when they both got promoted and were transferred to different cities away from Bangalore. They didn't want to restrict themselves in their careers and found themselves at loggerheads when they realized that their relationship had evolved to a level that was far deeper and more discomforting than they were both prepared for. Neither of them was able to take up alternate assignments within Pepsi to be with each other nor were they willing to leave Pepsi. They decided to get married, hoping that it would help keep their relationship healthy despite their rapidly progressing yet diverging career paths.

Agastya nodded.

'It's not as simple as that, M, but this is not the time to discuss that. Not that I need to either!'

'That's your call, Agastya, but I'm sure this would make for a very interesting conversation.'

He received a message on the messenger.

Sailesh: Check out TV21 News.

Agastya turned on the television and tracked down TV21. The reporter was standing outside the BCL corporate office.

'...we have unconfirmed reports that the BCL CEO Vikram Rajyavanshi has put in his papers and so has the CFO,

Abhishek Nanda. Other BCL senior management officials including their Chief Marketing Officer, Agastya may also be putting in their papers shortly. There are no clear details on what may have caused this, but rumours suggest that there may be some irregularities in the IPO issue of the BCL Metrics JV. Involvement of a cabinet minister is also under speculation right now. The BCL and the BCL Metrics JV stock prices have been taking a heavy beating in this trading session…'

Agastya put the TV on mute. He looked at Sailesh's message again. He had hoped that the news wouldn't hit the media till the press conference, but realized that it was now in the open. The press conference was a calamity in the making and now even he was under the scanner. Rumours were treacherous and unforgiving allies in corporate life, but their shadow remained even when they were squashed or proven to be untrue. Rumours and reputation were strange bedfellows and notorious allies. Agastya had been known to be an aggressive risk taker in all aspects in his life, but his integrity had been unquestionable. He was cognizant of the fact that his passions for the stock market would make him a natural contender for suspicion in the stock scam, and now Maithili's evidence against Nandita could prove to be professional death knell as well. The last few minutes had just increased the stakes. His personal battle was one that he had hoped to recoup with time, after all it was only about money. His professional integrity was now a lost, hidden dimension that could not be resurrected.

Sebastian called.

'Have emailed the new press release. Want to see it?'

Agastya shook his head.

'Please go ahead with it.'

There was a pause as Sebastian didn't speak a word.

'What happened, Sebastian?'

'The process requires your sign off on anything being released to the media.'

'Just go ahead with it for now! I'll respond when I can.'

His mobile rang.

'Agastya…'

'Yes?'

'It's Mark.'

'Yes, Mark?'

'Did Richard give you the approvals for the promotional offer?'

Agastya sensed that something was amiss.

'I got an email a few minutes ago.'

'Just hold on to it for now.'

'But, Mark, we need to head into the press conference in the next twenty minutes…there's…'

Mark interrupted him.

'Richard is under the scanner…'

Agastya froze. He wasn't sure how to react.

'I beg your pardon?'

'This scam seems to be more widespread than we thought.'

'Let's call off the press conference, Mark, and this product launch. This is not the time.'

Mark cut him again.

'It's under consideration right now, Agastya!'

There was a heaviness in his voice. He could sense the hesitation.

Mark continued.

'Agastya, I have asked Sebastian to overlook the operations for now…till we have some clarity…'

'I beg your pardon?'

'You've seen the news reports too, Agastya.'

Mark hung up. The screen on the iPad continued to post more reds with a few sprinklings of greens. The bloodbath was continuing. He couldn't focus. Mark's words felt like a stab in his chest. Waves of nervousness and uncertainty were sweeping across his body.

Sebastian waited at the door and knocked. Agastya opened the door and stood there, facing him.

It had been but a few seconds since they had spoken, but he could make out the difference in his body language and demeanour. There was a sense of triumph and even smugness in his gait. He wanted to tell him to hold back, but realized that this would be the ideal opportunity for his subordinate to usurp his position. The rug was being pulled from under his feet and he could sense the situation slipping from his hands.

'Boss, I just received an email from Mark asking me to connect with you. I am just following instructions.'

It was a stoic, yet polite tone.

Nitin walked towards them and Sebastian left.

'What happened, Nitin? Hearing quite a few things on the floor.'

Nitin led him to the empty cabin beside his own.

'Listen, hang in there. Some major crap is going down and it's getting out of hand. I've got over a hundred distributors who've just shut down on me. It's a damn nightmare. This has been orchestrated like crazy. Someone, or some people, are gunning for us. It's a whitewash. This is too much of a coincidence. I heard about you as well!'

Agastya was feeling numb. He wanted to run away from it all, undo his tie, get some fresh air and scream his lungs out, but realized that he wouldn't have that luxury for a while now.

'You've heard?'

'It's all over the floor. Mark asked me to cover your position for a while but I told him my hands were full. I heard that the internal auditors have already started scanning all our investments and business deals. A team from Singapore is also being flown in. It's getting totally out of hand.'

'What's your sense?'

'My sense?! I want to take a bazooka and blow the brains out of Sailesh Rao! That's my sense. What else do you think, Agastya?'

'You've heard about Richard as well?'

'Yup. I can't believe even Richard got dirty. This is outright insane. We're never going to recover from this.'

'Any luck on what we had discussed?'

'I can't do too much on that right now, Agastya. I've got enough fire on my hands.' Nitin rushed out of the room as his mobile began ringing again.

Agastya stood for a few seconds and then walked back to his cabin.

Maithili was now standing beside the iPad and pointed the screen in his direction as he entered the room.

'What happened?'

She pointed towards the BCL and the BCL Metrics–JV stock. They had been bludgeoned and had dropped over 12 per cent in a few minutes. The blue chip, ever reliable darling of the bourses, was being slammed and struck down to the ground. With that was vanishing the ESOPs that he had been holding precious for so many years as well. That had been one of the wealth options that he had been banking on outside his trading stocks, but those too seemed to be turning to worthless junk in a matter of minutes.

Agastya remained standing. He realized that he needed to up the ante and had to put into play something that would be much larger than the immediate product launch. The senior management team at BCL was now paralyzed and also vulnerable in the situation.

Agastya was amazed at Sailesh's calm. It was admirably discomforting. He didn't seem to be making any inroads and realized that he was throwing pellets at Goliath and he needed something more explosive. He needed something that would shake Stark out of its slumber. He was wondering if he had been playing this wrong after all. He needed something bigger, but possibly directed at Stark rather than at Sailesh, or maybe something that affected both? He possibly needed to change tact. Maybe there was something that didn't damage them, but in fact helped them.

He called up Vikram.

'Yes, Agastya?'

'Got a minute? It's important!'

'Tell me.'

'The situation is getting out of hand. We really need to do something. We can't be sitting here twiddling our thumbs.'

'What do you have in mind?'

'Can you reach out to Prem?'

There was a painful pause. Vikram and Prem Mehra spoke rarely and on most occasions stuck to exchanging pleasantries in conferences and other public events.

'Under the circumstances?'

'Yes, Vikram, under the circumstances!'

'Why don't you?'

Agastya was puzzled.

'I would need some leverage, Vikram. There must be something.'

'New Delhi could help them perhaps?'

Agastya beamed. 'Can we pull this off?'

'The minister doesn't want to be dragged into this. There would be too much collateral damage!'

'I'll give it a shot. Will call you back!'

Vikram hung up, but Agastya kept holding the mobile to his ear. He noticed Sebastian walking on the floor outside beaming. He had possibly leaked the news of his taking charge from Agastya and was now gloating.

He called Vikram again. 'Yes, Agastya ...'

'My position has been compromised, Vikram, and I'm sure Prem will know. I won't be able to influence the situation unless he's clear that I am the CMO.'

There was a pause.

'Why don't you have a word with Mark, Vikram?'

'Under the circumstances ...'

'I understand, Vikram.' He hung up.

'Would you like a hug?'

Agastya shook his head and smiled.

'You want to make love to me? Hmm ... it's a pity you don't have a comfortable enough sofa here, otherwise, you never know ...' Maithili walked across to him and patted him on the shoulder.

'Focus, my dear, focus. You're running slightly low on time. And by the way, Nandita called.'

'What happened now?'

'Oh nothing much. She just confirmed the meeting for today.'

'Good for you,' Agastya smirked.

The agency director called.

'Agastya, Sebastian told me to keep the campaign on hold again.'

Agastya wasn't sure if he could even react to the question considering the developments in the last couple of minutes.

'Just keep in touch with Sebastian.'

The director had been entertaining a never ending range of whims and fancies from the client for several days now, and he didn't have the appetite for it anymore.

'Listen, Agastya, I've been as supportive as anyone can ever be. I've spoken with my CEO and he is going to have a word with Mark.'

'What?'

'I didn't have a choice in the matter, you need to understand. For all we know, you'll just pounce on any goof up that can occur right now and we can't be held responsible for it.'

'You're doing this to me, now?!'

'It's not me, Agastya, it's my agency on the line right now.'

The director hung up. It had clearly been a difficult conversation for him and while Agastya understood, he didn't want to reconcile to the fact.

There was no respite. His mobile was vibrating again; it was his messenger.

Sailesh: Feel like a drink today? ☺

Agastya deleted the message, realizing that he would have been tempted to respond with something that would have shown his frustration and helplessness. It was all caving in around him.

He called up the journalist.

'What happened, Ajay?'

The journalist laughed. 'Your call worked. The ad sales guys are scrambling, trying to cover their asses.'

'And?'

'Check your email as we speak.'

He had been marked on a bcc. It was an email written to the CEO of Stark, by the journalist.

Dear Sir,

I am doing a story on the Nielsons' FMCG Index report. I have documents and evidence indicating that your team has been manipulating the stocks and sales numbers at some stores that are tracked by Nielsons in their market share reports. I have attached some emails and documents corroborating the same. I would like to have your comments.

Prem Mehra had been marked a cc as well.

Agastya read the email and wondered if that would be enough. He wanted to take it public and hit the news channels directly, but realized that he could use it as a bargaining chip if required later.

He then received another email, in which he had been marked a bcc again, but which had been sent from an alternate email id.

Dear Mr Mehra,

You will find attached trade reports of your CMO, Mr Sailesh Rao, where he has been trading heavily on BCL stocks. It would seem to be too much of a coincidence that such large volumes are being traded by a senior employee.

Prem Mehra, the CEO of Stark, was also on the cc listing.

The timing was almost deliberately obvious, possibly too obvious. He was sure that Prem would get the drift and take notice.

He smiled as he saw one more message on his messenger. It was almost instant. Was it even possible that Sailesh had received the email a few seconds earlier than him?

Sailesh: Not bad!

Agastya noticed Sebastian fidgeting and walking the

length and breadth of the marketing floor, shooting out directions and instructions, deflecting assaults from the larger team and the agency personnel.

He got a text message from the journalist.

'One more to go?'

He messaged back. *'Hold it.'*

Agastya walked towards the window and placed the palms of his hands against the glass. He took several deep breaths and closed his eyes.

'I know a good yoga instructor. He's done wonders for my back.'

Agastya clenched his fist and then realized that he couldn't hold back any further. The rage couldn't be contained. He needed to let it out. He just had to let go.

He walked across to the now seated Maithili, placed his right hand on her head and stroked her hair. He then went on to massage her neck.

'You know, Maithili, once all this is over…once we get away from all this madness…this mayhem…'

Maithili had closed her eyes as she submitted herself to the sheer pleasure and relief that his deft hands were delivering with the massage.

'Hmmm?' she was now rolling her head around her neck as he pressed gently yet firmly with his fingers and palms.

He then moved his hands further down her shoulders and continued pressing them and then moved them back towards her neck.

She had now pushed her head back and slipped down into the chair.

Agastya quickly grasped her neck with his hands and tightened the grip rapidly and firmly till she was gasping for breath. Her hands were soon clawing his and trying to push him back. She started kicking her feet against the carpet, trying to scream, but he maintained his firm grip. She swung her head vigorously trying to shake him off but he kept tightening the grip with his hands. She could feel his thumbs driving deeper into her throat. She tried to push herself up by slamming her feet onto the carpet, trying to get up and turn around, but she was pushed down. Her nails pierced his wrists, and he was in pain, but the pleasure of inflicting hurt on her far outstripped the agony her deep incisions were having on his wrists. The tussle lasted for over ten seconds, when his mobile rang again. He noticed that it was a call from Mark and he let go of her with a shove. Still breathing heavily, he held onto the chair with both his hands to regain his composure. She was now lying on the floor massaging her neck with her hands and gasping to fill her lungs with air. She was coughing and struggling to gain back her senses, which seemed to have been scattered by the lack of air supply.

His hands and legs were trembling as he walked across to the table. His heart was pounding and he was unable to collect himself. He wanted to let it ring, but realized that he had to take the call.

He connected the call and placed the mobile by his ear supporting it with his right shoulder.

He stuttered, struggling to utter the words calmly yet confidently.

'Yes, Mark?'

'I got a call from Prem Mehra...'

Had the emails worked?

'Yes, Mark?' he realized that those were the only syllables he was able to utter without making a mess of it in his anxiousness.

'It was a brief call but he said he would call back again.'

'What was it about?'

'He seemed to be disturbed with some news reports...'

'Why is he calling us?'

Mark laughed, and it seemed miraculous to Agastya that the global CMO had found the reason to even attempt a laugh.

'He thinks you have a hand to play in this.'

Agastya maintained silence, knowing that any false step in this situation could be detrimental to him.

'And...'

'He seemed to have been distracted by something else when he called and said he would call back. Your thoughts?'

'Got too much on my plate right now, Mark.'

Mark laughed again. 'Vikram spoke with me. I believe you wanted to speak with Prem?'

Agastya hesitated to reply.

Mark laughed again. 'You've just got a lease of life. Make the call.'

Maithili had now picked herself up and was standing with her back against the window. She was glaring at him when suddenly her face transformed. There was a sudden calm about her; it was an eerie silence. They just stood there staring at each other, both of them knowing that they wanted to lash out, punch and tear away at each other. These were moments of violent restraint and the gush of emotions paralyzed them.

Sebastian walked into the room and was startled at what he saw. Maithili's unkempt ruffled hair, one shoe fallen beside the chair and another one on the far side of the room, her blouse pulled out from within the neat confines of her trousers and her jacket button torn loose and dangling. He could see tear stains on her cheeks and her mascara running. He realized that he had walked into a situation between two agitated people and wished he could quietly disappear.

He walked across to Agastya and handed over the phone to him.

It was a text message from Mark: *'Connect with Agastya.'*

Agastya's eyes glowed. He was back at the helm.

Sailesh Rao's Office, Stark, Mumbai

Sailesh was reading the news reports. He was absorbed by the mercenary guerilla tactics.

His mobile rang.

'Hi, Shankar.'

Shankar, the Stark HR head had moved in from Gillette after the takeover. Shankar had been instrumental in negotiating the final offer for Sailesh at Gillette, before his CEO candidate had decided to abandon ship and join Stark instead. Theirs had been a strained relationship at the best of times and he was often, to Sailesh's chagrin, the CEO's messenger on sensitive issues.

'Hi, Sailesh. I need to have a chat. Good time?'

'For you, Shankar, I will have to drop everything else, won't I?'

Shankar laughed and then quickly adopted a formal and professional tone.

'Sailesh, these emails are putting us in a tight corner.'

'These are ramblings, Shankar. You know how the press works here.'

'I would like to say that I understand, Sailesh, but I've just spoken with Prem, and he's equally disturbed.'

'I'll speak with Prem.'

'Prem is busy on a few calls right now, so he asked me to have a word with you.'

'What's on your mind, Shankar?'

'As I mentioned, Sailesh, we have some major launches coming up and a fair amount of media coverage. We need to keep the reputation of the company in mind.'

'What are you suggesting, Shankar?'

'I'm not suggesting anything, Sailesh. It's just that these allegations are serious. You need to consider this. I was speaking with Prem, and this situation seems to be getting quite serious.'

'Serious? Yes, it is a serious matter, but we need to work towards resolving it quickly.'

'I understand. But this seems to be having some reputational implications as well.'

'And? Shankar, we know each other quite well. So, please don't beat around the bush!'

'Let's just say we need to take a sense of ownership on the matter.'

Sailesh paused.

'Sailesh, are you there?'

'What are you looking for, Shankar?'

'I wouldn't put it like that. But in a situation such as this, it is important to address the requirements of the business in a professional manner.'

Sailesh hung up and clenched the mobile in his hand.

Prem was hanging him out to dry. Sailesh had tried to ensure that he had gained Prem's confidence in the launch of Velvet, but also realized that he had gained a tremendous amount of visibility within the upper echelons of the Stark management, which had disturbed his CEO. He had discussed at length, the possible retaliation and manouveres that BCL was likely to make and especially Agastya, but was conscious of the abysmally short tenures of corporate memories.

He scanned the BCL stock price once again. The decline continued.

His mobile rang again.

'Yes, Shankar?'

'Sailesh. I think it would be best if you were to put in your papers.'

There was a deafening silence for several seconds, as neither party spoke.

'Thanks, Shankar. I'll speak with Prem on this one.'

He disconnected the call again.

He reflected on his tenuous position. He had to make it to the end of the day and gain Prem's confidence and support. They couldn't blink now. There was too much at stake. He had invested several months in planning, seeking support and executing the rollout of Velvet. They were missing the larger picture. His blueprint would bring BCL to their knees, if only Prem stood beside him. They couldn't dither at the slightest distraction. Had he created an ideal situation for Prem? A blueprint to decimate BCL was now the firm bedrock for Prem to extricate Sailesh from Stark and secure his CEO slot for a little longer.

Radhika walked into his room.

'Sailesh?'

'Don't tell me... I know, it's getting hot, right?'

'That would be an understatement.'

'Radhika, can I ask you something?'

'Sure, Sailesh.'

'How long have you been married?'

'Five years. Why do you ask?'

'Has he been faithful to you?'

'That's quite a personal question.'

Sailesh smiled. 'You've seen me drunk and collapsed in my office, Radhika. I guess that's why I take this liberty.'

'He's a good man.'

'That's good.'

'Why do you ask?'

'What would he do if you were unfaithful?'

Radhika had a concerned look. 'I think he would be very troubled … and possibly quite mad.'

'What would you like him to do?'

'I think I would like him to hold me tight.'

'It's as simple as that?'

'Anything but simple, Sailesh. Let's just say that we are not defined by the moments, but by the journeys.'

'Quite a philosophical approach?'

'Revenge is a natural instinct, Sailesh. But there's more often than not too much collateral damage and in most instances we miss the point in the process, and hurt ourselves.'

'And that's what I'm doing with Tanya right now?'

'It's for you to be true to yourself. Only you have the answers.'

'I don't know how Tanya and I got where we are today.'

'I think you do. You're an intelligent man. You just need to find the strength to have that conversation with yourself and then with her.'

'You think I made her do it?'

'I wouldn't know that.'

'Thanks, Radhika.'

'You're welcome, Sailesh. I hear that your job is on the line?'

'You don't hold back the punches. Do you?' Sailesh smiled.

'Now you know why my husband is faithful to me!' Radhika winked.

THREE MONTHS EARLIER

winds of sensual uncertainty
tantalize every breath
in the face of imminent death

The waiter served the LITs along with some snacks as accompaniments.

Maithili raised her glass. 'Cheers to making it to the list, honey!'

Agastya shrugged, but raised his glass nonetheless.

'Not you too, Maithili. That list is a load of crap!'

'Come on, Agastya. The Matrix List of Top 10 Marketing Professionals in India! Surely that's genuine.'

'Sure.'

'You're beginning to get on my nerves!'

'The person who comes in second is the first to lose ...'

Agastya sipped the drink and looked away. She could see his frustration and rage.

'So that's what's bothering you, that Sailesh Rao came up first in the list?' she giggled.

Agastya reflected on the day that had transpired. The sales numbers had been looking up, the Nielsens report had confirmed that their market share numbers were on the rise across categories, the preliminary market research findings looked encouraging for some of his new product launches and he had made a killing in the stock market. Vikram had made it a point to suggest that Sailesh would have achieved those results quicker and even more emphatically, in a conversation with Nitin.

Agastya had had a tumultuous couple of years at BCL. It had been a huge challenge to steer through the bureaucracy and dead wood that had crept within the organization, whereas Sailesh had found himself at the helm of a leaner and hungrier Stark. He had introduced several new products and rapidly increased market share across categories. He had been by far the more accomplished of the two in the eyes of the media and even several senior management team members at BCL.

The references to Sailesh had continued within BCL with Vikram leading the pack.

'Don't giggle...it's just not you.'

'Why? You don't think there is a little girl inside me? Or you don't think I'm feminine enough?'

Agastya looked towards the band. They were appalling! He looked around the room and noticed that it was a rather strange mix of people. A young couple that appeared to be celebrating their anniversary, a bunch of yuppies, who seemed to have just discovered the limits on their credit cards, a group of corporate professionals having a Friday evening drink together and on the other end of the room a gay couple in passionate embrace. Mumbai had changed; Agastya smiled.

'What's with the smile?'

'Nothing. Look at that couple there,' he pointed his finger in their direction and then quickly retracted realizing how rude it could appear.

'Hmmm...love is in the air...'

'I think it's more like the horny hormones have come out to party on a Friday night.'

'I can't figure you out, Agastya.'

He sipped the cocktail, placed the glass back on the table and smiled.

'Stop that irritating fake smile. It bugs me!'

'You're suddenly in a bad mood. What happened?'

'Listen, Agastya. I know you wear this enigmatic cloak about you, but sometimes it can be a bit too much. You seriously need to shake out of this obsession you have with destroying Sailesh. What's with that?'

He smiled again.

'It's just healthy rivalry, Maithili.'

'Seriously? You want me to buy that?'

Agastya sipped the drink.

'Do you know how it feels when the CEO remarks that Sailesh would have made for a better marketing head?'

'He said that? Or are you reading too much into it?'

'These are conversations that he has had in my presence, M! It's not heresy.'

'That's just small talk, Agastya. Don't let it get to you.'

'But it matters.'

'How does it matter, Agastya? Since when did others' impressions and perceptions affect you? Opinions and perceptions change by convenience.'

'This is not the time for philosophy.'

'This isn't philosophy, but maybe I've misunderstood you.'

'As in?'

'I didn't think you were someone to whom others opinions mattered so much!'

'They don't!'

'Then, you do know what it is, right?'

'What, M?!'

She smiled.

'You actually believe that he is better than you. And that's making you sick!'

Agastya shook his head and clenched his fist.

'You're quite a bitch!'

'That's not a logical response. You don't need to tell me, Agastya. It's a conversation that you need to have with yourself.'

'You're on some vendetta trip today, aren't you?'

Maithili laughed.

'What?!'

'Seriously. You've seen that I'm vulnerable today and you're drawing out all the daggers!'

'You've gone insane. Just get off your huge ego trip and get a reality check. You are bloody human. Deal with it.'

The band had finished playing a Bob Marley number and the audience broke into a reluctant applause.

Maithili decided to change the subject. 'This place really sucks, plus you've made a killing in the market today."

'You know, Maithili…'

'What?'

She could sense that Agastya was getting into one of his zones—one of those zones where nothing and no one around him mattered. It was only about him and nothing else when he got there. He could treat her like a piece of garbage or just completely indulge her so luxuriously that it would keep her going till his next tryst with the dark side.

'It's one of those days when I really want to indulge myself.' He was shaking his head.

She could sense him getting into it much quicker than she had anticipated, and she wasn't sure if she had the patience or the inclination to be around him. She had had a miserable day at work and her situation with her family only seemed to deteriorate with each passing day. She had nowhere else to go. She realized how hooked she was to him. Her entire after work schedule was now dependent on and a function of his availability, mood and intentions.

'I need to make some new friends,' she whispered to herself. She didn't want to be alone and she decided to stick around, because she was sure that ultimately there would be some excitement.

'You know, Maithili, I want to be able to do something wild… just get out of this straightjacketed existence…'

She didn't want to debate him on which particular aspect

278

of his life was straight jacketed. Was it his high visibility corporate job, the plush four bedroom apartment in South Bombay, the chauffeur driven cars, frequent international holidays, the holiday homes in Goa and Coorg or the designer watches?

'You're a jerk.'

He would never admit it, but he was turned on when Maithili took him on, when she challenged him.

'I know, but you still stick around with me.' he sniggered.

'It's an addiction. Don't read too much into it.'

He got up from his chair and sat on the one to her left. He placed his arm around her shoulders and held her hand with his.

'Look around you. Let's get you some action tonight!'

She tried to shake him off but she was held down by his firm grip. It was going to be one of those games for him. He wouldn't let her back down or lay off. She needed to play along, or he would just leave her and go.

She took a deep breath and decided to enjoy the thrill.

'So, what do you have in mind, darling?'

'How about a threesome tonight?' Agastya smiled.

Maithili's tolerance and patience for his dark humour and even darker mind had run its course for the evening. She had been having a miserable couple of days at work and didn't have the inclination to put up with any of his nonsense. It just wasn't amusing.

She pushed his hand off her shoulder and got up.

'I need to get some fresh air…'

'What?'

'Why? Do I need to take your permission?'

'Let me guess. You're going to go and make love to Ismail?'

'Do I question you when you make love to Nandita?'

'Does it bother you?'

Agastya wasn't in a mood to be refused. Not on this night. He needed to be with people. He had been feeling low. He needed the warmth of another human being, but the words coming out of his mouth were divergent to what he was thinking. He needed to feel powerful and didn't want to plead.

Maithili picked up her car keys from the table and left. Agastya sat on his chair watching the band play. He felt awkward. He had become used to Maithili and having her around. She seemed to understand him better than anyone else; even his insane streaks. He was angered by the fact that she had left him at the table, for no apparent reason. This had been his normal behaviour. It was nothing out of the ordinary. They had always played it differently. They weren't the everyday couple having an affair. They were different. It now didn't make any sense.

'How could the bitch leave?' he murmured to himself.

He had wanted to run out and chase her down. Possibly one of those high speed car chases again. Possibly one of those violent arguments!

But he was held back by his ego and his pride. He didn't want to be chasing her down.

He ordered scotch and drank quickly as the band continued spewing inane songs while the audience applauded each and every despicable rendition of the classics.

'Are these jerks on dope?'

His eyes were drawn to the bar and a woman dressed in a brown suit, around Maithili's height, but with brown eyes and what he considered to be excessive make up. He had consumed over four glasses of scotch in under twenty minutes and it had achieved its desired effect. His eyes kept steering themselves back towards the woman in the suit. She looked very familiar, but he couldn't recollect if he had met her, or if she was just a familiar face. He stood up, adjusted his tie and jacket, smoothed his ruffled hair and walked up towards her.

'Is this seat taken?'

She forced a smile, but was apprehensive as if she wasn't sure if she wanted any company that evening.

He settled down on the chair opposite hers and took a sip from her glass. She smiled.

'And…you are?' Agastya turned on his charm.

'Do we really need names? Would that make a difference?' It appeared as if she already knew him. There was a sense of familiarity with him in her tone.

Agastya laughed.

'A rather different opening bunch of lines…but refreshing nonetheless.'

'I hadn't planned it that way, but I say it as I see it!' he smiled at her and took another sip from her glass.

He noticed her wedding ring worn rather unapologetically. She was blinking furiously and her contact lenses seemed to be causing her much irritation. She had folded her legs and he noticed that they were silky smooth, long and fair. She had undone the top two buttons of her beige blouse and kept fidgeting with her short hair.

'Are you from Mumbai?' he asked

'Do you always ask so many questions?'

Agastya laughed. She was taking him on and he was increasingly enjoying this stimulating interaction.

'Only if I think it's going to be worth my while!' he took the glass from her hand and emptied its contents.

'Are you upset that your girlfriend left you or is it something else that's bothering you so much?'

Agastya sat back on his chair and stretched his tired legs. He loosened his tie and pulled it down and then unbuttoned his collar button. It also gave him time to take a closer look at her.

'Are you stalking me? I hope this is not going to turn out to be one of those cheap nightmare movies?'

'That's very amusing, coming from an intelligent man such as yourself,' she continued smiling.

'Why's that?'

'You should well know that if I were a stalker I wouldn't be the one declaring it to you, right?'

He laughed.

'Can I get you a drink?'

'No but maybe I can have some of yours? Let's reduce the clutter?'

Her sense of humour was both sharp and refreshing. Her confidence seemed deep and the words came out naturally. She was Indian, but seemed to have lived abroad or possibly studied there. A working professional to boot with her BlackBerry and the laptop in a pure leather bag. He couldn't place her accent and it seemed to have traces from several countries. He was getting increasingly fascinated by her and wasn't sure if the scotch was perhaps influencing him as it shouldn't.

They continued chatting for over an hour, but they both steered clear of their personal and professional lives. They spoke about politics, their trekking adventures and holidays and even discussed recipes to their mutual enthusiasm. It was getting to be a very comfortable and comforting conversation, and it troubled him that he was so at ease with someone he knew so little about.

They had consumed five large scotches between them. When the sixth one arrived, she emptied half its contents in one large gulp and got up.

'Room 203. Be there in five minutes or I'm locking you out!' she winked at him and left even before he could respond. He noticed that her steps and posture were both self-assured. She could hold her drink, and there was no doubting that.

He watched her leave the bar even as she didn't even turn around once. She was playing him and Agastya was in unfamiliar territory. He was always fascinated with his appetite for danger, but this seemed to be in a different league altogether. This woman had done something to him and he couldn't let it go, even though he knew that he was being played. She had the upper hand and she was making every move. She was always a few steps ahead of him.

He settled the bill and walked to the rest room. He looked in the mirror and noticed the blood red eyes and a stubble heavier and darker than he had imagined.

Had he aged over the last couple of hours?

His eyes veered towards the watch and noticed that he had barely a minute and half left. He wasn't even sure if he wanted to go up to her room. He wasn't sure if he wanted to follow her like a desperate puppy. He hated the fact that he was being played, but he couldn't take his mind off her plunging neckline and her long legs. He couldn't let go of the fact that a gorgeous woman had made an advance at him. He liked the attention and felt a childish delight at being desired.

He soon found his feet rushing to the elevator while his hands thrust themselves in between the closing doors. He pressed the button and waited impatiently for the elevator to make its way. As the doors opened on the second floor, he quickly walked to the door bearing the number 203 and stood still.

Had he thought this through? He checked his mobile and noticed that there had been no further messages or calls from Maithili or Nandita.

He knew that this could turn out to be one of the worst decisions that he had ever taken. His instinct told him to walk away and head home to his wife and children. There were some bets that were not to be played. This was one in which he should have just folded and walked.

He nodded his head and then a sudden streak of panic swept across his body.

Had the great Agastya lost his charm and penchant for risk-taking? Was he losing it? Surely, he still had it in him. And why should he not even consider making meaningless love to a desirable woman?

He opened the door and noticed that she had flung her coat on the bed, and had collapsed on the couch near the window. Her shoes were lying on the table and her bag had been dropped in the passage near the door. 'I hope you're not late in everything that you do!' she laughed out loud and he felt genuinely embarrassed. She seemed to have this power over him. He felt the pain of humiliation but didn't mind it. It was quite uncharacteristic of him and it surprised him. His mind couldn't process all the contradictions in his behaviour and even his actions. He wasn't in control. He wasn't the one calling the shots. He just didn't have his finger on the pulse. This was unchartered territory.

Playing with stocks had two outcomes. One either made a killing, making loads of money, or one crashed and burned. But the scenarios and outcomes had been played out in his life on so many occasions that they ceased to disturb or even exhilarate him as they used to several years earlier. Now it was a process and a series of cycles that he had become accustomed to as the thrills were marginalized with each trade, gain and loss.

But this? This was a new thrill.

She got up, walked towards him and flung herself at him. They both fell on the bed and lay still for several minutes just looking at each other, her body on top of his.

Suddenly he changed positions and deftly flipped her under him. He pressed down on her, his hands clasping hers, till he could make out that he was hurting her. She didn't resist even as the metal strip of his watch cut her arm evoking a sharp pain. He wanted to hear her plead, but she lay there without an ounce of resistance, looking straight at him through the pain. Agastya hesitated—he wasn't sure if he just wanted to wear out his lust or express his anger against Maithili and himself for missing her.

He let go of her arms, pulled the chain around her neck, leaving distinct scratch marks on her body, and proceeded to rip apart every piece of clothing and accessory that she was wearing. His feeling of a sense of triumph every time he flung an item from her body to different parts of the room was quickly followed by a crushing sense of vulnerability as she lay there smiling even as she was brutally assaulted.

He felt inexplicably angry. As rage mixed with passion overtook his senses, he grasped her hair with his left hand and slapped her several times with his right. Soon the loud whacks resounding around the room had drained the energy out of his body and he collapsed; his naked body across hers. While he breathed heavily, exhausted by his own anger, she rose to kiss him. She held him by his arms and gently slid him off her to her side and then lay on top of him, motionless for several seconds, just feeling each other's heavy breathing. A heady concoction of perspiration, perfume and sexual desire seemed to permeate the room.

She felt the bruises on her body with her fingertips and let out a soft sigh. She raised her head and bit his lip and progressed to kissing him all over his body. She kept kissing him for several minutes as he struggled with fatigue and dehydration from excessive alcohol. Her relentless kisses and the heat from her body seemed to stir Agastya. He suddenly changed positions and was on top of her in the blink of an eye.

They made love with wild abandon and moments after they had finished, they rolled from the bed to the rug and made love again.

After the second bout of extreme passion had subsided, he pushed her away and walked up and down the room, running his fingers through his hair and shaking his head vigorously. He wasn't sure if he was being disloyal to Nandita or Maithili or both? Or was he lying to himself? It didn't make any sense and he didn't want this to make any sense either! This wasn't like him. This should have been a random meaningless act.

She picked herself up, the pain evident as she walked to the mini bar and poured herself a drink. She sipped it and then walked across to Agastya who was standing beside the window staring at the Queen's Necklace. They both stood naked, pressing against each other and the French windows.

'Why did you do this?'

'Of what I recollect we did it together,' she laughed.

He noticed that there were tears rolling down her cheeks.

'What are you doing in this hotel?'

'I just needed some time away.'

He shook his head and sat down on the carpet with his back resting against the window.

She sat down beside him and placed his hand on her knees.

'Did you enjoy me?'

Chapter Twenty

3:15 pm
TODAY

in the face of subterfuge
aren't we all cannibals?

Sebastian walked out of the room.

Maithili tucked in her blouse and adjusted her hair. She dabbed her eyes with a handkerchief and walked back to the chair. Agastya wanted to apologize to her but wasn't sure how to go about it. He was overcome with a mix of emotions for her, but then held himself back and didn't want to fall prey to weakness or compassion. He wanted to ease out the situation and decided to focus on more pressing problems.

There was a sudden rush of blood as it occurred to him that he may have come up with something that could turn the situation around. The enemy had blinked. They were now taking notice and had realized that he and Nitin were the only persons who could quash any further countermoves by Stark. Agastya anticipated that there was more to come and he would have to go for the jugular to make it imperative for the competition to take notice.

Alliance was falling at a mellow rate and had breached the ₹428 mark, and not as quickly as he had hoped for. On a normal day, that would have been a commendable collapse. He also realized that he needed sufficient time for Mukund to cover and close his position. With under fifteen minutes of trading time left, he knew that he had undertaken an extremely high risk route by banking everything he had on just two stocks.

Spectra had however moved swiftly from ₹897 to ₹892. If it kept its pace, it would reach the target ₹880-mark in time for the kill. He wondered if he should have placed more on Spectra and diverted some of the funds from Alliance instead.

He messaged Mukund. *'Need some more leverage... pls.'*

There was no response.

'M! How do you fancy giving me some money for a few minutes?'

'You must be out of your mind!'

'No rules about that, right?'

She shrugged.

Agastya dialled Prem Mehra's number as he watched Maithili retreat to the conference room.

A deep voice responded, 'Yes, who is this?'

'It's Agastya from BCL. Can we speak?'

The silence hung between them. Agastya pushed on.

'Prem, I have your long term interests in mind when I make this call. A minute of your time?'

'Tell me.'

'You've been struggling in New Delhi.'

'I don't follow.'

'Your situation can be possibly influenced!'

'What situation?'

Agastya had anticipated an antagonistic response in their first conversation and especially under the circumstances.

'Your factories have been awaiting environmental clearances, right?'

'Yes. That is in the public domain.'

Agastya was struggling with words. He didn't have the luxury of time and neither the inclination to be politically correct.

'There may be an opportunity to expedite some of those clearances.'

Agastya realized that Prem's ego and the deep rooted rivalry between both the organizations, given the present circumstances, were making this conversation more difficult than usual.

'As simple as that?'

'Not simple by any means! We would need to have an understanding though.'

'Let me think about it, Agastya.'

Prem disconnected the call.

Agastya wasn't sure if he had made sufficient impact. He was certain that Vikram would have had a more immediate and possibly slightly warmer conversation.

He called up Mark.

'What about the press conference?'

'We are going ahead with it.'

This is insane, Agastya thought to himself.

'The press is going to lynch us. Let's just do a press release and go ahead.'

'I know what you're thinking, Agastya, but I am in conversation with the board on the matter.'

'We don't have the time, Mark. There are too many things that we need to finalize and rollout.'

He wanted to mention to Mark that in the absence of a senior manager, the ability of the organization to take decisions was severely impaired.

'I've been granted executive powers by the board to take decisions, under the circumstances.'

It was as if Mark had read his mind.

'I've spoken with Nitin as well. I'm going to be banking on both of you through this situation.'

'I understand, Mark. Just let me know what we can do.'

'Agastya, there have been rumours about your connection with Sailesh.'

Agastya didn't respond, wanting to mention instead his golfing association with the CMO of Stark.

'Agastya! Are you there?'

'Yes, Mark.'

'You need to pull something off on this one.'

'Mark, I would need some resources to influence the situation.'

Mark remained silent for a couple of seconds. He could hear him tapping away at the keyboard.

'Agastya. You'll need to give me some more time on the promotional discount offer.'

'But...'

'And what are these resources you are referring to?'

'Some funds for market development,' Agastya blurted.

An excruciating silence followed.

'I can't have any further scandals, Agastya.' While his words suggested otherwise, Agastya sensed consent in his tone. 'I understand, Mark.'

'Good!' Mark laughed and disconnected.

Agastya scanned his contact list and looked for a name from the BCL Metrics JV directory. He dialled the number and cursed himself for not thinking of this earlier.

'Hi, Agastya.' They had interacted briefly a couple of weeks earlier in a meeting for the product launch. Rakesh Srivastava was the operational head at the BCL Metrics JV and managed the logistics for the BCL account. He had been in the transportation and logistics business through his career, having worked in several Indian companies, before taking the plunge into the 'funny MNC set up,' as he termed it.

'Hi, Rakesh. Got a minute?'

'Can't say that I do. Nitin has been breathing down my neck trying to re-dispatch and reroute stocks because of this distributor mess that we are in.'

'I can understand. But this is critical.'

'Tell me...'

'How're your friends at Mahesh Roadways?'

Mahesh Roadways was the largest trucking partner for Stark and handled over 70 per cent of their supply chain from the factories to the warehouses and C&F agents across the country.

'They remain friends. Why?'

'Are they still facing payment issues?'

'From Stark, yes! But why do you ask?'

'You were in talks with them to come over and work with you. Right?'

'Yes, it's been in the pipeline for a while now.'

'Push it.'

'What?'

'Make it worth their while…'

'I don't get you.'

'How much, Rakesh? You would understand that right?'

'I spoke with them even yesterday. I needed some help with the new launch, additional volumes.'

Agastya was getting irritated with the unnecessary conversation.

'How much, Rakesh?'

'They've got over 7 crores stuck with Stark for a while now, and it's only growing. It didn't help when they got wind of the fact that they're having a chat with us.'

'So help them out.'

'What?'

'Have you finalized your terms yet?'

'Yes, that's been sealed and closed. We've got our board approvals as well. Even you know that.'

'Make a call. Cover them. Do whatever it takes, but they need to stop their trucking operations with Stark.'

Rakesh paused.

'Have you gone mad?'

'They need to freeze the Stark truck network. I want a total lockdown.'

'That's over four hundred trucks out there, Agastya.'

'Let's just say that their trucks are temporarily indisposed!'

'You've got to be kidding me!'

'What do you think?'

Rakesh had been trying to close the deal for months, and this was the latitude that he had been seeking from the management team to beat the impasse.

'Do you have the approval for this? In my previous company your word would have been enough, but here …'

'It will have to do or come and lynch me. You know where I stay!'

'Not as easy as that.'

'Follow your gut. Make the call, Rakesh, and then call me back.'

Rakesh chuckled.

'You guys are crazy…'

'But I need this to happen in the next sixty seconds, you got that?' Agastya disconnected the call.

He was disappointed with himself and felt he should have pressed harder, but realized that he didn't want to take Mark's name in the matter.

He was restless. Maithili was now staring at him again. He could see the mild bruises on her neck. He wanted to walk across, sit beside her and comfort her. It had been a moment of rage and he hadn't meant for it to happen, but then realized that the moment was gone and there was nothing he could do about it. One more moment of madness in their relationship. One more moment of incomprehensible rage that had overcome him.

He messaged Vikram. *'We may need New Delhi to step in.'*

Vikram responded instantly. *'Making the call.'*

The mobile rang again. He sulked. He wanted to ignore the call but then realized that that was a luxury he didn't have.

'Yes, Nitin?'

'What updates?'

'Stark called up Mark.'

'Yup.'

'What do you think is happening?'

'No clue, but I hope they are sensing the heat.'

'Is that all?'

'I don't know. What did Mark share with you?'

'Nothing much.'

They both realized that they were bluffing each other. Agastya looked at the time. He hated that Nitin was consuming precious seconds but reckoned that there was a purpose for the call.

'How's it going with your distributors? Any headway?'

'My guys have been calling and meeting with them. Stark had played them against us. I am trying to drill some sense into them, but some of the bigger ones are quite adamant.'

'But there would be a notice period and penalty clauses as well, right?'

'Well, it's tricky. It's easy for them to take up distributorship with Stark in another legal name and then transfer all their employees, if required. They would be serving notice periods, etc, but even they know that we need them more than they need us.'

'Why is Stark taking these guys? They have some strong distributors themselves!'

'They've been pruning down some of their non-performing ones, and our distributors make for easy pickings.

They know the markets and the retailers, and have been in those places for decades. It's invaluable really. Plus, with all their new product launches, they need more guys to take up the additional business.'

'Tough one!'

There was a silence for a brief period.

Nitin finally cracked. 'I heard that Vikram may be back ...'

'How?'

'It's more of a face save for the media, the stock price is taking a bludgeoning and they can't afford to have a scandal on their hands. Too much at stake.'

'Can they pull it off? I believe there's evidence?'

'There's one journalist who seems to have some material, but even he hasn't really disclosed it yet. All this is uncorroborated and speculative as of now. You know the terms that they use.'

'And the rest of the media?'

'They've just picked up on one of the rumours. It can be twisted if required.'

'Who's the journalist?'

'Some guy from News Times. Don't have his name though.'

It seemed too much of a coincidence for him.

'So how are they managing to stall the media leak?'

'I heard that Mark spoke with Goenka ...'

Goenka from News Times?'

'Yes. I heard that Mark assured him that all the rumours were baseless speculation. But I don't know what else was discussed.'

'But this journalist would have got the information from someone. Right?'

'Well. That's a mystery. Don't know that one yet. Listen, I've got to go.'

'Is this stuff about Vikram confirmed?'

'Under the circumstances, nothing is,' Nitin disconnected.

Agastya's messenger beeped.

Sailesh: You're being played…

Agastya: ?

He waited for a few seconds for a response and received none. It was enigmatic. Agastya felt the message was genuine, but wasn't sure if for some perverse reason it was more hope than reality. He wanted to believe that Sailesh was in fact a confidante, and that their bond hadn't been compromised, but the facts were stacked up against him.

He read the message several times over. Who was playing him? Was it Nitin or was it Mark? Or was it Sailesh playing with his mind? He wanted to ignore it, but those three words were having their desired effect on him. He had been on a roll for the last several minutes and now the brakes had been applied.

He still hadn't received a response.

Agastya called up the journalist, but couldn't reach him.

Sebastian walked into the room.

'Heard?'

'What now?'

'There are talks of appointing a deputy CEO.'

'A deputy what?'

'Yes, a deputy CEO. By the way, you do know we have about ten minutes to go, right? And we're all sitting here twiddling our thumbs.' There was a distinct frustration in his voice.

Agastya called up Mark.

'Yes?'

'Less than ten minutes… We need to take a call or it's going to be too late.'

There was a long pause.

'I am contemplating calling it off!'

Agastya was exasperated.

'The press conference?'

'No, the entire product launch.'

'I don't think I follow...'

'We need to get it right.'

Agastya's journey with the product launch flashed past him. The thousands of man hours, crores spent on research and design, the new factory line up that had been set up—all this for a damn detergent! It just seemed senseless.'

'Mark, there's quite a bit at stake here.'

'I know, Agastya, but Nitin has his hands full with the issue we are having with the distributors. We won't be doing a good job with it either way and now this discount. It's just not working out.

'*And what about the commitment to the board?*' Agastya wanted to ask but kept this thought to himself.

'Mark, I understand, but we have to take a call...'

There was a long pause. He seemed to be typing on his keypad.

'What's your view, Agastya?'

'We've committed quite a bit on this. Let the product hit the shelves and let's take it from there?'

There was another tense pause. Sebastian was crossing his fingers. He had seen more mayhem in a day than he had ever seen in his career.

'Go for it.'

Agastya wanted to shout and struggled to restrain himself.

'And... is it 20 per cent off or 15 per cent?'

He knew that the numbers appeared quite small in

percentages, but over the lifetime of the product it would in effect result in a difference of hundreds of crores of profits.

'Let's hit the party in style. 20 per cent?'

It had been a question, but Agastya was not going to let this opportunity slip by.

'We're going with 20 per cent, Mark.' He was polite enough to hold till Mark disconnected but had started scribbling "20" on a piece of paper that Sebastian had placed on the table. He had barely placed the mobile on the table when he saw Sebastian dashing out of his room and bellowing his lungs out.

'It's 20 per cent off! Let's get a move on!'

Agastya was tempted to call him a drill sergeant.

The entire floor erupted into a flurry of screams, shrieks, yells and cries, with instructions, commands, pleas and requests being hurtled across the floor. It had been a volcanic eruption as all the teams hit the floor, relieved with the break in indecision and thankful that finally they were going forward with the *'damned launch'*.

Agastya received another message on his messenger in a few seconds:

Sailesh: 20 per cent?

'Damn!' he muttered.

Alliance had stood still at ₹426.14 for several seconds. It wasn't moving quickly enough.

'Hit 420!' he screeched.

Sailesh Rao's Office, Stark , Mumbai

Sailesh tapped the table with his fingers. He had dialled Prem's number twice, but it had been busy. The commotion outside his room had resurfaced, and he was agitated by the disturbance.

He toggled to the screen with the chess moves and was impressed with the progress that Agastya had made in the game. Over the last couple of months, he had noticed a greater maturity and clarity in his moves. In the initial few games, Agastya had been on a predictable and perennial offensive, without hesitating to exchange or sacrifice pieces to move forward in the game, quite in contrast to Sailesh's cautious and overtly defensive approach. In the recent games, Agastya had retained his offensive streak, but had mastered the art of surprise.

Sailesh wanted to step out and spend some time with the team as they finalized the details for the launch later in the evening. There were many aspects to be ironed out and details to be completed, and he realized that he needed to be at the helm of affairs to provide them an appropriate direction.

Having worked closely with Prem and with the blueprint having been finalized, he also realized that he had possibly made himself redundant. The Stark board and the senior stakeholders within the Indian business had already bought into the blueprint. It was already on a roll, and with Sailesh's meticulous eye to detail and precision, each and every aspect had been defined immaculately. In his quest for revenge and supremacy, he had ignored the now obvious reality that stared down at him; his CEO was his albatross. His proficiency in game theory had been crushed to rubble with his slight oversight of the critical variable of having his CEO's true support. He was now vulnerable to his arch rival and, albeit in a convoluted manner, his assumed protégé Agastya. Disgust with Agastya's brash arrogance and access to significantly greater resources and influence than he had at his disposal had slowly evolved into an appreciation of the fact that Agastya was an equally astute genius who brandished his brashness deliberately to deflect attention from his intellectual brilliance.

Sailesh acknowledged that his animosity towards Agastya was for his qualities that Sailesh was envious of—his political astuteness and his belief in following his gut. He resented Agastya for having snatched the BCL CMO spot from him, but also realized that he shouldn't have taken the position for granted, relying solely on his proximity to Mark. He had doubts if he indeed had it in him to make it to the top spot of a large multinational and if in fact his decision to join Stark had been fuelled by his nervousness in taking on the role of a CEO, and not as much as the scale of the opportunity with Stark.

The mobile finally rang.

'Hi, Prem.'

'Sailesh. We have a rather sticky situation here, don't we?'

'We had discussed this, Prem. It's just a matter of time. The launch will address most of these matters.'

'It's not as simple as that, Sailesh. The press has me in a corner right now.'

'We can manage the situation, Prem.'

'Shankar would have spoken with you.'

'Yes, Prem.'

'You need to give it some thought.'

'Sure, Prem.'

'How're the preparations looking? Trust we're all set for the rollout?'

'Yes, Prem. We're on top of it.'

Prem paused. 'Sailesh, this situation is getting quite sticky with BCL.'

'It's as we had expected, Prem. But, I'm sure it'll work out fine.'

'I'm sure it will, Sailesh.'

Prem disconnected the call.

Sailesh reflected on the conversation and the thousands of hours he had invested in the strategic blue print and the launch of Velvet; the impact that it had had on him, his career his family.

He looked towards the family photograph once again and realized that he looked at it several hundred times each day. He missed his wife.

He received a call from his logistics head.

'Sailesh. Mahesh Roadways is holding us to ransom. All our trucks are coming to a standstill. It's a total damn lockdown!'

Sailesh hung up and burst into hysterical laughter, clapping his hands till he had tears rolling down his cheeks.

He received a text message from Tanya. *'Goa next month?'*

He replied, *'Sure!'*

'How're you doing?'

'Better…'

Chapter Twenty-One

TWO WEEKS EARLIER

through this curtain
of self-destruction
I long for someone, anyone
to recognize me...

This was the first time he was staying at the Burj, a magnificent hotel by any imagination. It was perhaps even too grandiose by his reckoning.

The BCL Global Marketing Leaders Meet was an annual event, and was proving to be more hectic than ever. Mark had been on the warpath, and rumour had it that he was in the midst of divorce proceedings with his wife of eleven years. Hapless chief marketing officers from across the globe seemed to be bearing the brunt of it. These meetings were largely short getaways, allowing them to network and have fun under the guise of a marketing conference, where they shared their marketing and communication strategies. However, Mark seemed to have come out with all guns blazing, ripping apart most of the presentations. He had asked for several data cuts, severely criticized slides and mocked their communication plans. He didn't seem to give his immediate team in the US a break either.

It was the last night of the conference. On most occasions, many delegates would plan to extend their stay by a couple of days to explore the local sights and sounds, and then head back to their respective countries. Agastya, however, had had a tormenting interrogation by Mark, and he almost got the feeling that he had been subjected to more irrational and unnecessary criticism than the other marketing heads. To make matters worse, Vikram seemed to have got wind of the conference proceedings and *suggested* that he return to Mumbai and update him ASAP.

Agastya opened the door to the suite, flung his bag on the couch and sat down on the large four-poster bed. He held his head in his hands, cursing out loudly into thin air. He needed a few seconds to calm down and then realized that he didn't have too much time to get ready for the evening cocktail and then take the night flight back to Mumbai.

He switched on his BlackBerry and noticed the breakfast meeting request for the following morning with Vikram. He would have had barely enough time to reach home from the airport, freshen up and then rush to the office.

He checked up on his portfolio, and fortunately there had been no earth-shattering or cataclysmic events that had unfolded in the previous three hours. His stocks seemed to be intact in an otherwise lacklustre day on the bourses.

He loosened the knot of his silk tie, pulled off his shoes from his aching feet and walked across to his suitcase in the cupboard in the dressing area. He felt the slight cut on his chin from his early morning shave as his nostrils picked up a rather familiar smell. It reminded him of a perfume. He didn't rate himself too highly on his olfactory senses, but there was something about it.

As he opened the suitcase, he could hear the water running in the bathroom.

'*Housekeeping must have missed this,*' he thought to himself.

He could hear the mobile ringing. He walked across and noticed that it was from Nandita.

'Hey, Nandita. What's up?'

'Where are you?' she screamed on the other end of the line.

'I just can't take this now…' he muttered to himself.

'What was that?' she screamed.

'What happened? All well?'

'No!' she screamed again.

He ran a quick checklist to figure out if he had forgotten something or buggered it up on the home front.

He remained calm, despite the day's proceedings. He spoke in a subdued and calm tone.

'Ok, calm down. What is it, Nandita?'

'How could you forget?'

He sat down on the bed and realized that this was going to be one of those conversations where he would be castrated and condemned repeatedly!

'Nandita, seriously, calm down and tell me what's happened!'

'You seriously don't remember?'

Nandita could get on his nerves and this was one of those precise moments. He rubbed his forehead with his fingers. He had thought of making a checklist for these domestic items that always seemed to get missed out between meetings, conferences, budgets and of course the stock market.

And then it struck him … had he forgotten her birthday? He had been living out of a suitcase for over a fortnight. The hectic preparations for the Sparkle launch had thrown his domestic life into disarray. Her birthday was not for over one more week, unless he had mixed it up in the midst of it all. He quickly shook his head, but drew a blank. He just couldn't recollect the date. The duel with Mark had worn him out and his brain had gone numb. The grey cells were not kicking in, they all seemed to have gone into a temporary hibernation. His mind had just frozen. He finally decided to risk it.

'Belated happy birthday, darling …'

He would buy her something at the duty free store on the way back.

'What!' was not the response that he was hoping for.

What had he done now?

'What do you mean "what"?'

'Well. That's another thing that you've forgotten then, haven't you?'

He seemed to be getting deeper into this quagmire. His patience was running low and he was tempted to take it out on her, but knew she deserved a patient hearing in the least. He hadn't been around for her and had meant to spend some quality time with her once work got a bit lighter and Mark was off his case.

'Listen, Nandita, I've had one of those days... I really can't take this, yaar, seriously. Gimme a break. I could really do with a hug!'

She laughed and then finally seemed to calm herself down. 'What was that about?'

'Hey...' she was still struggling to contain her laughter.

'I was just pulling your leg, sweetheart. You've been so busy of late, I haven't even had the chance to pull your leg, so just for kicks!'

Agastya managed to laugh, but didn't want to tell her that her humour was quite ill-timed.

'I really needed some cheering up. Thanks for shaking me out of it.'

'Hey, when you get back home from the sand dunes and those exotic Arab women, I was thinking you and I could re-enact some of those Arabian tales?' Nandita was gushing. She seemed to be really missing him.

He didn't want to disappoint her by telling her that he would barely have time to drop the suitcase at home before rushing for the meeting with Vikram.

'That sounds like a decent Arabian plan, Nandita! Listen, gotta run... but give my love to the kids!'

'Sure. Enjoy yourself... really missing you.'

'Same here…,' he disconnected as he saw the time on his watch. He needed to run.

He rushed back towards the dressing area when he noticed that the bathroom door was now open, but the sound of the running water had stopped.

The steam started swirling out of the room as he slowly opened the door.

'Hi, darling.'

He stood standing by door with his hand resting against the wall in the dressing area.

'You're not glad to see me here, Agastya?' She smiled.

She was dressed in a white robe and her hair was still dripping. He noticed bruises and scars on her face, hands and around her neck. They hadn't met or spoken since the call when Ismail had attacked her. Neither of them had reached out to the other.

'What on…?' His utter shock betrayed him.

'Agastya and surprised?' She laughed.

'What are you doing here, Maithili?'

She continued smiling and looked into his eyes.

'At least you can pretend to be happy to see me here?'

He just shook his head.

'Maithili, I don't know how you got into my room, or for that matter, what you're doing in Dubai, but this is not the best time.'

She laughed and shook her head.

'It's never the best time with you, Agastya, is it?' He could sense the irony and sarcasm in her tone.

'I've been busy, and…'

'Oh, come now, darling, it doesn't matter. All that matters is that you and I are here together.' She started walking towards him across the wet bathroom tiles. He could sense a slur in her voice and her gait seemed imbalanced. He wasn't sure if it was the wet floor that was making her walk cautiously, or if she was drunk.

He stepped back slowly, but it only made her move faster towards him.

'Listen, Maithili, as I said … not a great time. I really need to rush.'

His mobile rang and as he turned his head around to see where he had left it, she rushed forward and flung her arms around him.

He pushed her back and realized that he had applied more force than he had intended to. She fell back and crashed on the wet tiles, slamming the back of her head on the floor.

He stood frozen for several seconds and then rushed towards her.

She was lying on the floor, in pain but yet with a smile on her lips.

He kneeled over and supported her head with one hand and held her shoulder with his other.

She winked at him.

He wanted to let go and let her fall back on the floor but wasn't sure of the damage that may already have been done to her. He couldn't feel any injuries or bruises to her head.

He placed her head on his folded left leg as he kneeled down.

'What in hell are you doing here, Nandita?'

She smiled again.

'It's Maithili.'

He shook his head. He knew he had made the situation worse.

'Slip of the tongue. Now let's get you out of this bathroom.'

'It's more than that, Agastya …'

'It's just been crazy, Maithili, what can I say?'

'No explanations … no conditions … no strings … right?'

'Not now, Maithili …'

He picked her up and helped her stand on her feet.

She balanced herself by placing her left hand on the cabinet inside the bathroom beside the wash basin counter. She pushed him away and trudged back in towards the bedroom.

He followed ensuring not to keep more than a few feet behind her, lest she collapse again.

She collapsed on the bed with her feet still touching the carpet.

He moved up to her and then stopped when he noticed a bottle of vodka on the bedside table. Half its contents had been emptied.

'What are you doing here, M?'

She was looking up towards the ceiling and running her fingers through her wet hair.

'Agastya, I just need you to hold me for now … very tight. Just think of me as Nandita for now, but don't ask me anything else.'

'M, get dressed. Let's meet back in Mumbai. I can't be seen here with you. You know how it is. I've also got a flight to catch …'

'You left me there to rot. I didn't think you could be such a selfish bastard!'

He bent over and stroked her hair.

'We just needed to cool off, Maithili; just cool off for a while.'

She held his hand.

'He beat me to pulp, Agastya. He almost choked me to death. He treated me like an animal … he abused me … he showed no mercy...' She was panting. She suddenly raised her voice, 'But I didn't hold back! Even I gave it back to him! I managed to save Roshan. I got out of there. For a change I managed to protect another person, without a care for myself.' She paused to catch her breath.

'It felt good, Agastya, to love someone else unconditionally. I managed to protect Roshan and I didn't care about what could have happened to me. That's me, Agastya! I can give myself completely for what I love. Do you know what that is like?'

'I didn't mean to hurt you, M, or to see you hurt.'

'I don't mean anything to you, Agastya!'

'It's not like that, M.'

'You know, Agastya, I realized my love for you was not unconditional...'

'It's understandable.'

'I always thought that you would be there for me when I really needed you. I thought you would be man enough at least for that! I guess I had expectations.'

'It was just bad timing.'

'Do you know how long it would have taken for you to drive across and pick me up that day?'

'Let's not get into that now, M.'

'Sixteen minutes, Agastya, sixteen minutes. I know because I've calculated it so many times that I've lost count. On a good day it takes under seven minutes, even. And that day was a good day. I remember.'

'That wasn't a good day for either of us, M.'

She got up and pulled him towards the bed and kissed him. He resisted, but she held on to him.

'M, I need to go.'

'Agastya, will you do something for me?'

'What's that ?'

'I want to have your child. I don't want anything else from you, I just want to have your baby…'

'We can't, M, you know that!'

'Why not?'

Agastya looked at the time on his watch.

'Listen, M, we just had an affair… Get over it. Don't park all your problems and bad choices on this relationship! You're a strong, independent woman. This isn't like you.'

'I don't want you to marry me, Agastya. I just want to have a baby with you.'

She was getting delirious.

He shot up and stood beside the bed, realizing that the pleas for a baby would only continue. She could be adamant and this was just another manifestation of her obstinacy.

'Get lost!' she screamed and broke into tears.

Agastya picked up his shoes and his jacket and walked out of the room. He sat down on the chair outside his room, slipped on his shoes and rushed towards the lift.

He pushed back his hair and adjusted his jacket in the mirror in the elevator on the way down. He didn't approve of the ruffled and disturbed face that he noticed in the mirror. It was at times like this that he wanted to simplify his life. Maybe he couldn't juggle everything as well as he imagined.

His feet moved him towards the banquet hall where the delegates and some of their spouses had converged. The proceedings of the day hadn't diluted their appetite for the fine champagne and selection of wines, scotch and beers that had been laid out. He picked up a chilled glass of champagne and in a few seconds noticed that the glass was empty. He asked the bartender to replenish its contents and emptied that one as well. It just wasn't hitting him as quickly as he needed it to.

The bartender glanced at him, but politely poured more champagne into the fine crystal glass. Agastya moved away and walked towards a small group of five persons that had formed near Mark. He wanted to keep a distance from him but knew he would be better off by breaking the ice with Mark before he left.

Mark appeared to be more jovial and the turbulent exchange of the evening seemed to have been forgotten for the moment. The group was soon regaled with Mark's experiences and trysts with product launches, internship jokes, dark secrets of board members and liasons with prostitutes and comparisons of their performance metrics across four continents.

As the evening progressed, Agastya reassured himself that Maithili would have left his room, and hopefully the city as well.

As Mark called the team across to the main dining area, a hotel attendant walked up to Agastya and whispered into his ear.

'Sir, can I have a moment please?'

Agastya followed the attendant from the banquet hall into the lobby area.

'Sir, there is a matter that requires your personal attention.'

'I'm not sure I follow.'

'Sir, may I accompany you to your room?'

'My room?'

Agastya read his name on the badge.

'Wayne?'

'Yes, sir?'

'What's all this about?'

'We like to be discreet so it's best that you kindly accompany me, sir.' Wayne nodded his head and awaited a confirmation from Agastya.

They walked up to the elevator, and proceeded to the fifth floor without any words being exchanged.

As they approached the room, Agastya noticed a security guard standing outside. Wayne knocked lightly on the door, which was promptly opened by another hotel staff member. As Agastya entered the room, he noticed a doctor seated on the bed beside Maithili who seemed to sleeping.

He rushed to the bed and noticed a wide array of syringes and bottles lying on the bedside table.

'What the hell happened?' Agastya raised his voice and rushed to Maithili.

'Please don't raise your voice, sir. That is something we should be asking you.'

Agastya sat beside her and placed his hand on her forehead and looked at the doctor.

'What happened?'

The doctor appeared to be Indian.

'I'm the house doctor. One of the attendants heard some screams and glass breaking and entered the room.'

Agastya noticed that the glass on the table beside the sofa had been shattered and there were bottles strewn all across the floor.

The doctor continued when Agastya's eyes turned to his again.

'She appears to have taken some medication and had collapsed on the floor by the time I arrived. Who is she?'

The enormity of the situation struck Agastya and his mind was thinking through the various outcomes of the current situation. He couldn't afford to have a legal tangle and especially not in this country and with BCL staff all over the hotel.

'She's a friend.'

'I gather both of you had a disagreement of sorts?'

Agastya nodded. 'How is she, doctor?'

'You do know what just happened, right?'

Agastya struggled to find a response and dreaded the words that might just emerge from his lips. 'She drank too much?'

The doctor shook his head disapprovingly. 'Sir, your friend just attempted suicide and her condition is not stable. I've pumped some of the tablets out of her system, but I would strongly recommend that she be admitted to a hospital.'

'You're kidding!'

Wayne stepped across to Agastya and placed a hand on his shoulder.

'Sir, I gather she is not a guest staying with us?'

Agastya didn't respond.

Wayne continued.

'Sir, you do understand this is a police matter. I would need to call them in, and she needs medical care. I just hope we're not too late.'

'Police! Why?'

'Sir, that is the due process.'

Agastya was now clearly shaken and reached out for Maithili's wrist. He could feel her weak pulse and her shallow breath. She had turned pale.

'I'm sure we can maintain some discretion here. Wayne, I would like to make a call.'

'Of course. I understand, but you will have to hurry. I need to report this matter to my management. '

'Just give me a moment.'

Agastya scanned his mobile and searched for the number and dialled it.

'Something's happened. I need you to come across to the hotel right away.'

Agastya got up from the bed and walked towards Wayne.

'Wayne, I need you to manage this situation. I have a flight to catch, and I'm running late.'

Wayne raised his eyebrows.

'Pardon me, sir?'

'Listen. I have someone coming over in the next few minutes. He is a member of the Indian diplomatic corp. You understand, right?'

'Sir, I need to understand something, and I do hope you will understand why I'm asking this of you?'

'What's that?'

'Is she a lady you hired?'

Agastya raised his hand but realized that he needed to maintain his composure in the situation.

'No. A friend who is going through a tough time.'

'Is that all?'

Agastya was disgusted with his terse and brutal responses, but had to ensure that Wayne and the hotel staff were privy to as limited information as possible.

'Yes, Wayne.'

'I will need to make some calls, and this friend of yours will take matters into his hands. Our hotel will have no responsibility for your guest's welfare after your friend's arrival.'

Agastya nodded.

Wayne disappeared into the hallway and returned in a few seconds.

'You have thirty minutes to manage this private matter, sir.'

Agastya heaved a sigh of relief. He shook Wayne's hand and escorted him to the door.

'Sir, the guard will remain at the door and the doctor is at your service for the next thirty minutes. I trust your friend didn't visit you in our hotel on your current visit?'

Agastya nodded and closed the door behind Wayne. He walked up to the doctor who was checking Maithili's pulse.

'What's her condition?'

'She needs some IV fluids and I need to run some other exams on her. Blood work, some X rays, as she may have fractured her hand when she collapsed on the floor.'

'I get the picture.'

He looked at his watch. The doctor kept monitoring Maithili and Agastya sat down on the sofa awaiting the arrival of his first cousin.

Rishikesh Kumar, knocked on the door twenty-three minutes later.

Agastya opened the door and saw two security personnel walking in behind him.

'You're one son of a gun, Agastya...'

'I'm sorry to do this to you, Rishi!'

'Listen, I need you to leave this city this very instant.'

'Are you sure this is what I should be doing?'

'Trust me, Agastya, this is not a discussion.'

'I can't leave her... not like this... you must be raving mad!'

'I can't have you anywhere near this woman, you got that? I've spoken with some people here. I've got another room booked in her name at this hotel. She checked in two hours earlier, and that's what the hotel records will show.'

Agastya was taken aback by his cousin's meticulous but ruthless approach to the situation.

'Yes.'

'Now, get out of here. Don't call me on my mobile, I'll call you. Nothing about this in any of our communication, got that?'

'I owe you one.'

'Listen, this is not the time or the place, but you need to remember something—get back to India, clear your damn head, get your head out of your ass, and get yourself out of this mess.'

Agastya walked across to the wardrobe and stuffed his clothes into the suitcase.

The security guards picked Maithili up and placed her on a wheelchair that had been towed into the room.

'And, Agastya … ? Say hi to Nandita for me.'

Rishi closed the door behind him as he left the room.

Chapter Twenty-Two

3:20 PM
TODAY

in the midst of the lift
and the strike of my sword
I curse myself...
for having looked into his eyes

'Deputy CEO?' Agastya murmured to himself.

He received a text on messenger.

Sailesh: This is not over…

His mobile rang. It was Rakesh Srivastava from the BCL Metrics JV.

'Agastya, it worked!'

'What?'

'They bit the bullet. They're speaking with Stark as we talk. Now this will get those guys' attention, if anything ever did! In fact they've already started stopping the trucks.'

'Who are they speaking with out there? It's important!'

'My guess? They would speak directly with Prem. I even suggested it. Is that ok?'

'You're a champ, Rakesh! I just hope they get across to them quickly enough.'

'These guys are truckers! They find their way through. Trust me! I believe the Stark guys are already getting the jitters.'

'Thanks, Rakesh!'

'No, Agastya! Thanks to you, I've been trying to close this damn thing for ages. Couldn't have done this without you.'

'We're even?'

'More even than you can imagine. All the best for the launch!'

Alliance continued to tease him at ₹426. It wasn't moving from the spot. He was worried if it had found its support. He also realized that his calculations would have gone awry, as when Mukund would move in to close the position and pick up 4 million shares in the market, the price was bound to move up again. Alliance would need to breach far lower than ₹420 for him to have sufficient cushion to recoup his position. He realized that he wasn't going to make it with the existing mix.

Spectra however had moved rapidly towards the ₹885 mark, much closer to the ₹880 mark that he had been targeting. He was going to be well over ₹2 crores short. The balance in his other bank account was a tad below ₹40 lakhs. He wasn't going to have sufficient time to close his position. He had to do something drastic.

The time read 3:22 pm.

Mukund messaged, *'Close?'*

He called up Mark who answered after just one ring.

'Yes, Agastya. Aren't you on your way to the press conference?'

'I'm about to start. But, who's going to be on the dias?'

'Why do you ask? Vikram, Richard and I, of course.'

Of course! Agastya couldn't figure how that was remotely obvious.

'And the questions?'

'About Vikram?'

'Yes.'

'It's all just baseless speculation.'

'Great!'

Mark disconnected the phone.

Alliance moved up and inched towards ₹427. Were others covering their short positions as well? Spectra was however holding out near ₹885. His fingers were now fidgeting with a pen. Maithili kept staring at him and he resented her for distracting him. He had wanted to close out the position on Alliance, but couldn't get himself to take the call. He didn't have any other option either. Closing his position on Alliance would have meant that he had submitted himself to defeat. He decided to hold out for a little while longer.

Agastya sat and continued holding the mobile against his ear. It wasn't sinking in. He received a text message from Vikram.

'New Delhi inclined…'

Agastya called up Prem Mehra.

'We just spoke.'

Agastya took a deep breath and spoke slowly.

'Have you been able to consider what we had spoken about, Prem?'

'You could be bluffing. I know you, Agastya. But, I'm in touch with Mark. I can't be having two conversations.'

Agastya was tempted to enquire about the details of his conversation with Mark, but realized that Prem would not be forthcoming about the details.

'I heard about that…'

There was another painful pause. Each and every second counted.

'How would I get an assurance on this one?'

'That's a call only you can take, Prem. I can just tell you what's on the table.'

'Your expectations?'

'It's quite clear.'

'You could be bluffing.'

'Prem, I will assure you of one thing. A set of events is going to unfold over the next couple of minutes which should convince you.'

'I've seen your cheap tricks. I'm not going to blink because you sneeze!'

'Let's just say, I will ensure that you will have my attention.'

Agastya disconnected. He had wanted to be polite, but had got carried away by the moment.

Alliance again moved minutely downwards. But it wasn't significant enough. The trading volumes remained high and there seemed to be equal pressure on both the buy and sell sides. He was getting restless. He would have to leave for the press conference in a few moments. He bit his lip and sent Mukund the message.

'*Close Alliance.*'

Sebastian walked into the room.

'Agastya, we need to head out there. Aren't you coming?'

'How bad is it?'

'Let's get there and figure it out, but I believe the turnout is better than expected. We've got guys we haven't even invited turning up!'

Agastya looked at the financial impact. The new product was going to be a loss maker for its entire life. He shook his head. This wasn't the way it was to have worked out.

Sebastian placed the new creative for the 20 per cent off offer on Agastya's table. It had been a quick turnaround, but the advertising agency had done an exceptional job in the layout and the overall look.

Sebastian left the room as Agastya remained seated looking at the new creative.

He was distracted and couldn't get his mind off Nitin's appointment as the deputy CEO. He felt let down by Richard. Rage and hatred swept through him. He picked up the mobile and dialled Richard.

'Hi, Richard. Can we speak?'

'Yes, Agastya. I'm walking across to the venue. How about you?'

'What happened?'

There was a pause for several seconds.

'There's so much that's happened, Agastya. What are you referring to?'

'About Nitin...'

'Well, that is how it is. Don't think too much about it!'

'Is it final?'

'It has been discussed with the board. It was a call that we had to take under the circumstances. We realized that your hands are going to be full for now with this mess. But don't rush into anything for now, Agastya. I know the events may be getting to you, but let things settle down. Let's speak after the press conference?'

'Sure, Richard. I just thought I'd let you know that this is not over with Stark. We may still have some headway here…'

'I'm not following you.'

'All I'm saying, Richard, is that I'm not letting this go with Stark. You know me better than that!'

'Is there something that you want to share with me?'

'Just wanted to tell you that this isn't over.'

'I'll keep that in mind. I believe you've had a word with Mark on a market development initiative you had in mind?'

He could sense that Richard was smiling.

'You'll know if it happens. I just wanted to make sure you knew how it happened, and who made it happen.'

'Ok, Agastya.'

Agastya crossed his fingers and glanced at the stock prices again. The BCL stock price continued to tumble.

He received a text message from Nitin.

Sailesh may be resigning!

Agastya immediately clicked on the messenger icon and typed a message to Sailesh

Agastya: Why?

Sailesh: You crossed a line…

Agastya: ?

Sailesh: You slept with Tanya.

Agastya froze. His fingers went numb. Had Tanya done this to him deliberately? They hadn't met after that night. And, how did Sailesh find out? He deleted the chat from his mobile.

He looked at the time again. He had to give Mukund enough time, or he would have been in an even more awkward position. The funds needed to be remitted.

Spectra was nearing ₹883. He wasn't sure if it would go below the ₹880 mark, and even if it did, he wouldn't have time to close his position. His eyes kept veering towards the clock. Once the press conference started he would have neither the time to pass on any instructions nor access to any information. Defeat was slowly sinking in. He hesitantly typed, possibly, his last message to Mukund for the day.

'Close Spectra.'

He closed the messenger icon and placed the phone gently back on the table and then quickly picked it up again and dialled Rakesh.

'Yes, Agastya!'

'Call it off, Rakesh, call it off!'

'What the hell, Agastya? Are you out of your mind? You can't do this to me, you bastard!'

'It's not like that, Rakesh. You won't understand!'

'I won't understand?! You bastard! I've given my word and I did that based on your word. Your damn word, Agastya! You're a slime ball. What happened? Went weak in the knees? Or did you get cold feet? What happened? Nitin's becoming the CEO and now you want to cover your ass! I knew I should have checked with Nitin on this! You've made an ass of me!'

Agastya placed the mobile at a distance from his ear as Rakesh started screaming.

'Listen to me, Rakesh. You've still got my word. The money is there. But you need to call this off for now... you just have to!'

'I will take you down, Agastya. I will drag you to the roads and feed you to the dogs. I knew you would be just another MNC jerk covering his ass. I thought you may be different, but you've just shown your colours. You're one jack ass!'

'Cool down, Rakesh. Something has just happened. Will explain it later.'

'Later? You bastard! Go to hell!' Rakesh yelled and disconnected the phone.

Next, Agastya called up the journalist.

'Ajay, take it easy.'

'What do you mean?'

'No more... just no more!'

'It doesn't work that way, Agastya, you know that!'

'Listen to me. You need to pull back...'

'You made a deal with Goenka, Agastya!'

'I'll make it up some other way, but for now... just let it go!'

'You don't want front page now?'

Agastya shook his head. He had been overcome with emotions. Revenge, anger and trust were each vying to trump the other. He was perplexed. He wasn't sure if he wanted to wipe out Sailesh any longer. A sense of guilt engulfed him. He wasn't sure of his moral compass any longer. Right and wrong were now blurred.

'I'll call you back, Ajay.'

Agastya slipped on his jacket and adjusted his tie. Maithili rose from her chair and patted him on his back.

'I hate to see you going broke! But I have a feeling I'm going to enjoy the journey!' Maithili smiled and pecked him on his cheek.

'It's not over, M!'

'It isn't?' she laughed.

'It's not over till it's over, M!'

'Let me walk with you?'

He smiled.

'That would be a pleasure, my dear.'

'What have you decided, Agastya?'

'About?'

'Your money or your wife?' Maithili laughed.

'Let's see, M...let's see.'

They walked out of the room and he received a call from Nitin.

'Where are you?'

'On my way.'

'Mark has been asking for you. Something's brewing out here. He's been on a long call with Prem.'

'What's going on?'

'I don't know. He has been pacing up and down the hotel lobby on this call. And now Richard is also with him. Any idea what this could be about?'

Agastya wasn't sure if he should share his escapade with Rakesh or discuss the stunt he was trying to pull, by bringing down the Stark trucks to a standstill. The situation and dynamics had changed.

'I'll be there in a few minutes.'

'Are you sure you don't know what this is about?'

Agastya wondered if Rakesh had been able to swing it so quickly with the trucks.

'There's been so much happening. I'm getting into the lift. Let me call you back.'

Rakesh called him.

'Agastya!'

'Yes, Rakesh. I'm sorry…'

'I spoke with them. They haven't been able to get through to Prem yet. He seems to be on some call and they've kept my guy on hold for several minutes. What do you want to do?'

'See if you can call it off…'

'But they've already spoken with their logistics and sales heads. The ball is in play.'

'But Prem would be the main one, right?'

'Under the circumstances, yes. '

'You seem to have cooled down.'

'It's not that, Agastya. I need this job more than you do. I still need to make my mortgage payments. That's my reality! These games that you guys play... I can't be the one who gets burnt between you and Nitin. I'll have my time and we'll have our conversation then!'

'I understand, Rakesh. For now call if off though.'

'I can't promise. I'm not able to get through to them. They're on wildfire right now. They had gone delirious when I spoke with them. But there is one thing, Agastya.'

'What's that?'

'You have to keep your word, whatever happens… My credibility and career are at stake. I've been in this business too long. It's slimy and thankless, but one's word counts for everything. I stuck my neck out for you. I had my own interests in this as well, but don't make me regret backing you on this one. You need to do that for me!' It wasn't a request as much as it was a veiled and polite threat.

'I will, Rakesh. Let me know what happens?'

They were about to enter the lift when his mobile rang again.

'Yes, Sebastian?'

'Nitin accosted me.'

'For what?'

'He was grilling me on the financial impact of this 20 per cent off!'

'Ok ... I'll be there. Just hold on.'

'And there's one more thing!'

'What?'

'There's some talk about you as well!'

'What is that, Sebastian? Just be direct!'

'There are rumours that you may be asked to put in your papers.'

Maithili walked up to him having sorted herself out and combed her hair.

'I've seen you disturbed, but this is new. What happened?'

'Give me a damn break, you mad woman! You're squeezing every last penny out of me, screwing up my marriage and, to make things worse, now my career has gone down the drain. You've really screwed me this time! Why did you have to pick this day for all this? We've fought before ... we've had our differences ... what in hell's name happened? We were just having an affair, M! What the hell did you expect? What in god bloody hell tipped you over the edge? I just can't take this anymore. I need to know. Nothing's making any sense. Just damn you! Damn your money! Let all this go down the damn tube! I really don't care anymore. I'm not giving you the damn money! Do whatever you like!'

She continued holding his hand.

'Feeling better? Now that that's out of your system?'

They remained standing in the lift lobby.

'Can I ask you something?'

She nodded.

'Are you delusional, or have you just lost your brains? Haven't you heard anything of what I just said?'

She smiled.

'Are you upset?'

Agastya didn't respond and stood motionless.

Sailesh Rao's Office, Mumbai

He received a call from Shankar.

'Sailesh. Have you thought about it?'

'Shouldn't we be focusing on the issue at hand?'

'We are.'

'And you think if I were to put in my papers, the matter would resolve itself?'

'It would address the issue at hand.'

Disgusted with the sarcasm, he hung up.

His phone beeped the arrival of a new message.

'Agastya's head on the block.'

He deleted it with a reluctant sense of retribution. A sense of fatigue had overcome him. He remained seated in his chair and looked at Tanya in the family photograph again.

He had heard that Prem was under tremendous pressure with the breakdown of the trucks and the Stark senior management had been grilling him on the two emails that had been received from the journalist at News Times. The allies had turned instantaneous detractors. His team was maintaining a distance from him and he hadn't been marked on any emails for several minutes now, quite unusual considering that they had been on the verge of a product launch.

Nikhil Mathur, the strategy head and his key ally in formulating the strategy blueprint, walked into his room.

'Hi, Sailesh.'

'Hi, Nikhil.'

'I've just met Prem.'

'Give me a minute, Nikhil.'

Sailesh had received a message on his messenger from Agastya and was now typing furiously.

He placed the mobile back on the table and switched it off.

Sailesh smiled, 'Yes, Nikhil. Any further thoughts on the blueprint?'

'The vultures are hovering.'

'I've heard. Who's the prey?' Sailesh laughed.

'Word has it that it's a stocky little gentleman with yellow suspenders.'

Sailesh slid his thumbs below the suspenders and moved them up and down.

'Do you wear suspenders?'

'Come to think of it, that would be the missing piece in my wardrobe!'

They both laughed.

'Sailesh, Prem is in touch with Mark at BCL.'

'I heard…'

'There were some discussions with Agastya as well.'

Sailesh was now curious. 'Agastya?'

'Yes. Prem was very disturbed after the conversation.'

'Agastya can do that to people. He has a knack for that! You think Prem will hold out?'

'He's a tough cookie. I don't see him crumbling too quickly.'

'What else did he speak with you about?'

'About you, Sailesh.'

'What about me?'

'He asked if you were indispensable.'

'And?'

'I told him as it was.'

'And ... that is?'

'You're a great strategist, Sailesh. Possibly one of the best thinkers I know of in the game right now.'

'But?'

'I think you got distracted with Velvet. I don't know what was running in your mind. Everything else in the blueprint made sense, but this, even I couldn't figure out. I just don't get it. It was never sustainable. We have to sell large volumes and at that price point it's always going to yield losses.'

'But this was clear all along. We had all bought into it. Why all these doubts and questions a few hours before the launch?'

'The dynamics have changed.'

'And how's that?'

'Nothing much. Prem has a reason to be rid of you now. This couldn't have played out better for him.'

Sailesh smiled. He clicked on a folder and searched for an email. He forwarded the email to Prem marking a cc to Nikhil.

Nikhil opened the email on his BlackBerry.

'What's this?'

'I'm taking Prem head on!'

'A.K. Enterprises? '

Chapter Twenty-Three

3 DAYS EARLIER

in these tattered palms
is me, shredded and torn
weave me with threads
of your love

His finger kept compulsively pushing the bell. He didn't want the door to open and yet the finger persisted. He was torn by guilt and fear. He didn't want to see her and yet he needed to hold her and comfort her and know that she was still his. There was no noise coming from the apartment, but he could see strains of light seeping from the gap between the door and floor.

And then, the hesitant footsteps were audible. His heart began to race and he was feeling breathless. The stench from the smoke and alcohol on his suit and his perspiring body repelled him and he had a desperate urge to run when the footsteps drew closer to the door. He had wanted to call her several times but realized that he wasn't prepared to complicate his life. He needed space and some time to reflect on the relationship, his marriage and the new product launch. He had been overwhelmed on the flight back from Dubai to Mumbai and had been consumed by panic that he may never see Maithili again.

The door opened and he was startled to see Priyanka standing at the door. He had seen her picture on Maithili's mobile several times, but they had never met. He knew that Maithili had ensured that they never meet and he hadn't wanted to encroach into her personal space and the one relationship that truly meant something to her. They had spoken several times when he and Maithili had had disagreements or when Maithili would vanish and remain incommunicado, but these conversations remained privy to both of them. A quaint yet deep bond had been formed between them during the course of their conversations, and she had deftly played the role of the mediator between two sparring and strong headed lovers.

Maithili had been maniacally overprotective of Priyanka whenever she mentioned her briefly in conversations and almost felt as if even the utterance of her name in front of him would harm and corrupt the sanctity of the bond that she had with her.

Priyanka held the door open and stood poised and calm. And yet he could sense the disapproval in her eyes.

'Is Maithili there?' The syllables were uttered in a gradual manner, knowing that if the words emerged at his normal pace, the slurring would be apparent.

She shook her head.

'Is she at Ismail's place?'

'You don't know, do you?'

'What?'

'She's still in the hospital.'

'I heard that she came back from Dubai ...'

His legs were finding it difficult to keep him upright and he had to place his palm on the wall to support himself.

'How drunk are you?'

Agastya was surprised at being embarrassed, an emotion that he had not felt for several years. There was a calm innocence in her voice and demeanour even though her resentment was unmistakable.

'Would you like to come in?'

He was startled by the cordial invitation but could neither muster the strength nor conviction to enter her apartment. She stepped out, placed her soft hands on his and led him in. He had been to Maithili's apartment several times and the moments and memories flashed by him as they walked to the couch. It then struck him that she had ensured that Priyanka would never be in the apartment whenever he had been there earlier.

He stared at the quaint cuckoo clock that hung on the wall. He had driven to her apartment straight from the airport on his return from Switzerland, made passionate love to her on that very couch and handed over the clock to her as he left the apartment. He could still remember her naked body perched on the sofa as her fingers toyed with the cuckoo, urging it to come out of its enclosure.

'Why don't you sit down?'

He turned around and sat down on the rug beside the sofa afraid that he would be overwhelmed by the memories of that night if he sat on the couch.

Priyanka walked into the kitchen, returned with a glass of cold water and handed it over to him. He noticed her long legs and the yellow shorts and couldn't help thinking to himself that shapely legs seemed to be a family treasure. He sipped the water and placed it on the rug beside him, rested his head on the couch and stretched his legs. He was finding it difficult to subdue the fatigue and exhaustion and the energy drained instantly from his body.

She sat down beside him and rested her back against the couch as well.

The cuckoo jumped out from its ensconced shelter and yelled three times before it mercifully muted down and disappeared.

'Why do you guys hurt each other so much?'

'I don't know, Priyanka.'

She smiled.

'I think you do…you just don't feel like admitting it to yourself.'

'What do you think it is?'

She rested her head on the couch and took a deep breath.

'You're just like every other man she has been with…'

'What do you mean?'

'She can't be with anyone who respects her, because she doesn't respect herself.'

Agastya uneasily shifted his weight.

'Why is she still in the hospital?'

'She developed some complications.'

'How is she doing now?'

'She would have been home by now, but relatives have made her life miserable. It's pushed her into a deeper depression. She doesn't know where to go. I think she feels safe there.'

He sipped the water and his eyes veered towards the drinks cabinet.

'Shall I get you a drink?'

He nodded as he was too guilty to speak.

'Scotch, right?'

'She seems to have told you quite a bit about me.'

She stood up, walked up towards the cabinet, pulled out the bottle of scotch with one hand and the crystal tumbler with another.

'There's no ice at home, is that ok?'

He nodded.

She poured him a large and deliberately unmeasured portion of scotch and handed it over to him. She then walked back and poured herself a drink and came back to sit beside him. He could feel her elbow brushing against his arm.

She raised her glass.

'Cheers?'

He nodded and sipped the drink.

'When is she going to be back?'

'Should be soon…'

'Do me a favour.'

'Sure…'

'Don't tell her that I came to check on her.'

She smiled.

'Why did you leave her there in Dubai?'

Agastya gulped down the drink and was frustrated that it didn't calm his nerves.

'Would you like another one?'

He nodded and realized that he needed a few moments to gather his thoughts. He hadn't been prepared to be accosted by her sister and was wondering what had provoked the insane urge to meet Maithili. He had held himself back and immersed himself in his work on returning from Dubai, ensuring that he didn't have even a few spare moments to reflect.

He had hurt her on several occasions before, but it had been the inherent code of their relationship. There had been a maniacal belief that the deeper the hurt and pain, the more resilient and fulfilling their relationship would evolve into and even greater the power he would wield over her. He didn't want to acknowledge to himself that he had perhaps crossed the line when he left her at the Burj in Dubai.

Priyanka returned with the glass and handed it over to him. He noticed that the glass was filled even more than on the previous occasion. He sipped it again as she assumed her position beside him.

She turned around and stroked his hair.

'Do you think you'll ever love her?'

He realized that she wasn't pressing him for answers.

'That's between Maithili and me, don't you think?'

'Don't you think I deserve to know?'

'It's not that…'

'She is very precious to me, Agastya…'

'I know. She is very protective of you.'

'That's one thing I don't like about her. She can be over protective.'

'I wouldn't blame her under the circumstances.' Agastya paused realizing that he had ventured into a terrain that he should've steered clear of.

'What circumstances?'

'Nothing.'

She smiled and pecked him on his cheek.

'She told you about my uncle?'

Agastya turned towards her and his lips brushed against hers. He pulled himself back but she remained poised and still. She didn't move away from him but extended her arm further and continued stroking his hair.

'No, what about your uncle?'

She smiled. 'Don't worry, Agastya, it's ok. I know she is close to you.'

'I'm sorry… I didn't mean to raise the subject.'

'Don't worry, it's a struggle that M and I go through every living moment. Your mentioning it doesn't change anything.'

She picked up her glass with her left hand and sipped from it.

'He came to visit her at the hospital.'

'Who?'

'The same uncle, Agastya. Why do you think she's so disturbed?'

'The ruthless bastard!'

'Why are you getting so worked up? Do you see me getting restless?'

'Why did you let him meet her?'

'I didn't have a choice. He came in with papa.'

'Is your father still in town?'

'No, they left a couple of days back. I convinced him that it would be better for both of us.'

'He just left?'

'Let's just say I didn't give him a choice.'

'What did you do?'

'I threatened to expose my uncle for everything that he had done to Maithili and me. I don't think we will ever be seeing them again. For a change I stood up for her.'

'I'm not sure what to say'

'It's complicated, but she has been looking out for me all these years. I needed to show up for her this time around. You know this incident has actually been good for me. Maithili has been looking out for me ever since I came into Mumbai. I don't think we were ever this close even when we were children in Delhi. It's just a wake-up call for me I guess.'

'That's good to hear...' he was struggling to utter the words.

She gazed at the cuckoo clock and laughed.

'What happened?'

'She keeps looking at that clock when she is feeling low.'

'I gave it to her.'

She turned towards him. 'You think I didn't know that? Why don't you finish your drink? There's something I need to do.'

She placed her hand below his glass and guided it to his lips.

'Now, drink it slowly, but leave the last few drops.'

He found himself submitting to her instructions and gulped down the scotch. She slid the glass out of his hands, emptied the contents, and slowly moved her body above his, seating herself on his legs. She pushed back her long hair and kissed him. He tried to resist but she held his head and ensnared him in a tight grip. She bit his lips before kissing him repeatedly.

He tried to push her back with his hands, but she lunged forward and pushed his hands back onto the couch with an intensity and strength that overpowered him.

'Just think about Maithili...' she whispered into his ears and kissed him on his neck.

She gently stretched his arms on the couch, sliding her hands towards his, till their fingers were clasped tightly together.

He could smell the perfume on her skin, a bottle that had been gifted by him. It plunged him into memories of his intense and wild love making with Maithili. He had wanted to feel the warmth of her body and re-experience the power and authority that he felt over her. The initial spurts of intense aggression, stark ferocity, sadistic abuse swiftly followed by an insane turn of passive submission and meek surrender when she did everything to please him.

'Just have me as you have her...'

He found himself in a trance. His eyes were unable to focus as she pulled off her blouse revealing her naked body with a brazen abandon.

She placed her hands around his neck and held it in a tight grip, but seemed confused.

'Do you know why I'm doing this?'

He found it difficult to speak and shook his head.

'I need to understand Maithili, and you need to make me a promise.'

The distinct resemblance to Maithili, her voice and smell, and the violent streak aroused him and he did not have to try too hard to convince himself to believe what she was saying.

'What?'

'You will never mention this to Maithili.'

She released the grip around his neck.

He pushed her back on the rug with a torrid force, and could hear a soft thud as her head hit the rug. He took off his jacket, ripped the shirt off his chest and pounced on top of her and whispered into her ears.

'I promise…'

Chapter Twenty-Four

3:25 PM
TODAY

what if...
amidst deception
and blackmail
stood naked remorse

The lift doors opened and Maithili followed Agastya inside. As it started moving, she pressed a button that abruptly halted the lift.

'What do you think you're doing?'

'Do you remember Dubai?'

'Yes! Is that what it's all about?'

'It's not as simple as that, Agastya! Can you feel the pain I was feeling?'

'You were upset, M, but you really can't compare the two situations.'

'You didn't answer my question. Can you feel the pain?'

'What frigging pain, M? You wanted to meet me and I was just busy, and then you take an overdose in a hotel room in a godforsaken foreign country! What did you expect me to do?'

She held his hand again and began stroking his hair.

'Darling. I just wanted you to listen to me.'

'Stop these games. Just tell me directly. What was it?'

'I lost our baby, Agastya!'

Agastya looked at her. Her eyes were moist and she was trembling.

'What baby, M?'

'And…then Priyanka…'

'What about Priyanka?'

'You couldn't spare the one person who you knew meant the world to me?'

'What are you talking about?'

'You raped her, you sick bastard!'

She tilted her head and smiled wryly at him.

'That's going to cost you much more than money, Agastya. Unless you close this in the next five minutes!'

Beads of perspiration were rolling down his forehead.

'I didn't rape her, M!'

'You're one lying piece of work. I'm going to ruin you... have no doubt about that! 'I couldn't protect the one person in my life who counted on me, Agastya. The one person...'

'You're not going to go ahead with this, M!'

'I understand, Agastya. If that's the way it's going to be, then what can I say? I'm sure Nandita will have much more to talk to me about than you do.'

'Go to hell, M!'

'I just might. But I thought I should let you know, that your journalist friend Ajay will be receiving some of our photographs in a short while from now. That should make for some interesting reading in some publications. It would only add to your page three allure, don't you think?'

He screamed, 'You're mad! Priyanka is lying, M. It wasn't like that!'

She moved her hands away from his hair and pressed a button, and the lift resumed its descent. She looked at her watch.

'You have less than four minutes, Agastya... make it happen. If I don't have the funds in my account before 3:30 pm...'

As the lift doors opened, she walked out quickly, away from him.

He glanced at his mobile. There was a text message from Nandita. Agastya's heart skipped a beat.

'*All the best for the launch. Let's meet for a few minutes if you're free after it gets over?*'

As he finished reading the message, his mobile rang again.

'Hi, Rakesh. What happened?'

'They managed to get through to Prem. Their trucks have come to a standstill across the country. They've just

344

stopped. I spoke with a guy managing logistics at Stark. He's confirmed it. They've gone mad over there. They don't know what's hit them. They first thought it was a problem with their GPS tracking systems. It took them a while to realize that this was for real. It's a complete lockdown, Agastya. They will be crippled if those trucks don't move for some more hours. Hello? Agastya? Are you there?'

'Will call you later, Rakesh.'

He disconnected and walked briskly outside the lobby, and ran across the road and reached the Oberoi in under a minute. He walked towards the main lobby, frustrated with the intrusive and often exasperating security check by the staff. He moved quickly through the security area, glancing at his watch the whole time. The lift doors were open when he rushed through them. His restlessness showed as he tapped his feet impatiently for the lift to come down. Deciding he had no time to waste, he ran across the lobby, up the staircase and through the shopping arcade into the connecting passage to the Trident hotel.

He stopped abruptly when he noticed Prem Mehra calling on his mobile.

'I need to speak with Vikram.'

'You can call him, Prem...'

'Did you have something to do with what just happened?'

'What just happened, Prem?'

'Don't play smart, Agastya.'

'I'm not... and have you heard from your union leader?'

'What union leader? What's this about now?'

'Then let's connect a little later, when you are a little more apprised of the situation.'

'What situation, Agastya? What slimy tricks are you up to now?'

'I think you should speak with Vikram.'

Agastya disconnected and sprinted across, perspiring furiously. He still wasn't sure if he could inflict any more damage or pain on Sailesh. He reconciled to the fact that he had crossed the line. He had been the one to have breached the bond they had. He had been brutal with Maithili and outright callous with Nandita. And then he realized that beyond all this, he was still thinking of how to keep his job, the only thing that made some sense to him at this time.

Maithili had won the challenge. He was running well over ₹3 crores short. He realized that he had spent too much time deliberating instead of making moves. He could have pulled it through if he had taken the call on Alliance earlier and had not wasted too much time offloading Infitel and DSQ. It then struck him that in the rush he had forgotten about Nectar. He stopped in his tracks and called up Mukund.

'What about Nectar?'

'You hit a gold mine on that. It went up over ₹12!'

That was at least ₹60 lakhs! Was he still in the game?

'Go up any further?'

'Yes, but you don't have time.'

He clenched his fist.

'Close it!'

He tried calling Sailesh, but couldn't reach his mobile. There was a deep sense of guilt that consumed him and he had an urgent need to shake it off. He couldn't carry it with him any longer. It had to be shorn off that very instant. He was finding it difficult to breathe.

As he reached the end of the passage way he found himself near the staircase that led to the main lobby area at the Trident.

He paused for a few seconds and typed a message to Prem Mehra. He read it twice and then pressed the send button.

He rushed down the stairs and noticed Mark, Vikram, Richard and Nitin entering one of the lifts.

He screamed out, 'Nitin! Hold up!'

The over two hundred staff and guests in the lobby turned their heads towards the smartly attired man who was soaking with sweat and jumping three steps at a time.

Nitin turned around to see Agastya racing towards them. He stopped in his steps as Mark, Vikram and Richard also turned around to watch their suave Chief Marketing Officer panting as he ran towards them.

It took him a few seconds to reach the lift and he held on to Nitin's shoulder as he caught his breath.

'Agastya, what happened?'

'Vikram…you'll be getting a call from Prem…'

'Prem Mehra?!'

'Yes, Vikram…'

'What happened?'

Agastya smiled as he caught his breath. 'Their trucks have come to a standstill.'

Richard stepped into the conversation, 'How?'

'They are down on their knees right now.'

'That would be temporary though?'

'There's more to it…'

'What?'

'They may have union problems as well…'

Vikram smiled. 'Do they?'

Agastya didn't react.

Richard stepped in. 'So, what are you suggesting?'

'There just might be an opportunity here, and a reason for Vikram to take the call…if he does call.'

The four of them stared at each other and Nitin's restlessness in the situation was evident.

Agastya looked at his watch. They had less than two minutes for the press conference to commence.

'Mark, can we postpone the conference by a few minutes?'

'That would not be possible. We have one of the board members connecting via video conference.'

Richard looked stunned. 'When did this happen? I wasn't informed about this!'

Mark glared. 'Under the circumstances, Richard, it would just add a sense of credibility to the situation. Don't you think?'

Vikram's mobile rang. He let it ring three times and then connected the call.

'Hi, Prem, I'm in a bit of a rush. Is this urgent?'

Agastya noticed two women walking into the reception from a distance. He narrowed his eyes and noticed that it was indeed Nandita and Maithili who had walked in together.

Vikram nodded his head as he listened to Prem.

Agastya opened the messenger. It was a message from Manish.

'The buddies have a little surprise for you!'

He replied, '?'

Mukund messaged, *'Manish and co have passed their trades to you…'*

He was ecstatic, *'How much?'*

'1.85 crore!'

He wanted to hug them, but he smashed the keys with his fingers.

'Remit!'

Vikram concluded his call with Prem Mehra.

'Let me get back to you, Prem?'

Vikram shook his head.

'What was that about, Vikram?' Richard asked

'Give me a minute, guys.'

Vikram walked away from them and for about twenty seconds there was an excruciating silence as he spoke in a muted voice on his mobile.

He walked back towards the group as he disconnected the call and pulled Richard and Mark away from the group and walked into the main lobby area, deep in an animated conversation.

Nitin broke the tense silence. 'Agastya, what's all this about?' The desperation was evident.

The conversation between the three gentlemen lasted for over twenty seconds. Agastya kept looking at his watch and didn't attempt a response to the evidently agitated Nitin.

The group walked back towards them and Mark pressed the lift button.

'Agastya'

'Yes, Mark.'

'You want to launch Sparkle?'

Agastya grinned. 'That would be nice.'

'So, what are you waiting for?'

'What the hell is going on?' Nitin's frustration finally broke through his veneer.

Agastya placed his hand on Nitin's shoulder '"What next", would be an obvious question?'

Mark turned around and laughed, 'What do you think?'

'We could do with a beer after this damn press conference.'

Mark laughed, 'That round would be on me!'

The elevator doors opened.

Agastya noticed Nandita and Maithili seating themselves in the lobby area.

He messaged her. There was a sense of euphoria that had swept through him.

'Funds remitted!'

'And would any one of you three gracious gentlemen be kind enough to tell us what the hell happens next?' Agastya laughed.

'No change in pricing, Agastya. We go for it as originally planned. Am surprised you even ask these basic questions!' Mark smiled.

Agastya nodded.

'And there is one more thing, Agastya...'

'Yes, Mark?'

'Let's have some fun?'

Mark looked into his eyes, urging him on.

'I was thinking we could do a buy one and get one free offer.'

Three of them stared at Agastya as he thrust his hand out to keep the lift doors from closing.

Vikram spoke, 'But...'

Mark shot back 'Let's blow these bastards out! Vikram, when is our 100 year anniversary in India?'

'That's day after Mark.'

'What time is the press conference for Stark?'

'I think it's at 5...'

'Then, let's give them something to ponder about over the next one hour! Let's do a buy one get one free offer on all our products, day after, and keep it running on Sparkle for a while!'

Agastya smiled. 'That should do well.'

'Now let's stop this childish squabbling. Let's show Mr Prem Mehra how the big boys play. Shall we leave for the press conference gentlemen? It is 3:30 pm!'

Chapter Twenty-Five

THREE WEEKS LATER

hanging each other
out to dry, relishing
descending moisture
from the sky

Maithili stepped into his car, smiling.

'You're looking good, M!'

'Aren't you in a good mood.'

'Managed to take a few days off from work…just chilling for a change.'

'How's the stock market doing?'

Agastya laughed.

'I've taken a break from that as well.'

'You're not keeping well?'

Agastya shook his head.

'I just needed to take it easy and find myself.'

'A philosophical side—that's a new one!'

'I'm full of surprises, M, you should get to know the new me better.'

Maithili laughed.

Agastya started the car, shifted into first gear and was thrilled by the stunning sound emanating from the engine.

'Are you thinking of buying this?'

'I already have.' He looked at Maithili.

She glanced at him briefly and then looked back towards the road.

'How's Ismail?'

'He dropped me to the airport.'

'…and Roshan?'

'He's doing well.'

They both looked towards the road and the restless yet cautious silence was apparent. There was much that they wanted to say but they struggled with expressing their emotions.

Do I still surprise you, Agastya?'

'Sure, you could say that.'

He was now speeding at over 120 km/h in the Porsche Cayenne.

'Why are you driving so fast?'

'Because I can, M?'

She laughed.

'How's Nandita doing?'

'Let's say your conversation with her was a little more than she could digest. She's taken the kids to her mom's place.'

'What's happening with both of you?'

'What do you expect, M? After you burned me...'

'C'mon, Agastya. You asked for it. And it was bound to happen some day.'

'I was short by 10 lakhs, M. 10 frigging lakhs!'

She laughed. 'A deal is a deal. But I did cut you some slack.'

'How's that?'

'I didn't release the photographs to the press.'

Agastya nodded.

'Yup. That was very kind.'

Agastya pressed down on the accelerator and the SUV now hurtled past 150 km/h.

'And how's the Colonel taking it?'

'We've had a long chat...'

'And?'

'He's lying low.'

'That's not like him. What happened?'

Agastya smiled.

'Let's just say he had some skeletons in his closet as well.'

Maithili winked.

'You still haven't answered my question, Agastya. You and Nandita; what's the story?'

'It's going to be a rocky road.'

'Have both of you discussed what you're going to be doing?'

Agastya now pressed down on the accelerator taking the

SUV to over 180 km/h.

'She's leaving me, M. She's leaving me…'

'I would like to say that I'm sorry, Agastya.'

'But you're not really, right?'

'I guess not…' she paused.

'And you?'

'As in Ismail and me?'

'Yes?'

'We're giving it one more shot. Let's see how it goes.'
Agastya smiled.

'How do you know that baby was mine?'

'You're really a piece of work, aren't you?'

'How's Priyanka doing?'

'You don't have the right to utter her name, Agastya.'

'I didn't rape her, M, you know me better than that!'

'I don't know what to believe any more, Agastya.'

'Why did you even meet me?'

'What do you think?'

'I have no clue, M, I have no clue.'

'You're a precious wound I can't let go off.'

'And?'

'It really doesn't matter anymore.'

'As simple as that?'

They didn't exchange any words for a few moments as
Agastya fidgeted with the panel of the music system.

He pulled out two miniature bottles from his jacket
pocket with his right hand and handed over one to her.

'You're kidding me, right?'

He took his hands off the steering wheel, opened the
bottle and extended his arm towards Maithili.

Maithili asked, 'A toast?'

'Crash and burn!' he smiled.

Chapter Twenty-Six

FOUR WEEKS LATER...

what have we become...
questions unanswered
against a setting sun

Agastya walked up towards the hammock that was swinging lightly in the warm gentle breeze. He noticed the prominent paunch in a red T shirt, with a straw hat above it. He could hear the man humming an old Hindi song, distinctly and consistently out of beat.

'I think you should stick to Mathematics!'

The surprise was hastily concealed as Sailesh Rao stepped down from the hammock and seated himself on a cane chair. He looked towards the sea and Agastya settled himself in the hammock.

Sailesh stroked his belly and smiled.

'On vacation, Agastya?'

'Not quite sure, really.'

Sailesh laughed.

'Rum?'

Agastya nodded and Sailesh handed over his glass to him. Agastya emptied the contents and returned the glass to Sailesh.

'I can see that some things don't change!'

'They never will, Sailesh.'

'You didn't tell me… Who told you where I was staying?'

'Radhika.'

Neither spoke for some time as they both looked towards the sea, admiring the setting sun. A masseur was massaging a woman as she lay naked face down on a towel that she had laid down on the sand.

'How's your leg doing?'

Agastya tapped the plaster on his right leg.

'You must autograph this before you leave.'

'In an SUV as I hear?'

'You've been keeping tabs on me?'

'Old habits die hard. There doesn't seem to be much space on the cast for my initials.'

'You need to get some glasses!'

'Tanya insists I need to get a pair too. Age catching up I guess.'

'Where is she?'

'She's taken the kids out shopping.'

There was a restless silence that hung between them.

'I am sorry, chief.'

'Why, Agastya? Because you slept with my wife, or because you got caught?'

Agastya got off the hammock and gestured towards the shore.

'Let's walk down the beach. It's a great day for a walk.'

Sailesh followed Agastya as he limped on the warm sand towards the sea.

'So, did you enjoy her, Agastya?'

Agastya stopped in his steps and turned around and faced Sailesh.

'You need to know something, Sailesh. I could see the regret in her eyes; it didn't mean anything to her.'

Sailesh smiled.

'How's Nandita? Has she left you?'

'We're not clear right now. We're just going with the flow.'

Sailesh chuckled and shook his head.

'When is Vikram leaving?'

'Before the end of the year. He comes into office, has a drink, warms his chair and then heads home for lunch. Hectic schedule. Poor bugger!'

'Why would you say that, Agastya? He was guilty like hell!'

'I know that. But he was a good man and is still a good man!'

'To that I agree. He is.'

'Why did you frame him, Sailesh?'

'What?'

'You were the one that leaked his stuff to the press. Right?'

Sailesh took a deep breath.

'I wasn't alone. Sebastian was the one who gave me the information!'

'You're kidding.'

'Nope.'

Agastya shook his head.

'And then?'

'Mark and Richard are not the best of buddies. It had been brewing for several years. And Vikram was struggling to get into China, which Richard had been resisting. And then the BCL Metrics joint venture was formed. You know all that about the IPO and the pre placement of stocks etc. Nitin was getting restless, and he didn't have a great equation with Richard. You on the other hand had Richard's blessings and were coming in his way.'

'So, both Nitin and Sebastian leaked it to the press?'

'It was Sebastian who leaked everything to me. I was the mere messenger. Your aide de camp Sebastian.'

Agastya laughed. 'Well, what can I say? Let bygones be bygones?'

'Sebastian gained Mark's confidence, so Mark was in the know.'

'But why leak it to the press?'

'It had to be a situation that got out of control and set the cat amongst the pigeons. And Mark had to be the visible saviour of the day. Simple as that really.'

'Sebastian? Really?'

'Yes, Agastya. Sebastian. And let's not forget your journalist friend Ajay! He played both of us.'

'What did you feed the journalist?'

'Some details on the Metrics JV and what happened over there.'

'But that didn't hit the press?'

'That was the game played by the journalist and Goenka.'

'What game?'

'Goenka got some additional advertising budgets from you?'

'How did you know about that?'

'Well, Goenka got some from me as well, to cover my ass! He cashed in an additional 175 crores between both our companies. Not bad for a couple of calls. And we both gave in to save both our companies and ourselves from the media glare.'

'Goenka played us both?'

'Why do you think that incident played out so smoothly? Else that stock trading scandal would have blown the living daylights out of BCL! Goenka told his TV channel folks to stay clear.'

'That's why that apology that was announced subsequently...'

'Yes. It was touted to be a misunderstanding. The same for us as well. Both BCL and Stark came out clean.'

'But, to be honest, I wasn't sure if Prem would buckle.'

'You unleashed that bunch of stuff on me... Prem got cold feet... and the rest is history.'

'But it's not like Prem to back off.'

'I'm sure your conversations with him had something to do with that?'

'Vikram is the one that closed it with Prem,' Agastya smiled.

'You were playing with their egos. Give me some credit for understanding you. Prem is serving his last few months, and he didn't want to leave with a mess and a bunch of scandals on his hands.'

'But, Sailesh, he also got something that he wanted so badly.'

'Yes. Your friendly minister cleared some projects for Stark that had been stuck in the pipeline for years. But tell me, what was that stuff about some labour union problems that you mentioned to him?'

'What union problems?'

Sailesh laughed. 'You bluffed?!'

'You should play poker, Sailesh. Let me give you some lessons some day! So tell me this, Nitin had nothing to do with any of this?'

Sailesh smiled.

'Even Nitin has a messenger service on his mobile, you know?'

'You bastard!'

'The need of the hour, my friend. Don't get personal! And don't tell me you're jealous?'

'You're a slimy…'

Sailesh cut him. 'Hold on to the pleasantries. You're feeling cheesed off and possibly even humiliated. You got played, fair and square, my friend. Take it in and move on.'

They didn't speak for several minutes, and listened to the music being played on the cheap radio.

Sailesh broke the silence. 'So, what's next for you?'

'Surprisingly enough, Mark seems to have taken a fancy to me. He still thinks I'm a maverick.'

'Rumour has it that you've got a plum posting!'

'Well, let's see how it works out… But, I've started brushing up on my Mandarin!'

'Not bad!'

'They're splitting China into two zones, so I've been asked to take on the CEO position for one of them for now!'

'How did you pull that off?'

'My charm, Sailesh? But it wouldn't have been possible without you!'

Sailesh laughed. 'You know, Agastya, you're not too bad a guy.'

'Why? Coz I slept with your wife?'

'You son of a gun!'

Sailesh got up and extended his hand to Agastya to help him get up and stand on his feet.

'Did I tell you?'

'What now, Sailesh?'

'I quit.' Sailesh was smiling.

'Why, congratulations!'

'It wasn't as much fun without you!'

They started walking back towards the bar.

'Why did you guys play foul and still launch the promotional offer? I still don't get that.'

'That was a neat one, right?!'

'That was a blood bath, Agastya. We had to retaliate. We must have both shelled out over ₹150 crores on that damn offer.'

'I think we wanted to make a clear statement and send you a message.'

'That set you back by over 100 crores! That's quite a statement to make.'

'You see, Sailesh, sometimes size does matter!' Agastya winked and laughed.

As they settled down on the bar stools, the waiter promptly served them their drinks.

Agastya raised a toast.

'To your success Sailesh…'

'See you in China!' Sailesh winked.